So Shine

By Andrew Martin Walker

Andrew Martin Walker lives and works in southern Spain.
When he is not writing he enjoys a parallel career as an
art teacher and professional artist.

You can find him online here:
www.andrewmartinwalker.com (writing)
www.andywalkerart.com   (paintings)
www.artclasspro.com (learn to paint online)

and interact with him on facebook on these pages
www.facebook.com/andrewmartinwalker (writing)
www.facebook.com/artclasspro (painting)

or on twitter here: @AndyWalkerArt

Dedication

To my gorgeous wife, Donna, who has put up with me typing away for many months, and to all those who gave their lives to enable us to read the Bible in our native tongue. Thank you.

Acknowledgements

My very grateful thanks go to a small number of people without whom this book would not have been published. Thank you to Mark Hart, Director of Operations at King's school, Ely, for showing me around the Porta and helping me locate the original prison, and for the tour of the Prior's chapel and the monastery grounds.

Thanks also must go to Lord Melvyn Bragg for kindly allowing me to use the quote from his book, 'The Book of Books', which gave me the initial inspiration for this novel. I would like to acknowledge Arman Zhenikeyev for the use of the cover photo.

I would like also to thank my wife Donna for helping me straighten out some of my wayward plot ideas, and for all her encouragement along the way, and to Lynn Murrell and Marian Preston for proof-reading the manuscript and picking up all my grammatical mistakes.

Thanks also must go to all the people who have published websites that have provided me with much of my historical research. There is now such a wealth of brilliant information online that fact-finding becomes a joy!

'The medieval Oxford scholars, long-woollen gowned, staff in hand, took to the mud tracks of medieval England with their concealed manuscript Bibles in English. They travelled secretly through unculled forests and barely inhabited wild lands, hiding in safe houses, forever fugitive. They were a guerrilla movement and they were called Lollards. Their mission was to give people access to the Word of God in English.

The authorities would not endure it... Wyclif's Bibles were outlawed. Anyone caught with a copy was to be tortured and killed. Yet the Lollards persisted, for more than a century they roved the land and passed on the Word.'

Extract from *The Book of Books* by Melvyn Bragg

Prologue

Holy Innocents' Day, December 28th, 1384

The man with the long white beard sat hunched on a wooden bench in his study, a stone's throw from the parish church of St. Mary's in Lutterworth. He was wrapped in a thick woollen cloak that masked his thin frame and kept out the worst of the biting cold, and on his head he wore a flat cloth cap. Spread before him on a well-worn oak table was a book, the thin vellum pages recently bound and stitched in secret.

Only he knew how many months it had taken him to write the chapters lovingly by hand, trusting the eternal truth he believed they contained. Hour by hour and day by day he had sat on this bench and copied studiously from the only other book of its kind that was still in his possession. This was a precious work of art, beautifully ornamented and coloured and yet still, after all these years' labour, not completely translated from Latin to English. But now at last he had copied it word for word, and this copy would be a gift for someone else.

He leant over wearily, the left side of his body weakened by a stroke that had disabled him two years before, and reached for his quill. He dipped it in the inkwell, opened the book cover and scratched inside it in an unsteady hand. It was too dangerous to write the recipient's name, for he would surely be found and condemned, but he could make some mark that only the messenger would understand.

He blew gently on the ink to dry it, closed the cover and kissed the book. Slowly he rose and fetched a small wooden box belted with straps of iron, and tenderly placed the book inside. He paused a moment to pray and then closed the lid and locked it with a small iron key. Stepping outside into the winter chill, he drew his cloak closer around him, concealing the box, and pulled the hood over his head. He made his way towards the churchyard, walking slowly and carefully on the uneven path, which was already smattered with Christmastide snow. A steady stream of villagers was heading to mass. He bowed his head in acknowledgement of one or two of them, and then went into the vestry to change.

This small room had always been a favourite of his ever since he had taken up the parsonage of the church; it was a place to pray and calm oneself before ministering to God and the assembled congregation. He had spent many hours there, and knew the secrets of the room. Closing the door behind him he took the box and placed it on the floor. He knelt down stiffly and pushed his fingers against a small wooden panel in the wall. It slid easily under his touch, revealing an opening just large enough to receive the locked box. With another prayer he slid the panel shut, climbed unsteadily to his feet, and breathed a sigh of relief. The book was at last safe, and only he knew where it was hidden.

The congregation had all but filled the pews, a people expectant and willing to hear the great man speak. He was something of a champion, this man who had withstood persecution for his beliefs. He had experienced so much, and had been sorely tried and tested, and so his sermons were always a challenge to the hearer. He coughed dryly to clear his throat and rose slowly from his seat and made ready to speak. He began to read, his voice clear but with a broad Oxfordshire accent, and he read in English, not Latin.

"O almighty God, who out of the mouths of babes and sucklings hast ordained strength..."

He paused mid-sentence and screwed up his eyes in pain. He loosened his grip and the book dropped to the floor with a heavy thud as a terrible agony swept through his head and the church around him blurred. He felt himself fall, as if floating and tumbling into a deep well, and then blackness. He slumped to the floor as the stroke took effect.

A gasp went up from the congregation. Someone ran forward, and then another, and soon a small crowd had gathered around him, flustering and shouting at each other. They tried to rouse him, but to no avail. Then a chair was brought and upon this they carried him from the church and back through the graveyard to his cottage. Two days later, on December 30th, 1384 John Wyclif was dead, and his secret died with him. Or so it was thought.

Chapter 1 - The Hound of Hell
Tuesday February 21st 1401

"Don't do that, you'll rile him!" Adam hissed angrily at his younger brother. He turned his head to stare at him, his steely blue eyes flashing with annoyance and just the slightest hint of fear. Richard laughed and rattled the stick one more time on the wooden fence.

The bull mastiff growled deep in its throat, a long low rumble that chilled the bones. Its eyes narrowed and fixed on the two young men. It was tethered by a long rusty chain to a post that had been hammered into the frozen ground, and as it now rose to its feet the chain clanked heavily on the hardened earth.

Adam Wolvercot took a step backwards. "Look what you've done now!"

Richard looked at him in amazement. "Ha! He's just that old bear-baiter. Look at his scars and the way he limps. He'll not bother us, he's chained up." In defiance he rattled the stick once more.

The dog growled again, this time more forcefully, its breath visible in the cold morning air. Then, without warning, it charged towards them barking loudly. The chain tightened around its neck, yanking it back and flipping the dog onto its side with a dull thud. It yelped in pain and clambered to its feet again. Both brothers jumped back into the road, their hearts beating fast. Richard laughed once more. "See, I told you! That chain will hold." He put his hand on his older brother's shoulder as if to calm him. "Come on, let's go. Don't be such a coward."

The dog was now barking incessantly. Over and over again it leapt towards them, only to be floored each time by the chain around its neck. A white foamy froth dripped from its jowls.

"Let's go! Run!" shouted Adam above the noise. He started off at pace up the road, his thin leather soles scratching on the frost hardened mud. Richard followed, a little slower and a lot more carelessly. He wasn't afraid of a chained up guard dog.

The road they were on ran alongside the old manor house, which was guarded by the bull mastiff, and then wound gently on past a handful of single storey hovels. Wisps of smoke curled upwards from soot-stained holes in the thatch, and slowly merged together to form a grey shroud that blotted out the pale winter sun. The ancient village of Wolvercot then petered out and gave way to common land that had been used for as long as anyone could remember for grazing cattle and geese.

And it was for these geese that Adam Wolvercot and his brother Richard were searching on this frosty morning in February 1401. Or rather they were searching for their feathers. Goose feathers made excellent fletches for arrows, the feathers plucked from the same wing so that they would all curve in the same direction and spin the arrow in flight. There were always plenty to be found on the common, having dropped out as the birds moulted, or left in a ragged pile after a kill.

Adam was a good archer in a time when all young men were encouraged to shoot for sport and in preparation for battle. From the age of seven he had begun to master the longbow, practising with other children alongside the men every Sunday after church. Then every weekday between chores he would load and fire, load and fire, until his muscles tired and his shoulders ached. But through all this he now had an innate sense of where to aim. He no longer needed to look along the arrow for sight; he just kept his eyes on the target and let the familiarity of his movements direct the shot.

His longbow was the pride of his few possessions. Made of Mediterranean yew and capped with a yellowing horn that was notched to take the string, it was beautifully supple and had seen service in the wars in France. It was well worn and had a smoothness to it that came from years of handling. And it had been gifted to him by his father before he died. That was ten years ago when he was just 13. A young man coming of age.

His one other prized possession hung on a string around his neck. It was a small iron key that his father had called the 'Key of the Kingdom'. It came with a warning never to let it out of his sight.

"The Key of the Kingdom," repeated Adam as his father placed it over his head, "will that make me a king one day, like our King Richard? He is only a little older than I am. Perhaps I too could rule the country like him. Will the key help me do that?"

"Perhaps, perhaps," replied Jacob with a smile. "Perhaps it will and perhaps it will not, but come a day when it will save many lives. Never lose it; never tell anyone of it, for it must remain a secret until it is called for."

"And how will I know when that time comes?" asked Adam.

"You will know." Jacob de Wolvercot looked deeply into the eyes of his son and held back a tear. "You will know," he whispered.

Adam fingered the key, now hidden beneath his tunic. It was warm where it had lain on his chest, and it seemed so familiar that it had almost become a part of him. He had never once removed it from his neck in all those years.

Though painful times had struck him, and so many loved ones had been lost, he never forgot the words his father had spoken that night so long ago. "It will not keep you from evil", his father had said, "and it may even bring evil to you." Yet to Adam this small key had become almost a talisman, keeping him safe. Somewhere deep inside it even gave him hope. To be a king? Could that be possible? Would he grow up to just be a simple farmer like his brother and his friends, or was there something more?

"Look," cried out Richard.

Adam jolted from his thoughts. "What?"

"Look over there. In the rough grass under that tree. I think it's a dead goose. There will be plenty of feathers to pluck and maybe meat for the pot." He pointed to a clump of white and grey that was half hidden by a bank of long damp grass.

They ran to where the mangled creature lay, its neck broken and its body ripped and bloody.

"Probably killed by a dog or fox," said Adam, "I wonder why it's not been eaten."

Richard grinned, "Well, the fox's loss is our gain. Let's take it home and we'll eat meat tonight."

Adam looked about him furtively to see if anyone was about, and then quickly opened the drawstring on his bag and thrust the dead goose inside. He checked once more that no-one had seen. But the common was quiet on that cold winter morning and nothing stirred around them. The pair started on the way home, Richard leading the way, his stick in hand, and Adam following on behind, the heavy bag slung over his shoulder, now dreaming of a hot stew.

The dog heard them before they saw him. It smelt their stale odour on the wind and then caught the smell of the dead goose. A gobbet of sticky saliva hung from its mouth, and it bared its yellow teeth. As the pair approached, it raised its head and then lumbered to its feet and growled once more, a low rumble that came from the back of the throat. It yanked at the chain. The post it was tied to moved very slightly in the icy ground.

Richard swung his stick and tapped it on the road as he walked. He was happy and content and began to sing a rude minstrel song that had suddenly come to mind. The mastiff lurched forward, tightening the chain around its neck and tugging at the post. It loosened a fraction more, but still the dog was held. Then, with one final effort, it hurled itself at them. The chain tautened and strained and then, with a loud crack, the wooden post flew out of the earth.

Adam and Richard froze for an instant in disbelief, then turned and ran for their lives. The dog bounded after, dragging the heavy chain and post behind. Adam could hear the clanking of iron on the icy road drawing ever closer. His smooth leather soles slipped on the hard and rutted mud, throwing him off-balance and making it difficult for him to run faster. Ahead he could see the great oak, the old tree that for centuries had been the playground of many a young boy in the village. If only he could make it there he would be safe. His heart pounded within his chest.

Richard ran on ahead, racing for his life. He dived at the tree, scrabbled his foot onto a low branch, and swung himself up. "Throw me the goose," he shouted.

Adam turned his head to see the dog closing in on him, its teeth bared. He grabbed the bag from his shoulder and swung it towards the tree. As the heavy goose left his hand, he overbalanced and his foot slid on a patch of ice. His ankle twisted and he fell clumsily to the ground. The mastiff closed in on him, hungry for the kill. Adam cried out. All of a sudden the wooden post that was dragging behind the dog bounced high and became entangled in the branches of a thorn bush. For an instant the mastiff stopped. It twisted and pulled. Then there was the cracking of a branch and the post flew free. But this was all the time Adam needed. Somehow he clambered to his feet again and limped the last few feet to the tree. The dog snapped at his heels.

"Grab hold," cried Richard, reaching his arm down for Adam to catch. As their hands met he pulled, and Adam was jerked up into the bough. The bull mastiff leapt high and clamped its jaws around Adam's twisted right ankle. It hung there, its teeth ripping through his hose and the thin flesh inside, its full weight tearing at the bone. Adam screamed in agony. Richard swung the stick and struck the dog a blow across its head. It yelped and let go, falling to the ground, where it leaped and snarled at them.

Richard quickly pulled his brother up higher to safety. Blood dripped from Adam's damaged leg onto the frozen ground below. He gently prodded his blood soaked ankle with his finger and winced. "Hell's teeth! I think it's broken." He squeezed his shin with his strong hands trying to stop the searing pain rising further up his leg. "What do we do now?"

Richard looked around. They were safe in the tree for the moment, but the bull mastiff was still scrabbling at the trunk and trying as best it could to reach them. It showed no signs of giving up the chase. Nobody was about, and the chill February air began to penetrate their shaken bones.

"Throw the goose to him." Adam's voice cut through the barking.

"Are you mad? How many days has it been since we had meat?"

"I don't care! Just throw the goose!" shouted Adam. "Please, just get the dog away."

Richard looked at the goose and then at the pain on his brother's face and realised he had no option. He pulled the dead bird from the bag and then, holding it by the neck, he swung it back and forward, gaining momentum. With a final thrust, he let go and the goose curved through the air and landed with a dull thud some distance away. The mastiff heard it land and caught its scent. It turned from the tree and lumbered over to the bird, sniffed it and then tore into it hungrily.

"Quick! Down!" whispered Adam. Richard clambered over him and jumped the last few feet to the ground. Adam twisted in the branches, keeping his injured foot clear, then dropped down. He flinched in pain as he hit the ground, and clamped his jaw tight, trying not to cry out. Richard pulled him up and ducked his head under his arm to support him. With one last glance at the dog that was now ripping the goose apart, the brothers hobbled homeward.

It was the next day that the fever hit. Adam's mother had washed and then bound his ankle with an old cloth torn into strips. She fed him a warm broth and told him to rest. He had slept fitfully, tossing and turning and trying to ignore the throbbing pain from his leg. And then, as dawn broke, the fever began. Every joint in his body burned with an intense fire, and he shivered and shook even though covered in thick blankets. His mind wandered through hazy mists, in and out of consciousness.

There was a knock at the door. Isabel rose from her place next to her son and quietly crossed the room to open it. "Oh, it's you. What do you want?" she said, her voice full of poison.

The pretty girl waiting outside lowered her eyes. "I thought I might see him. I heard he was ill."

Isabel looked her up and down, unable to disguise her disapproval.

"And what is it to you if he is?" she said.

"I … I just thought … perhaps I could help…" The girl raised her eyes a little in the hope that she would find mercy.

"Oh, you did, did you? And how might you do that, I wonder? Do you think that I cannot give him all the help he needs? Am I not able…"

"Hush, mother!" Richard's voice cut through the darkness of the room, "Let her come in if she so wishes, she can't do any more harm than has already been done".

Isabel grunted and turned from the door, her back to the girl.

Agneta stepped gingerly across the threshold and waited a moment for her eyes to adjust to the gloom. She glanced around the room, making out the few pieces of plain furniture that lined the walls. Finally her eyes alighted on the mound of blankets on the pallet in the corner. Adam stirred beneath them and let out a moan. Agneta took a step towards him, her heart thumping, but then caught herself and stopped. She needed to remember where she was.

Isabel seated herself on the low wooden stool next to the bed. "Richard, bring me a damp cloth."

Agneta watched as Richard soaked a rag in a basin of cold water, wrung it out and handed it to his mother. Isabel laid it gently on Adam's forehead, patting it down with her fingers.

Richard walked over to Agneta, who seemed frozen to the spot with fear. He pressed softly in the middle of her back, urging her forward. She took a hesitant step towards the bed, watching Isabel for any sign of threat, but Isabel did not take her eyes off her son. Agneta drew closer then stopped and stood awkwardly at the bedside. She looked from

Isabel's hard features to the fevered yet handsome face of her Adam. Her eyes began to fill.

"Stop snivelling, girl," muttered Isabel. "It will do you no good, nor him either."

"I just want him to be well."

"Oh, and I know why that would be."

Agneta reddened. "I should not have come." She spoke in no more than a whisper.

"No, you should not." Isabel's voice was sharp. It cut the air.

Agneta could take no more. Suddenly she turned and ran for the door, desperately trying to hide the sob that was rising from within. She flung the door open and ran outside. Richard chased after her and caught her up a few yards down the road. He reached out his arm to grab her, but she pushed him away. "Leave me! Let me go!" she cried, and wiped the tears from her cheeks with her hand. "Please, just go."

"Agneta, I am so sorry. Just ignore her, she has no right to talk to you like that."

"Doesn't she? How do you know?"

Richard looked puzzled. "What do you mean?"

"Nothing. Nothing at all. Now leave me. I had best be away home." Agneta stepped away from him and headed down the road, still wiping her face.

"He loves you, you know," Richard called after her. She hesitated for just a moment, then continued down the street.

The fever continued for two more days. Isabel and Richard never left his side; there was always one of them watching and praying over him. At times he woke briefly with a start and cried out, at others he seemed to slip from them into another world. He dreamt of wild beasts and fire, of ice and storms. He dreamt of Agneta. Isabel kept a cold damp cloth on his head to stem the raging temperature, and checked his ankle often for signs of healing. The swelling began to go, and the raw ripped flesh caked over with a dry brown crust. And then, on the third day and quite suddenly, the heat in his body abated and he woke with a shiver. He opened his eyes and tried to focus through the gloom. Someone moved, a blurred body close to him. His mother reached out her hand and stroked his forehead.

"Hello, my son," she said tenderly. "Welcome back."

Chapter 2 - The Crow-black Gown

The following two weeks saw Adam return to full health. Whatever poison had entered his body through the bite of the dog had now surely gone, but his ankle would never mend. At first he was unable to put any weight on it, and hopped from one wall to the next in an attempt to get around the house. Richard cut him a fine forked branch that served as a crutch, and bit by bit he began to stand on his foot.

But the damage was done, and his ankle would never be the same again. He would live his life with a limp, for there was no way of healing the scars and strengthening the twisted joints. It was not a bad limp – he had seen many worse in the village and more so in Oxford town; results of accidents or of deformities caused in the heat of battle, soldiers returning from Scotland or France with a limb missing, or blinded or disfigured of face – but his crooked foot was enough to mark him out from the majority of his friends and would always affect his gait.

Agneta saw him often in that fortnight, stealing away with him when he left the house to exercise. She would take his arm and put it around her neck, supporting him as he painfully tested out his weight, and enjoying the nearness of his body against hers. She cajoled him when he was down and encouraged him to walk further and further each day.

Adam brooded much, often saying nothing and trying not to catch her eye. She tried to console him, but the very thought of limping throughout his life made him angry. When he did speak it came out in self-pity. Richard tried to make him laugh, but what they soon all realised was that it would take much more than a few silly jokes to lift his heart. What he needed was a challenge. And this came one day in the form of St. Austel's Fair.

The fair had been held at Oxford for as long as anyone could remember and it always generated a buzz of excitement in the villages around. Everyone went to the fair, to buy, to sell, to be entertained, or simply to get drunk. Every year troupes of entertainers, hawkers and minstrels travelled in from all the outlying towns to gather in the castle grounds for three days of festivities. And each year amidst the music, food and acrobatics there was an archery competition.

One day Richard approached Adam as he sat rubbing his ankle. "Shall we go to the Fair?" he asked. "It is only a few days away."

Adam carried on rubbing his foot. "And how do you think will I get there? It's four miles to Oxford. I can't walk that far." His voice trailed off as disappointment came flooding in.

"You could ride Beatrix and Agneta and I will walk alongside. Come on, it will be fun! Besides there will be an archery competition. And you *are* the best archer around!"

Adam knew this to be true and he knew also that it would be an opportunity to prove himself. He was becoming bored of sulking and he needed to get on with his life again, and what better way than by beating the competition with a longbow.

"Fine," he said. "I will go, and I'll win the prize for Agneta!"

"And for me," laughed Richard, and punched him on the arm.

Two days later they saddled the old nag Beatrix and made their way along the well-worn track to Oxford. Richard held the reigns and walked a little in front, allowing Agneta to walk alongside Adam. The day was cold and they walked as quickly as they could to keep warm under the leaden sky.

They rounded a corner just outside the city walls and stopped in their tracks. There at the gallows hung the bloated bodies of two men, swinging lazily in the gentle breeze. Richard called to Agneta to hold the reigns and ran up to them to see if they were anyone he knew, but Adam turned his head away. He had never been able to look at these swollen and decaying corpses, set up as a warning to the illiterate population that thieves and murderers would not be tolerated. Just as the paintings and sculptures in the churches reminded the faithful of the torment of hell and the beauty of heaven, so these cold naked figures, twisting on their ropes, reminded people of the eternal dangers of sin. The law was in charge, and the law was severe. He crossed himself and looked at the sky.

By the time they reached the castle the festivities were in full swing, and the air was filled with the clamour of the crowds and the smell of cooking. Large throngs of onlookers clustered around as jugglers in bright coloured chequers threw flaming torches high into the air, acrobats spun and danced, and mummers in wonderful costumes played tricks on the unsuspecting.

A group of dwarfs and humpity-backs ran and jumped through hoops of fire, making people laugh. A woman wobbled precariously as she balanced upside down on the sharp point of an iron sword; a man clothed in rags told stories to a jostling group of excited children. Here and there young women in scarlet hoods plied their trade, winking at every young man that passed.

A large mob had gathered around a large tethered bear which was being bated by a pack of dogs. It bellowed as the dogs growled and rushed in, lashing out a great claw and tearing into them as they mauled at it with gaping jaws. And all around were people dancing to the tunes of the musicians. After such a winter of hardship, the people of Oxford were out to celebrate.

"Over there!" shouted Richard, above the noise.

Adam looked to where a small group of archers had assembled. The longbow competition was already well under way, and Adam watched as a stout red faced youth braced himself and fired uncertainly at the target.

"Come on, let's go!" cried Richard, tugging at his sleeve. They tethered Beatrix to a rail and raced over as quickly as Adam's foot would allow. Richard introduced his brother to the judges and Adam bowed low. There were about a dozen archers but only one that he recognised. His name was Hugh Cooper and he came from a small-holding just outside Wolvercot. Although about the same age, he stood a full three hand-spans taller than Adam and he was broad across the shoulders with arms muscular from farm work and fighting. He had an ugly face with a whispery beard. His eyes were set just too far apart for comfort, and his nose, broken on more than one occasion, now pointed somewhat to one side. He was surrounded by a small gang of fawning youths, each swigging from a tankard of ale.

One of the gang lifted his free hand high in the air and pointed to Adam. He said something to Hugh Cooper, who stared for a moment and then walked slowly over to Adam, faking a comical limp by dragging one foot on the ground. His companions laughed and jeered, making Cooper act up even more. Adam felt his face redden. Hugh Cooper stood too close and towered over him. He glared down and the smell of his breath rankled.

"Well, well, look who's here!" His voice was heavy with ale. "And who are you aiming to impress, crook-foot? Your girl? She won't be wanting you for long!" He motioned towards Agneta, and leered at her. She turned her head in disgust. For a long moment, he stood and stared at her, then with his finger and thumb he flicked Adam on the cheek, as though brushing away a bothersome fly. Adam flinched, and Hugh laughed. Then with a snort of contempt he walked off and joined his smirking friends. Adam looked in embarrassment at Agneta, not knowing what to say or how to defend her. This was not the first time he had lost out to Hugh.

All of the other contestants had now fired their three allotted arrows. The small flat disk of straw that made up the target was a good two hundred paces away and not easy to hit, let alone the red painted circle in the centre. Many of the arrows missed completely, or clung to the outer rings by their tips. Despondent archers muttered together and took consolation that none of them was very good. Hugh Cooper, in contrast, had done well with his first two arrows hitting the mark, though not quite in the centre. The official nodded at him, and Cooper sauntered up to the toe line. He smiled at the crowd around him, soaking up the adulation and recognising that he was about to win the prize. He loaded the bow, paused and then shot. His arrow landed on the very edge of the red centre circle, and stuck fast. A ripple of applause greeted him and he bowed toward his admirers.

"You are late and can have but one flight," said the official to Adam. "Better to be on time next year."

"Go on," nudged Richard, "You can do it." Agneta kissed him on the cheek.

Adam bent a little over the bow and gripped the arrow and string in the first joint of his fingers. As he straightened his back, he pulled the goose feather fletching of the arrow to his ear. He felt the incredible tension in the bow string straining in the muscles of his arm and across his shoulder blades. He aimed at the centre, at that small red area the size of a man's heart, and focussed his hatred on Hugh Cooper. He was about to loose the arrow when he stopped. He had a better idea. He closed one eye and just touched his cheek lightly on the feather. He needed to be more accurate than ever before. He wanted to hit more than just the target, and for that he needed all the concentration he could muster. He slowed his breathing, closed one eye and focussed with the other down the straight shaft of the ash wood arrow, past the iron-sharp head and then across the courtyard to the target. He inhaled gently then held his breath. Time stood still. The crowd were motionless. He waited. Someone cried out, "He's lost his nerve!" and a peal of laughter rang through the onlookers. Adam ignored them. He felt a surge of anger rising within him, and he reacted to the twin injustices of being crippled and being bullied. Very slowly he moved his bow arm a fraction to the right, his eyes narrowed on the protruding wooden shaft of Cooper's arrow. He gently loosened his grip and let go. There was a whistle as the arrow shot through the air and then a crack of splintering wood as it split Cooper's in two down the centre and lodged itself in the target. A gasp went up from the assembled crowd. Richard laughed and patted him on the back.

The officials ran to the target and began a heated discussion. Hugh Cooper staggered over to them and started shouting angrily, stabbing a wild finger at Adam. The debate went on for some time, but eventually one of the judges walked towards the archers, now lined up on a dais, and cleared his throat.

"Today we have seen a fine display of archery from across the region; archers have come from Aylesbury and Missenden, from Chalgrove and Wallingford, and of course from Oxford." He paused while the crowd hooted and applauded. "But there is one outstanding archer, even though his method is … unconventional. I hereby proclaim a winner, and give you…" he paused to build the tension, the declared majestically, "Master Adam Wolvercot."

He raised Adam's arm in the air and a cheer went up. Those nearest to him grabbed at his arms and legs and threw him up onto their shoulders to parade him around in victory. The crowd waved and shouted all the more. A minstrel joined the parade, playing a feisty tune on his pipes. Hugh Cooper continued to shout at the judges, but then stormed off with his gang in tow. Finally the mob became bored, dropped Adam to the ground and went in search of ale.

Adam stood a little dazed and caught his breath. Then out of nowhere he heard a thin cold voice from behind. Something about it made his blood freeze.

"Well done, well done indeed, my archer friend."

He turned and saw a man much taller than him, dressed in a long crow-black gown and a hood that completely covered his face. "I have something for you, which I am sure you will find of interest. Call it a gift from my master."

The man reached inside his gown with a pale thin hand and drew out a velum roll tied with a black ribbon. He took Adam's hand and placed the vellum in his palm, then folded his fingers over it. His nails were bitten to the quick. "Read it with care for it contains your future."

Then the thin man stepped backwards and began to turn away. Someone brushed against him in the jostling crowd and for a brief moment his hood was pulled back from his face. Adam stared in disbelief at a kind of face he had never seen before. It was so pale that it looked like winter, and was topped with a short-cropped dusting of snow-white hair. The face had no beard or moustache to mark the strange creature as a man. But what struck Adam most were his eyes. They were no ordinary eyes; they were pink.

And then the stranger turned and was gone, melting mysteriously into the mass of bodies. Adam clutched the vellum roll tightly in his fist and pushed his way after him, but to no avail. The man had somehow dissolved in the crowd, as snow melts in the sun. Adam shuddered as an icy fear coursed through his veins, and the hair on his neck bristled. Suddenly, a strong hand gripped his shoulder. Adam yelped and swung round, striking out with his fist.

"Watch out, brother!" cried Richard, catching Adam's hand. "It's me. I thought I had lost you. Come on, I'll buy you an ale."

Chapter 3 - Seek the Plowman

Adam stowed the vellum roll in his bag, and they headed off to the nearest tavern. His heart was still thumping as Richard banged a tankard down on the trestle table in front of him, slopping ale onto the table, and slid another across towards Agneta.

"Did you see that man?" asked Adam.

"Who?"

"The man with pink eyes. He was tall – a head and shoulders above the crowd." He hesitated. "He gave me this." Adam pulled the vellum from his bag and laid it on the table. The three looked at it in silence.

"So are you going to open it?" asked Richard after a moment.

"I... I don't know. He said it would be my future."

"Don't be so stupid!" retorted Richard. "He was probably some poor fortune teller trying to make a fast penny. It will be some nonsense or other."

He grabbed at the roll, but Adam shot out his hand and stopped him. "No. I must do this."

He held the soft calfskin in his palm and looked at Agneta. Then he pulled gently at the black ribbon, the knot untied and the thin vellum unrolled. On it were written words in a dark brown ink. The lettering was written neatly as if with a practised hand, and formed a poem.

"What does it say?" asked Agneta. Adam read it slowly out loud:

> *In Merton's find a book to see*
> *The secret opened with a key*
> *The plowman digs in furrows deep*

But canst thou now the treasure keep?
A priest that's poor in misery
He now awaits his gift from thee
Give to this man and feed his sheep
So raise your father from his sleep.

"I told you it was nonsense," said Richard.

Agneta scowled at him, "It's a poem, and poems hold mysteries."

Adam read it again to himself. Something in the last line pulled at his heart. *So raise your father from his sleep.* Was this a reference to *his* father, Jacob? His father who disappeared all those years ago, who his mother said had died of the pestilence, whom he had loved and missed through all his years of growing up. Why had some stranger given him these words that said he could be raised from his sleep? He was dead, so how could he be raised? What did it all mean? Adam closed his eyes and tried hard to concentrate. Could it be that Jacob was not dead after all? For the first time in many years he felt hope rise in his heart. Was he alive? Could he, Adam, find his father again? He blinked back a tear.

"Are you alright?" It was Agneta.

Adam opened his eyes and nodded. "Just the cold wind." He supped at his mug, and re-read the poem.

In Merton's find a book to see
The secret opened with a key

A key. His key. They knew about the key around his neck. No, this was not nonsense. This was a puzzle that needed to be solved. And somehow or another it had to be solved by him. He read the poem again, looking for clues. What did he have to do?

Agneta came and put her arm around his neck and sat on his knee. "Don't let it worry you," she said, "It's only a poem. There's no harm in a bit of poetry now and again."

Adam shrugged her off. "No, this is serious. I have to find my father. He has sent a message to me."

"How? He's dead!" said Richard. "He can't speak from beyond the grave. You've just been scared, that's all."

"This poem is telling me something. I have to do something."

Richard snatched the vellum from his hand. "Why not start at the beginning?" He read slowly, his finger marking the words one by one as he concentrated on forming the words. He read out loud, "In *Merton's find a book to see.*" Then he lifted his palms nonplussed.

Adam spoke up, "Do you remember where father used to work? It was at the library at Merton's College, where all the books were kept. *In Merton's find a book to see.* We need to go to Merton's College."

"The library is huge. It must hold many thousands of books," said Richard. "How do we find this one?"

"I don't know, but we must go and try. If we do, we can maybe find him and bring him home. I don't know what we are looking for or what it means, but something tells me we must at least try. The college is just down the road and we could go there now." Adam looked from Richard to Agneta and back, hoping to find some sense of adventure in their faces, but there was none.

Eventually Agneta smiled at him. "Come on, Richard, let's finish here and go with him. He'll not rest until we do."

Richard grunted. He was never keen to finish his ale in a hurry, or to leave one half-drunk. He needed an excuse to stay. "But we don't even know where the library is. All we know is that it is inside the college but we can't get in. We are not college fellows."

Agneta stood up. "Leave this one to me," she said, and disappeared into the murky smoke filled room, squeezing her slim figure between drinkers who had been there too long. After a little while she came back. "Let's go. I've found out something of use." She took Adam by the hand and then coaxed Richard from his stool. "Those men are blabbermouths when they are soaked in ale. They speak too much and too freely, especially to a pretty girl!" She laughed.

They headed down the cobbled High Street away from the castle, and turning right at the church of St Mary the Virgin they saw the spire on the chapel of Merton College straight ahead of them at the end of Magpie Lane.

Merton College had already stood on the edge of Oxford for over one hundred and thirty years; a solid house of learning for those wealthy enough or educated enough to benefit from it. Behind its grand exterior was hidden the quadrangle, and in this lay the library which was already famous as the first in all academia. The original old library had been outgrown and a new one was built to replace it. The new library had only been completed in the year that Adam was born. This library was their goal, and one of the books within it.

The entrance of the college was guarded by two large iron gates that were closed and locked. Behind these sat the well - rounded figure of the warden, who was contentedly picking pieces off a greasy pie and shovelling them into his mouth. He held a pikestaff in his free hand and every now and then wiped his other on the filthy robes that once had marked him out as a man of office.

Richard left the others a little away behind and approached him. "My good man, may we have access to the Quad?"

The Warden looked him over, noting his tired and well-worn clothing. "You do not seem to be a Fellow of this college," he said, "and I am not authorised to grant access to anyone who does not study here."

"I thought you might say that," said Richard, and he dug deeply into his bag and pulled out two pennies. "Perhaps you would care to look after these for me?"

The Warden raised himself from his seat with some effort and looked down his nose. "If that is a bribe, Sir, then you had best be on your way before I call the constable and have you locked up. Now be gone!"

Richard opened his mouth to say something, and then thought better of it. Instead he made a great show of pocketing the pennies and turning on his heel to re-join Adam and Agneta.

"He won't let us in, so we are going to have to find some other way to get to this library of yours. Let's look around and see if there is a wall we can scale." He headed off down the street, leaving Agneta and a hobbling Adam a short way behind.

They had not gone far when a commotion broke out. Suddenly there was a great uproar, and they turned to see a mob of angry young men standing in the street, rattling at the gate and shouting abuse. They were obviously drunk and in a fighting mood and had appeared out of nowhere to throw a few punches at the chamber-dekkyns who were gathering inside the gates. These were students from the rough end of life who had somehow begged or blagged their way into the college against all the odds. The youth of the town knew they carried grudges and were easily provoked. Goading them into fighting was a favourite sport.

A rallying cry went up within the college grounds and more dekkyns ran from all directions across the square towards the gates. The warden tried to calm the situation by waving his pike at them, but one of them grabbed at the weapon as it swept past him and twisted it out of the older man's grasp. Another student shouted at him to get out of the way. The warden, quickly seeing that all was lost, seized his opportunity, and ran for his life towards the safety of the college door.

The dekkyns, now unhindered, faced the town youth across the bolted gates. Each side jeered at the other, throwing insults and curses. "Come and get us then!" shouted one of the youths from the town. With a great roar, the dekkyns pulled open the bolts and swung wide the gates. All hell was let loose. Knives and daggers were drawn and the flash of metal blades caught in the fast-ebbing winter sunshine. Blood was soon flowing and fists flew in all directions as the fighting gathered in ferocity. The dekkyn with the pike swung it like a scythe, driving the town youths back from the gates and into the street. For just a moment the gates were wide open and deserted.

"Quick," cried Richard, "Now is our chance. Run!" He grabbed Agneta by the arm and ran with her towards the opening. Adam hobbled after and just squeezed in as two youths grappled each other to the floor, one with his hands clenched around the other's throat.

They ran as fast as they could past the end of the church and into the small passageway by the entrance to the Hall. Agneta pointed to a small archway in the wall and they tumbled through this and into the Quadrangle. They found themselves in the relative peace of a square courtyard surrounded by the honey coloured walls of four stone buildings.

"Where now?" asked Adam, looking about him at the courtyard. There were a number of doors, any of which could have opened into the library.

"Over there, opposite the church – that's the library!" cried Agneta. "The man in the tavern told me where to look," she added with pride in her voice.

They ran across the empty Quad towards the nearest of the two wooden doors that gave access to the building. By the time Adam got there, Richard had already tried the handle.

"No good," he said, "It's locked. Try the other one in the corner."

Adam hurried to the second door, and wrenched at the handle. There was a slight squeak of hinges that needed oiling and the door opened a fraction. "Come on," he said.

"Wait a minute," whispered Richard, "we should leave one of us on watch just in case somebody comes. Agneta should stay here. I have a little learning, but she has none, so I can be of more use to you. I know my letters and could help find the book."

"Alright," replied Adam. "Here, Agneta, hold my bow and keep a guard. If anyone comes then run and find us."

Adam and Richard opened the door just enough for them to squeeze inside and disappeared into the dark. Agneta pulled her hood up against the evening cold and looked about her. She could still hear the noise of battle from the gatehouse; everyone was over there, and the Quad was empty.

Once inside the building, the two brothers took a moment for their eyes to adjust to the gloom. In front of them was a large wooden staircase leading upwards, and to their left a corridor with doors opening from it. As they took all this in, they heard the squeak of wooden floorboards above them. Distant muffled voices were becoming louder as the speakers' footsteps drew closer to the top of the stairs.

"Hide. Quickly!" Adam's hushed voice was tense. They crept along the corridor, trying door after door until they found one that opened, and silently slipped inside. The voices in the corridor grew clearer as the bursar and his student descended the staircase.

"Thank you Master Radle, you have been a great help."

"Oh, not at all! If you have found the book you need, I am well pleased."

Adam heard the door to the Quad open and then slam shut, followed by the unmistakeable clank and grind of a large key being inserted and turned in the lock. The voices receded as master and scholar walked away.

"Hell! We're locked in!" exclaimed Richard. "Some treasure this must be!"

"Then let us go and find it."

They climbed the carved wooden stairs and found themselves in a long L-shaped room, which followed the shape of the corner of the Quad. On both sides stood rows and rows of bookcases, each one set at right angles to the wall and lit by thin windows which, as the sun was setting, let in shafts of golden light that striped the floor. Between the cases were benches for seating and shelves on which to stand the books while reading them.

And what books they were! Written on parchment, rough paper and vellum and encased in wooden covers, their ragged page ends jutted out from the shelves, the backs of the books hidden from view. Each had a long metal chain dangling from its cover and linking it with a ring to a metal bar that ran horizontally the length of the bookcase. These manuscript books were not intended to be removed from this building. They were expensive treasures which had taken many months or even years to hand-write. They needed to be kept locked up.

"Where on this earth do we begin?" said Richard as he stared open-mouthed at the sight in front of him.

Adam had taken the vellum roll from his bag and was reading it once more, searching for clues. He read aloud,

> *"In Merton's find a book to see*
> *The secret opened with a key*
> *The plowman digs in furrows deep*
> *But canst thou now the treasure keep?"*

Richard wandered over to the window and stared out at the courtyard, looking for Agneta. But she must have been directly below him and out of sight, for she was nowhere to be seen.

Suddenly Adam exclaimed, "The plowman, the plowman digs in furrows deep. I think we need a book with something about a plowman. See, the bookcases are arranged in order – there is *philosophi* and there *mathematici*. Look for something to do with farming, but I do not know what word they would use to describe it."

Adam limped off in one direction and Richard shrugged his shoulders and wandered off in the other. He stared up at the large capital letters carved on the top of each bookcase, describing the nature of the books contained on the shelves below, but struggled to make any sense of the Latin words.

"Come here, Richard. This may be it!" Adam shouted in excitement. He was standing by a case with the word *agricultura* carved above it and was reading a board fixed to the end of the bookcase, which showed the titles and the order of the books. Richard joined him and together they studied the list looking for the word 'plowman'. Many of the books were in Latin and some in French and only a few in the newly accepted language of English.

"It's not here," admitted Adam eventually. "What now?" He slumped to the floor in a patch of light and pulled the vellum roll out once more. "What is your secret?" he muttered to himself. "What a riddle you pose! You and your poem."

Suddenly Richard called out "That's it! That's it! It's a poem! We should be looking for a poem!" and he began to run down the room. "What is the Latin for poem?" he shouted.

"I don't know, but look for anything like it."

They scoured the bookcases, and before long Adam came across a bookcase marked *Poesis*. He ran his finger down the list of books on the end of the case. In the second column he came across a title that made his heart thump. *Piers Plowman*. He counted the number of books in the column above it, fourteen, fifteen, sixteen, and then swung himself around to the front of the case and counted the books off until he reached number sixteen. It was a small book with neat edges and thin pages made of parchment. He pulled it out and began to flick through it, looking for any signs. Somewhere near the middle of the book, deep in its furrows, he saw an inscription written diagonally across the page in three or four short lines and for Adam the hand that wrote it was all too familiar. His breath caught in his chest.

"It's father. He has written in this book. I have seen his writing many times and I know that this is his hand. But I can't make out the lettering, it's getting too dark in here and the words are faint."

Richard rushed up to him. "Then let's take it with us," he suggested.

"And how do we do that?" asked Adam looking at the chains that held it bound.

"You have a key," replied his brother, "perhaps that is why father gave it to you. He said to keep it for a special time, and this could be it. It could unlock the book."

The metal rod that held the books in chains was itself fastened to the end of the bookcase with a metal strip containing two small locks. Adam pulled the string at his neck and the key came loose from his tunic. He held it for a moment in his hand, feeling its warmth and familiarity. Richard pulled at it, "Hurry up, we need to do this quickly!"

Adam took a deep breath and put the key in the bottom keyhole. It slid a little way in and then jammed. He jiggled it around and tried to force it in. But it caught on the metal barrel of the lock and would not turn. He pulled it out and tried the key in the top lock, but again he could not make it fit. He swore beneath his breath. So what was the key for, he wondered, if not for this?

A high-pitched scream cut through his thoughts. Richard ran to the window and looked down. Agneta was below but there was also someone else; a large thick-set man dressed in a woollen tunic and hose, his mantle cast to the ground. Hugh Cooper had one arm around her shoulder and was trying to catch her by the hand as she tried to fight him off. She looked up at the window with fear in her face and screamed again. Cooper just smiled through a beery haze and clapped his hand over her mouth.

"We have got to leave. Now!" shouted Richard at Adam and he began to run towards the staircase.

Adam reached for the book that was now lying on the shelf. It was open at the page with the inscription. Without a further thought, he took his knife from its sheath and cut through the page at the binding, and tore it out. Clutching it in his hand, he hobbled after his brother.

Richard was by now at the foot of the stairs and was hammering on the thick wooden door.

"Leave her alone!" he shouted. He put his shoulder to the door but it was locked fast. He looked around him in panic, acutely aware of the sounds of struggling coming from outside, and then ran up the corridor to the only other door which led to the Quad. He barged at it with his shoulder then tried stepping back and kicking with all his strength. Nothing moved. He ran back down the corridor to find Adam who had finally made it down the stairs.

"It's no good! We are locked in!" his voice was heavy with desperation.

Adam looked around to see what else could be done. There in the corner of the hallway sat a heavy oak chair. They dragged it over to the window and Adam lifted it above his head and launched it at the glass. It smashed through one of the small panes of lead crystal that made up the window. He smashed the next one and the next, breaking glass and wood until the hole he created was big enough to squeeze through.

Richard pushed him out of the way and climbed through first, dropping to the ground outside with a crunch. He leapt at Cooper, grabbed him by the neck, and pulled him off Agneta who by now was sobbing with distress. The two men stumbled and fell to the floor, but Richard was sober and faster and jumped quickly to his feet. As Cooper struggled to his knees, Richard drew his sword and held it to his opponent's throat. Adam had by now climbed through the window, landing painfully on his right foot. He yelped and hobbled over to where they stood immobile. Richard was panting heavily with short furious breaths. A rivulet of sweat ran down his face, and he stared through eyes full of hatred at Cooper. Agneta let out a sob. In that moment, time stood still. Then Adam acted. He clenched his fist and with all his might struck Cooper a blow across the face. Cooper put his hand to his cheek and shook his head to clear it, but before he could react further Adam laid him another blow and he crumpled to the floor, weak, drunk and battered, and lay motionless upon the cold earth.

Adam glowered at him for an instant and then ran to Agneta. He caught her in his arms and they embraced.

"You are safe now," he promised. "He will not hurt you again." She nestled her head against his neck and he could feel the soft warmth of tears on his skin.

A crunch of footsteps on the gravel path alerted them to a figure approaching through the gloom. Master Peter Radle, the bursar, was making his way towards them, his hand nervously fingering the pommel of the dagger at his belt.

They inched back from the body on the ground, Adam reached for his longbow, and then they turned and ran as fast as they were able across the Quad to the archway and safety. As they passed through the arch, Adam looked back and could make out the bursar kneeling over the dark prostrate form of Hugh Cooper.

Once outside, they slowed their pace and headed home through the shadowy streets. As they neared the castle they could hear the sounds of singing and music as the townsfolk danced and played. There was a hum of chatter and laughter as people enjoyed the festivities and drank in the atmosphere. Then out of the castle gate streamed a great procession of men, women and children, all following a raggle-taggle line of dancing mummers dressed in bright coloured clothes. Each wore a mask; a dragon or an angel, a swan or perhaps a baboon. There were stars, pheasants and snakes, and all mingled together to create a chain of riotous colour and noise. Torch bearers lit their way as they jumped and danced, their costumes flapping as though themselves alive.

Ahead of them played a band. A man playing a sackbut and another on a shawm played a melody with haunting notes, the strings of the rebecs and citoles jangled behind them, and all this was accompanied by a rhythmic beating of the tabors. Together they played tunes that in turn excited and then soothed the onlookers. The procession snaked its way down the street, delighting the adults and scaring the children.

The three friends stopped for a moment to watch, caught up in the frenzy of the scene. The mummers were playing with the crowd, talking to those they recognised as friends, making wild gestures at others, waving at the children.

And as they passed by, a tall man masked as a bird of prey with hooked beak and piercing eyes reached over and tugged at Adam's sleeve. He pulled him close in so that the evil beak scratched against his face, and spoke in a whisper, just audible above the noise.

"You have it?" he asked. Adam nodded involuntarily, as though forced into admission.

"Good." The mask moved away, but as it did Adam could just make out the hint of pink behind the eyeholes. Then the mummer turned and joined the rest and danced away down the street. It all happened in a moment, and was over.

Chapter 4 - Ale at the Angel

Early the next morning Adam shook Richard awake, then took a burning ember from the fire and with it lit a tallow lamp. By its flickering flame he studied the page he had torn from the book. He called Richard closer. "Look at this," he said, pointing. "A part of the text has been marked with ink."

"What does it say?" Richard stretched and yawned and feigned interest.

Adam read aloud:

"I teach every blind buzzard to better himself
Abbots, I mean, and priors, and all kinds of prelates
and parsons, and parish priests, who should preach and
instruct
all men to amend themselves, with all their might.
Unlearned men may say of you that the beam lies in your
eyes
And the speck of filth has fallen, by your fault, mainly
Into all manner of men's eyes, you maledict priests!"

Richard scratched himself and tried to concentrate. Adam held the page nearer to the light and studied the page more closely, trying to make out the fainter marks of a hurried pen, the marks made by Jacob de Wolvercot. He slowly read them aloud to Richard. *'Adam, my son, not all priests are bad... At the church in Lutterworth … is a book. Find it and it will lead you to a … Poor Priest who is good. He needs your help.'*

"What in the name of mercy is this all about?" asked Adam staring at the scrawled words, willing them to reveal their secrets.

The door opened with a cold blast and Isabel came in from the street carrying a large jar of water. Adam tried to hide the page under the blanket, but she had already seen it and let out a gasp. She set the pitcher down and held out her hand.

"Let me see that, if it is what I think it is."

Adam handed her the sheet and she studied it for a moment, recognising her husband's handwriting, but not the words. Her shoulders sagged and she slumped wearily onto the bed.

"So you have it at last," she whispered. "I hoped and prayed this day would not come." She held the page in both hands and Adam could see that she was trembling. "What does it say?" she asked.

Adam took it from her and read it out. Isabel turned her face from him as the shock set in. Then she checked herself, shook her head to regain her composure and sighed. "Tell me how you came by it."

Adam recounted the story, avoiding any mention of Agneta whose name was not welcome in the house. Richard butted in at times to give his point of view. At sixteen it was all an adventure to him, and as he told of his part in finding the book and fighting Hugh Cooper, he was blind to the pain it was causing his mother. But Adam could see, and so he spoke gently and carefully, watching her face for signs of distress. He pulled the vellum roll out from his leather pouch and read the poem to her. There was a time of silence, of decision making that came hard, and then Isabel spoke.

"There is much I must tell you. I have not wanted to do so until the time was right because you are both so precious to me. I have tried to protect you from the truth, for I fear what will be. But now the time has come and the matter is forced upon us. It concerns your father and what he was accused of."

Isabel inhaled deeply to steady her nerves, and then continued, her voice quavering. "Many years ago your father was involved in a matter of faith. He became caught up in a movement of men who stood against the law of the land and of the church, and as such he was hunted. I do not know all the details of what he did, for he kept it from me, but I know that his life was in constant danger. I pleaded with him many times to stop, but he said that there were greater things at stake than his own well-being and that he could not go back.

"He writes here of Lutterworth, and indeed he travelled to Lutterworth much and was often away for days. Over time he changed and he no longer was the carefree man I married. But then one day his travelling suddenly stopped and from then on he spent more time at home. He still worked at the Library, but he always had a hunted look upon his face. At night he took to barring the door of our home. And then one night ten years ago he disappeared, and I never saw him again."

"He died of the pestilence, that's what you said." Adam's face was white.

"Yes, that is what I told you. But you were so young and you would not have understood the truth. No, my son, they took him. I know they took him. And they will have tortured and then killed him. And now, as though from the grave, this comes back to haunt me." She shook the paper in her hands violently.

"Who are they, these men that took him?"

"The authorities. The lawmakers. The men from the church at Rome. Or at least those authorised by it to clean the land of heretics. And now I fear they will take you too. Oh Adam, be careful, for they have eyes everywhere and nobody is safe who dares to stand against them. Your father had business he could not finish, but do not do finish it for him. For my sake I beg you, do not do it." Isabel threw the paper to the ground and clasped Adam's hands.

Adam looked bewildered and stared at the floor in silence, thinking hard. Eventually he spoke gravely and slowly. "I think he may still be alive. If so I must find this book and deliver it and then find him and bring him home. If he believed in this cause so much that he was willing to risk his life for it, then I must honour his name and complete his task."

"But that was so many years ago. It is all in the past now and that is where it must stay! Again I beg you, do not go."

"Do you not want to have him back with you?"

"But Jacob is dead! I am sure he must be dead."

"Do you really think so? Can you really be so sure?"

Isabel wrung her hands and the anguish on her face all but hid the tiny flicker of hope that was birthed in her eyes.

Adam continued, "I have to go. It was my father's wish, and I have to go now because they have contacted me."

"And how do you know who they are? Do you think they are his friends? How do you know they are not his foes? My son, trust no one, for these are evil days. Even those you think are friends may turn upon you, for many are not what they seem. Adam, please stay. I need you here."

Adam looked about him. "So I am trapped like a bated bear! If I stay here I honour you and if I go I honour my father. Which is it to be? How do I choose between you?"

Richard jumped to his feet, his face red with excitement and his eyes blazing. "I'll go with Adam," he blurted, "and we'll find father. Don't you see? We must do this. It won't take long. We will go tomorrow, find this book and deliver it and we'll be back before the week has ended. It'll be an adventure. Trust us, mother. You need to trust us. We will be alright."

Isabel looked from one son to the other, her face drawn and pale. She knew that they had the same fighting spirit as their father Jacob, and that no words from her would ever change their minds. She looked from one to the other and then reluctantly nodded her head. "Come back soon," was all she said.

All that day they scurried about collecting together bits and pieces for the journey. They saddled their horse, Beatrix, a tired old nag that had seen better days, and loaded her with panniers, which they stuffed with blankets and a few items of extra clothing. Under these they hid a purse containing a few coins. They wrapped some bread and cheese in a cloth and stored them alongside a goatskin of water. And then they sharpened their daggers on a stone and checked the edges of their swords for damage. The roads would be dangerous with thieves and bandits, and who knew who else would be lying in wait for them. Eventually all was done, and Richard announced that he was off to the alehouse to muster his courage. Adam had other plans.

The board painted with the image of an angel creaked as it swung in the wind outside the tavern. As Richard entered, he could see that the place was full and there were no seats near the fire where he could warm himself. Revellers from the fair had taken the best places and were now noisily regaling each other with stories and anecdotes. Most were unknown to him and had likely come in from towns and villages nearby. He bowed slightly to the one or two that he did recognise and then took his ale and found a spot in a dark corner where he could lean up against a beam and watch the merriment. He drank deeply from the jug and thought about the day to come. He had never been further than Oxford –

indeed he had never in his life needed to go any further than that. What was beyond, he wondered, and what tales would he have to tell when he came back from this adventure?

A young man in his early twenties and sporting a few days' stubble on his chin pressed into the corner and stood beside him. He removed his cloak and Richard could tell that he was wealthy by the cut of his clothes. He was wearing a very short bright blue doublet over what seemed to be a fine braided tunic, and on his legs he had tight yellow hose. His feet were encased in expensive soft leather boots with the longest pointed toes that Richard had ever seen, and his head was protected by a dark blue hood which ended in a rat's tail of a liripipe, so long that it was tucked into his belt. Even his face was handsome in a way that spoke of a wealthy upbringing; he was not pockmarked or scarred like so many others. The stranger nudged Richard with his elbow.

"What a crowd tonight!" he said, and even with these few words Richard knew that he was not local. "No room here to swing a cat. Everyone has come from far and wide to the fair, and what a sight they are! Great for the picking. Did you see the bear-bait today? Three dogs fought off in one go; he was such a great beast. Never seen one that big before, or that strong. They say they feed them on blood to give them a taste for it, but I don't believe that." He sipped his beer. "Oh, pardon, I forget my manners. May I introduce myself – Master Randulf Payne at your service." He extended his hand in a friendly handshake.

"Richard Wolvercot," said Richard with a smile. "So you have travelled here for the fair. Where are you from? I don't know your accent."

"All over really, although I was brought up in the noble city of London. Have you ever been there? What an astonishing place! Full of life, just like this tavern." He laughed, and nudged Richard again, then sighed, "But the ladies are so much prettier in that city. You should see them, I tell you! You would never want to come back here again." He paused for breath. "Do you have a girl?"

"Not right now. At least not for want of trying."

"Aah, you have been spurned. I can tell, Richard when a lad has been spurned. You have that same dejected look that a dog has when he is ordered to his bed. Who was she, eh?"

Richard blushed a little. "I don't want to talk about her."

"But you still love her?"

"I ... I think so."

"Then reach out for her again. A woman is like a wild rose. The petals are soft to the eyes and perfumed to the nose and she will catch your attention and capture your heart. But in order to pick her you have to handle the stem. And the stem is so often covered in a mass of prickles that cut and tear at the flesh. But grasp the stem, Richard, go through the pain of winning her back and grab her tightly. That is the only way to make her yours."

Randulf sat back in his chair and looked smug. He had so much wisdom to dispense, and these country folk knew so little of the world and the affairs of men. Richard kept his thoughts to himself.

They fell to talking about this and that and the evening passed slowly but amiably. Randulf talked much yet drank little, and kept Richard amused with remarkable and fanciful stories. A steady flow of drinkers walked in and staggered out of the inn, putting a smile on the face of the hard-working innkeeper as he scurried to and fro with mugs of ale.

"Hold this a moment," said Richard at the end of yet another unlikely story, and he gave Randulf his empty wooden mug. "I'm just off around the back." He squeezed his way through the crowd and made his way to the stinking trough that acted as a latrine at the rear of the building. At least the flies aren't so bad at this time of year, he thought.

Meanwhile in the tavern Randulf refilled Richard's mug with ale and then withdrew a small linen pouch from his tunic. He glanced around the room to see if anyone was paying attention, but all were slowly getting drunk and were involved in heated debates and noisy conversations. Quickly he poured a small quantity of a fine brown powder from the pouch into the ale and swirled it around. He lifted it to eye level to make sure it had dissolved, and then added a touch more. He looked quizzically at the pouch, wondering how much to use, then shrugged and tipped the whole of the contents in, swirling the tankard again to remove any trace. Richard suddenly reappeared. "Ah, you have more ale! Thank you my friend," he said with a smile.

"Yes, this one is on me. I got lucky at hazard earlier today." Randulf nodded in the direction of three men who were sitting around a low table throwing dice. "Well, not so much luck – more a calculated knowledge of the odds that can help you to win every time. Oh, and loaded dice! I remember one time, playing a certain man, let's call him Master Nobrays, anyway I bet him all he had and on the final throw of the dice he gained but a one to my six and lost all. And I mean all! He left the tavern that night in nothing but the clothes he was born in! And I gained a fine set of yeoman's attire that I sold handsomely at market. " He chuckled in a childish way.

"Well, thank you for your kindness," said Richard, and lifted his mug to acknowledge Randulf.

"And to your future – whatever that may hold." Randulf watched Richard very closely as he quaffed a large mouthful of ale.

Adam left the house wrapped in his cloak and with his hood pulled well over his face to counter the bitter night wind. He had arranged to meet Agneta by the village barn, a place well known to them and to all of the other young men and women of Wolvercot. Inside he knew it would be sheltered, warm and quiet, apart from the crackle of hooves on straw as the horses and cattle stirred.

By the time he reached the barn he could see that the door was ajar. Agneta was already sheltering behind it from the wind, her arms wrapped tightly around her body. Adam squeezed through and closed the door behind him. He reached over and caressed Agneta on the cheek, then took her by the hand and led her to the ladder that climbed to the hay store above. This was to be their last night together for a while – who knew how long – and he did not want to waste it.

+

It did not take Richard long to finish his ale, and Randulf called for another.

"No, I think I have had too much already," slurred Richard, "I feel a little sick and my head is swimming. I think I should be heading home. But thank you Master Payne for your company this night. I bid you farewell." He stood to go, but the room span and he sat down again heavily.

"I think you may still need my company!" said Randulf, and he lifted Richard up and helped him towards the door. Once outside he caught his breath in the sharp wind, shivered, and said "Now which way is your home. I think I should take you there my friend, you look unwell."

Richard pointed in the direction of the cottage, and clung on to Randulf, his head thumping and his face white. Randulf unhitched his horse from the rail and heaved him on to it. Richard clutched at the reins and held on as best he could, slipping to one side or the other as the horse jolted on the rut-ridden lane that led towards the house, a warm bed and sleep. Along the way his stomach heaved and he threw up violently at the edge of the road. The short journey seemed to be taking forever, and it had begun to rain.

Chapter 5 - Warm Pottage

Randulf knocked at the cottage door, introduced himself to Isabel with a bow and quickly explained what had happened. She helped him pull Richard from the horse and between them they half-dragged him into the house and onto the bed.

"Silly child," muttered his mother, "he never could hold his ale." She looked at Randulf. "But thank you Master Payne for all your kindness. I am sure we can find some way to repay you."

Randulf, brushed his sleeve with a wet hand and shook droplets from his fingertips. "I don't suppose I could stay here and warm my bones by the fire until the rain ceases? It's starting to pour out there."

"It would be the least we could do for you," said Isabel with a smile.

"Thank you, that is kind. I am wet and cold and a warm fire would keep away the chills."

"Please, sit here." She motioned to a wooden stool set by the red embers of the fireplace and he gratefully sat down, rubbing his hands together and holding them to the warmth.

"I have some pottage in the pan and can soon heat some for you. I'm sure you must be hungry." Isabel brought a pan near and hooked it onto a chain above the fire and they waited until steam began to rise and the thick broth bubbled. She filled a wooden bowl with the hot pottage and handed it to Randulf. He ate quickly, for it had been a long time since breakfast, and she watched him with pleasure. Her plain food was not always so gratefully received or eaten with such relish. The wind had begun to strengthen and now and again the wooden shutters shook against the windows. Somewhere in the distance a dog howled.

"It is rough weather out there," said Randulf.

"Yes, and my other son is still out. No doubt he will be home soon, and dripping wet."

"In that case I suppose I must be away," said Randulf quietly, "as I do not want to burden you anymore." He rose very slowly from his stool as a heavy shower of rain clattered against the door like stones thrown from an angry hand. He paused near the door, and shivered, waiting.

"Do you have anywhere to go?" asked Isabel.

Randulf shook his head.

"Then this is not a night for being outside. You'll catch your death out there." She motioned to the room, "will you not stay here with us for the night?"

"I think I really should be off."

"Nonsense! There is room on the bed for you alongside Richard if you don't mind. Adam can sleep on the floor when he gets in. You would be most welcome here as an honoured guest. Our home is quite simple, though comfortable enough."

"It is I who would be honoured," replied Randulf with a bow. Isabel felt her cheeks redden slightly. He looked around the small room that served as kitchen, living space and sleeping chamber, with its baked mud floor and simple furniture; the two beds of straw mattresses on wooden frames, one half hidden behind a heavy curtain, a couple of low stools, a small table on which sat another cooking pot and a few vegetables cut that day, and a chest for clothes. He had never been in such a hovel, let alone slept in one. "You have a good home," he lied.

"It is suitable for us now in our station. We have known better," replied Isabel.

"And is there no husband for you?"

"No, he...he died of the pestilence. It was a few years ago now and I have brought up the boys by myself. Of course we had to move back here from Oxford and turn from the life we had there. I sometimes miss it — we always had food on the table then." She looked sadly around the room. "And what of you Master Payne? What is your story?"

"I have no story as such. I have done nothing special with my life thus far, just helped in my family business, trading this and that in London, and sometimes moving from town to town to find commodities that would interest us."

"And what brings you this far from London?"

"The fair. I have bought and sold at fairs many times, so I have an interest in them. You never know what might turn up at a fair..."

They talked for a while longer as Richard tossed and groaned on the straw mattress, and then as he finally lay still Isabel excused herself, extinguished the lamp and climbed wearily into her own bed concealed behind the heavy curtain. Randulf waited awhile, his face warmed by the glowing embers of the dying fire, his brow furrowed in thought, and then at last he lay down beside Richard and fell into a deep and contented sleep.

Adam returned in the middle of the night and crept into the house as quietly as he could. He cursed when he found that there was no room in his bed and considered waking the stranger up, but thought better of it and settled into a corner of the room, pulling his cloak around him to act as a blanket. And as he drifted into sleep he heard his mother's bitter voice saying, "That whore Agneta..."

Next morning Adam arose early and lit the lamp. He took it from its holder on the wall and carried it over to see who had taken his place in bed. There in the soft glow he could make out his brother, looking pale and still, and alongside him the stranger, snoring gently. Adam put the lantern nearer and the snoring stopped as the figure began to stir. He opened first one eye and then the other and then threw his arm over his face to shield them from the light. "What…?" he mumbled drowsily. Adam took a step back and the stranger pulled himself up and sat blearily on the mattress.

"Who are you?" asked Adam. "And what exactly are you doing here in my bed?"

Randulf looked at him wearily. "Is that a way to greet a guest in your house?" He shook his head to clear it of sleep. "I was welcomed here last night, and allowed to use this bed because there was space. I think I have not caused offense."

Adam knew the rules of hospitality well enough, and now and again as a family they had entertained travellers who were passing through the village on their way to Oxford. But he had always taken the precaution of checking them out before allowing them to stay, for it was dangerous to let some people in. He had no idea what his mother must have been thinking to let this complete stranger stay overnight. And in his bed too! But he could see by the cut of his clothes that this man was wealthy and well-spoken and was therefore unlikely to cause trouble. He softened a little. "What is your name?" he asked.

"Master Randulf Payne. And you?"

"Adam Wolvercot." The two eyed each other guardedly. "And what has happened to my brother?" he asked, tilting his head in the direction of Richard.

"Ah, too much ale last night I believe. I had to carry him home from the tavern."

Adam leant over and looked closer at Richard, who was still sleeping deeply. "He looks unwell," he said, noting his pallid complexion. "This is more than the effect of ale. I'll wager he is sickening for something, and today of all days! We were about to embark on a journey, but it seems we will have to delay it for now. There is no way he can travel like this."

At that moment Isabel appeared from her room, water pitcher in hand and made for the door, her daily round just beginning, as always, with collecting well water at first light. Adam avoided his mother's stare, but Randulf bowed a little and beamed at her. She inclined her head. The movement was almost unnoticeable and was accompanied by the smallest of smiles.

The morning wore on. Richard remained unwell. He refused food and complained of his heart beating wildly and his vision blurred, and he continued to vomit. At times he shook all over as though with the ague. There was no way that he could get out of bed, let alone begin a journey. The rain continued and Isabel persuaded Randulf to stay until it ceased, which he easily agreed to. Finally at mid-day the rain abated a little and turned to a steady drizzle and Adam decided to go in search of firewood as the little they had would not last another night.

"I'll come with you," said Randulf, "I could do with stretching my legs."

Adam led the way, hobbling as fast as he could to beat the cold and dodging the large drops of water that rolled from the low thatched eaves of the cottages. They found one or two dry patches under the dark fir trees just inside the forest and each collected a small bundle of branches and a few logs, carrying them in bent arms as they made their way home. They had just entered the village when Randulf nudged Adam and hurried him along.

"We need to move faster, my friend, I think we are being followed. I have heard footsteps for a while now, close behind and keeping pace with us. Whoever is on our trail has been there for some time. Let's get back to your home quickly."

Adam turned to see who might be behind and just caught a glimpse of a tall hooded figure in a crow-black gown darting between two cottages as though trying to hide. Adam froze for an instant.

"I know that man," he said. "I have seen him before, he was in Oxford at the fair, and he has been tracking me. He gave me…" Adam let his words drift away.

"Do you know who he is?" asked Randulf.

"I do not know, but I do not like him. There is something about him that chills my soul. I don't know who he is or what he wants, but why should he follow me here? He keeps following me. Come, we have to get away." He felt fear rising within him and in panic he dropped his firewood and started to limp back towards the safety of home. A coldness that was deeper than the winter rain had entered his bones. He felt his twisted foot slip and slide in the slimy mud, and the memory of the bull mastiff flooded his thoughts. All he knew was that he had to escape, and fast.

He dived inside the house and pulled Randulf in behind him then slammed the door and leaned against it to keep it shut.

"I have to go now. As quickly as possible," he announced breathlessly to his mother as he began to bundle up his bag.

"They are here already? They have followed you from Oxford?" Her face was ashen. "Oh, mercy, my son, what have you done? They will not stop now."

"And I cannot stop or we shall all be in peril. If I stay I will endanger us all. It is me they are after, I am sure of that. Once I am gone they will leave you alone." He looked at his mother. "I am sorry that I have brought this upon you."

Randulf cut in, "You cannot journey alone and you will need help as your brother is not able to travel. So if you allow me to I will go with you."

Adam tried to interrupt, but Randulf continued, "We can ready the horses and be out of here fast. Come on, there is no time to lose."

There was a knock on the door; a heavy thump of a fisted hand. Adam jumped and stared wide-eyed at Randulf. He decided quickly. "Very well," he said, "follow me." He clasped his mother in a hug, and looked into her troubled eyes. "Don't worry. I'll be back, and this business will be soon done. Look after Richard. Agneta can help."

The door rattled on its hinges as a wooden staff crashed against it. Once, twice, then silence. Adam pulled at Randulf's sleeve and motioned to the small shuttered window at the back of the room. He opened the shutters and, with one last glance back at his mother, climbed out into the cold wet yard.

Chapter 6 - The Fire and the Phoenix

Sir Osmund Clarke sat behind a large oak table, cluttered with papers and books, and drummed his ringed fingers in annoyance. How much longer did he have to wait? He stared at the door, willing it to open to reveal the King's messenger, but it remained resolutely shut. A log tumbled in the large open hearth and a stream of sparks cascaded from the roaring fire. He rose from his chair and paced the room. Damned messengers! He should not be kept waiting like this.

He paused to look around the room. He had had it decorated in the new fashion; the cold stone walls had been hung with tapestries showing woodland scenes and a depiction of the battle of Crécy. His furniture was large and grand and carved with intricate geometrical designs and the curls of leaves and flowers.

On his table, amidst the piles of papers, rested a book that recorded some of the wonders of the world beyond the London he knew, and far beyond the borders of England itself. It was full of curiosities; beasts of such diverse and strange designs that it was hard to believe that one God made them all. He had commissioned the drawings to be made whenever he heard news of sailors or travellers returning from overseas. He would arrange for them to meet him and tell him their wondrous stories, and then to describe the beasts they had seen to his artist, John Wryte, who faithfully drew them out and filled the pages of this magnificent book.

He flicked through the pages. Here were gold-digging ants that were as large as dogs and just as savage. Wryte had depicted them attacking a man. On another page was a snake with dragon-like wings and a head at each end flying through the sky, and on another a beast they called the onocentaur with the upper part of a man and the lower part of a donkey.

Clarke turned the pages more slowly, looking for his favourite, the great unicorn. This beast had been seen all over the world in one shape or another and Wryte had tried to combine the descriptions he had heard into one fantastic animal. Osmund Clarke ran his finger over the strange form laid out on the page. It had the body of a horse, but from its neck grew the head of a stag. Its legs ended in the feet of an elephant, and the horse's tail was replaced with that of a boar. But strangest of all, and fabled for its magical properties, was the three feet long black horn in the middle of its forehead. Such savage beasts as this had been seen and hunted in far distant countries. He smiled. This bestiary, this collection of strange animals, was a source of amusement to him among the seriousness of his work.

Osmund Clarke went to the window and looked down into the manor courtyard. A dozen young boys and a few young men milled about, throwing a leather ball to each other and shouting with excitement. One was running awkwardly with a twisted back, another was mute and communicated with hand gestures, another had but one arm. These were his protégés, the ones he had salvaged from the streets, those starving wretches that it was his duty before God to rescue and add to his collection. He had made sure they got an education, and had even personally taught them the doctrines of the church, sometimes beating it into them to save them from going astray. He looked down on them now, playing in the yard, and allowed himself a moment of pride.

There was a knock at the door, and he turned to face it. "Enter," he said in a loud clear voice. The messenger came in wearing the livery of the court of Henry IV and bowed low. He held a roll of parchment, tied and sealed.

"Give it to me." Sir Osmund Clarke's voice was brusque. He had no time for courtesy. The messenger handed him the roll, and as he straightened up his eyes began to wander around the room.

"You may go."

The messenger hesitated a moment too long.

"I said go! Now, damn you, get out!"

"Is there a reply for my Lord the King?"

In response Osmund simply pointed to the door. "Leave."

As soon as he was alone, he sat down at his table and, using the point of his dagger, prised off the King's seal and unrolled the parchment. The document was headed *De Hæretico Amotio* - For the Removal of Heretics. This was a first draft from the King for him to study and adjust as he saw necessary. He read it carefully. Would the King be too soft on the heretics, those who were slowly but surely destroying the power of the holy Church? Or would this law allow them to be rounded up and disposed of, their heretical English Bibles destroyed and the rule of Rome brought to bear once again on a grateful, if subdued, population.

He knew it was dangerous to put the word of God into the hands of common men and in their own common language. This precious word was to be kept for the Priests who could understand it and interpret its meaning to the rest. This kept the power where it should be and the country restrained and in order. What danger there would be, what unrest, if the uneducated man could hold the Word of God in his own hands. He shivered at the very idea.

As he read through the document, his first thoughts were proved correct. The King had not gone far enough. Henry had not demanded enough of the law. He could stamp out this heresy before an uprising occurred, as King he had the power to do as he chose, but he had chosen instead to curb his powers. The law was too soft.

No. Something more was needed. Something more brutal was required. Something that would put the fear of God into the heretics and into the hearts of anyone else foolish enough to think of joining their cause. But what? Sir Osmund pushed the parchment to one side and began to turn the pages of his bestiary with his ringed fingers, looking for inspiration in the monsters that dwelt in the hidden lands of the earth. Lions, bears, gryphons and centaurs filed past his eyes in a parade of terrible creatures, each more fearsome than the last.

And then he saw it. There on the open page was a drawing of a bird rising from a fire – a Phoenix. It was said that after dying in the flames of its own funeral pyre, it would reappear as a worm on the following day, crawling in the ashes, and then on the third day it would rise again as a new bird, to live for five hundred years before dying in the flames once again. He regarded this as nonsense, for surely no creature on earth could withstand the flames. No, neither an animal nor a human could withstand fire. This was what he was looking for. He banged his fist on the table and slammed the book shut.

Sir Osmund Clarke filled his quill with ink and scratched on the surface of the parchment. He would make sure the land got the law it deserved, that Rome kept her power and that all hint of insurgency would be crushed at birth. He wrote quickly and with zeal, crossing out sentences and scrawling notes in the margins. And then, when he had finished with the text, he made one final alteration. With a stroke of his pen he crossed out the title and wrote a new one: *de Hæretico Comburendo* – For the *Burning* of Heretics.

He knew that the King would not proclaim and enforce this law unless it was tested first. He would need proof of its power, to see if it had the desired effect of paralysing the crowds with fear. He, Sir Osmund Clarke, would hunt down a man, a heretic, and put him to the fire, and prove to the king the power of the flames. This Phoenix would not rise again.

Chapter 7 - Deep Runs the River

As soon as they were outside the house Adam motioned to Randulf to untie the horses, which were stabled under a leaking thatched roof in the yard. A chicken squawked and scuttled out of the way as Randulf ran to get them. Adam looked around nervously to see if they had been heard. There was a brief silence, and then, once again, the hammering of the wooden staff on the front door. Adam jolted and for an instant worried that by deserting his mother, he was placing her in greater danger. Was this cowardice to run away? Perhaps he should go back and face this man, whoever he was. Perhaps he should stand up and fight.

He looked over at Randulf who was throwing the loaded bags over the horses and tying them to the saddle trees so they hung loosely from either side. As he finished he led the horses over to Adam, grabbed him by the arm and thrust the reigns into his hands. "Ready?" Adam looked uncertain. "If you stay, your whole family will also be under threat. It's you they are after, but they will certainly take every one of you if you stay. Quickly now, let's go." Randulf mounted his horse, a fine white palfrey he called Henry. Adam hesitated a moment longer then reluctantly put his good foot into the stirrup, climbed a little clumsily onto his beloved packhorse, Beatrix, and nudged her into action.

The horses walked across the yard, their hooves clattering on the stones, and emerged onto the lane at the side of the house. Suddenly, Beatrix whinnied and reared up, her eyes wide and showing white. Adam caught sight of a shadowy figure lurching towards them. He slipped a little in the saddle, then righted himself and pulled on the reins to steady his mount. In panic he slammed his feet into her side, wincing with the pain this caused him. Beatrix bolted forward, her neck outstretched. Randulf chased after, and as they neared the bend in the lane they looked back to see the tall black-gowned man standing still and waving his staff in the air as though in farewell.

After a mile they slowed their pace to a trot, and passing by the pond, stopped to allow the horses a drink.

"So where are we going?" asked Randulf. "You had better tell me what all this is about."

"I can't do that because I don't understand it myself. All I know is that I am being followed and that our lives are in danger. It involves a …" Adam hesitated, remembering his mother's words that he should trust no-one.

"Go on. It involves what?"

"Nothing."

"It doesn't sound like nothing."

"I cannot tell you."

"Do you not trust me with your secrets? I am willing to place my time at your disposal, not to mention my life, and you cannot tell me why I should do this!"

Adam blanched. "It's not like that. But I have been told that there are people who would have my blood, and so I must be careful."

"And the man back there – the one who scared you so – who is he?" Randulf was searching for information.

Adam thought for a moment. "I do not know that either, but he seems very strange. He makes my flesh creep, and yet it is he who has started this whole affair. I thought at first he was a friend of my father's but I doubt that now. He is not the sort of company my father would keep. And he is not quite human; his skin is almost ghost-like."

"Oh I think he is human well enough!" said Randulf with a laugh. "They call his kind Albino, and they are all too human when you get to know them."

"You have met them before?"

Randulf did not answer, but instead suggested that they needed to remount their horses and continue with their journey. "With all your secrets you can tell me *where* we are going I presume," he said as he reigned his palfrey in. "After all we do need to be heading in the right direction."

"It is a place called Lutterworth. I have no real idea where it is, but my father used to go there often. I was going to ask the way as I went and hoped to find it by that means."

"That is a common way to travel, I admit," replied Randulf, "but better by far if your travelling companion already knows the way."

"You know where Lutterworth is!" exclaimed Adam.

"I have heard of it in my travels. I believe it to be near Daventre, and I know that that town is to the north of us. So that is the way we should head."

Adam looked at him in amazement. Randulf smiled. "I have journeyed much in my line of business. Come countryman, I will take you under my wing and together we will find this Lutterworth of yours."

They rode on, sometimes talking side by side, sometimes silently one behind the other as the lanes narrowed between wooded embankments. As dusk fell and the light began to fade they climbed a small rise and, looking ahead, could see the flickering lights of a small hamlet. Somewhere in the distance a dog howled and Adam jerked in his saddle.

"Afraid of dogs?" asked Randulf.

Adam drew breath. "No. No, of course not."

"Then this will do us for the night," said Randulf.

They came to the first cottage and knocked on the door. A man with a bent back opened the door, and after some discussion, admitted them into his home as the rules of hospitality dictated, making sure they left their swords in his keeping for the night.

+

Isabel tried to keep the fire burning as best she could, but the room did not seem to get any warmer. She pulled the few spare clothes she had from the chest and piled them onto the shivering body of her son, who was already smothered in a layer of blankets. Richard's pale face was wet with drops of sweat, but his skin was cool to the touch. Every now and again his body convulsed and shook dramatically.

Isabel began to panic. This was not the result of too much drink; she had seen those effects too often in Richard. No, this was far more serious - a malady caused by something else. Some evil humour was at work and she did not know how to counteract it. And how could she cope alone with her son so sick? Now that Adam had gone so suddenly she felt insecure and frightened. She damned the past and what it had brought with it. What had Adam said? Look after Richard, and Agneta would help. Agneta. That girl who had stolen the love of her son from her. That girl who had bewitched her son and lead him astray.

"Agneta." Even her name was hard to say, but she found herself saying it again. "Agneta." Adam had wanted her to be the one to help, and that wish must be granted.

She found her in a room near the barn, weaving cloth with her mother and some of the other women. "It is Richard." She said, "Come quickly." Agneta looked startled, but she dropped her threads at once and followed Isabel outside.

"I need your help with him, for he is very sick. Do you know the yarrow plant?"

"I think so. It grows down by the meadow."

"Then run and fetch me some. I have used it before to treat his drunken head, and perhaps it will work now. Run, girl, run! We may not have much time."

Agneta raced off and Isabel hurried back to the bedside. Richard was still tossing and groaning and one pale limp arm thrashed in the dank air. After a short while Agneta flew into the room, her hands full of green stems and leaves. "I found these," she panted, thrusting them at Isabel.

"Bring me a bowl of hot water," said Isabel, pointing to the cauldron over the fire. "I will brew the yarrow and together we will help him drink it." She tore the plant into small pieces and stirred it into the water, mashing it down with a knife. A bitter-sweet aroma filled the room.

Agneta stepped over to Richard and peeled back the corner of a blanket to look at him. "I do not know what to do," she said.

"You just need to sit with him...and with me."

"Where is Adam?"

"He has had to leave in a hurry. I do not know when he will return, but he asked for you to help."

Agneta looked startled. "Is he safe?"

Isabel did not answer, but turned her face away.

An hour passed in awkward silence. Isabel allowed the brew to cool and then tried to make Richard drink, but he could not swallow and it ran from his parched lips and spilled onto his clothes. They laid him down again and let him sleep. His breath was faint and shallow, punctuated every now and again by a weak cough, like that of a baby. His eyes rolled in his head. And then, just as Isabel and Agnes were nodding off, he coughed and shook violently, his limbs flailing about like a rag doll. He groaned, let out a long sigh that faded to nothing and then lay still. Very still.

Isabel rushed to him and clasped his hand, and screamed his name "Richard! Richard!" over and over again, as if trying to wake him. Tears rolled down her cheeks and she clutched his body to hers and rocked him back and forth. But it was too late. She knew deep within her heart that he was already gone. In an awful moment of stunned silence, the shock hit her and then in her deep anguish she let out a long low moan. Agneta hesitated and then gently laid a hand on Isabel's shoulder. Isabel said nothing. Did nothing. Finally Agneta reached over and unclasped her hand from her dead son.

"Leave me now," wept Isabel. "There is no more you can do."

"I could stay a while..."

"Girl, get out! I said leave me!"

Agneta looked back as she closed the door. Isabel had her back to her, and her shoulders shook with the sobbing.

+

The next morning was bright and clear, and there was a cold crispness in the air that spoke of a starlit night and a good day to come. The rains that fell the day before had long since ceased and there was, at last, a hint of spring in the air. Adam sat down with their bent-backed host as he waited for Randulf to finish his toilet.

"Do you know the town of Lutterworth?" asked Adam, as he chewed on the crust from a hardened loaf.

The man studied Adam's face for a moment, then drew his blade and thrust it deep into the bread.

"Now why would you be wanting to go to Lutterworth?" he asked.

"That is my business. I cannot say more. But it is urgent and important business and if you know the way then tell me, please."

The man scratched his head with a dirty brown finger. "Never been there."

"Well, do you know of any other town to the north where we might stay the night?"

"There is a place a day's ride from here called Banbury. You could make it by nightfall."

"And can you show us the way there from here?"

"Maybe I can and maybe I cannot." He looked around the squalid room. "Life here is hard and there is so little reward for it." He turned back to Adam and held out his palm. At that moment Randulf appeared in the doorway.

"Randulf, do you have a coin for this man. I think he can help us."

Randulf looked uneasily at the scene in front of him, and then drew a coin from the heavy purse hung at his waist. Adam hid his surprise at the amount that Randulf must have been carrying. Where did a young man such as he get such wealth? A fine horse and fine clothes and valuable coins do not just fall into one's lap. Was he really just a merchant?

The man snatched at the coin and bit it to test its worth. He grunted his approval and then led them outside. "Head over there," he said, pointing to the East, "and you will meet a river. Follow the river upstream and at the end of the day you will be in Banbury." He smiled greedily at them, his one tooth glimmering in the sunlight.

"Is that all?" Randulf was incredulous. The man nodded.

"And I gave you money for that! I could have told you that myself! You, sir, are a thief."

"And you, boy, could have spent the night in the cold."

Adam could feel the tension rising. "Come on Randulf. Leave him. He has served us well. Let's just go." He put his hand on Randulf's shoulder, but he shrugged it off.

"Thank you for your hospitality," said Adam, bowing to the old man. "Randulf, let's go – now!"

Randulf collected his sword, waved it at the peasant, and then sheathed it with a flourish, as if to show that he, Randulf, had won the argument. Then he mounted Henry and spurred him into a canter towards the woods.

They travelled east for a mile or two, until the trees grew thicker, and then descended a slight incline to meet a river winding through the damp undergrowth of the wood. The day wore on, and the path was easy enough to follow, although painfully slow as it wound its way northward, following the meanderings and twists of the river. For many hours they rode through deep woodland, unable to see exactly where they were going, or how far it would be to the town. They ate the bread and cheese that Adam had packed with his brother, and he wondered how he fared. It would be good to get home and see him again. He hoped his mother had been able to get Agneta to help out, although he knew that it would have grated with her to do so. But just a few days more and he would be home with them all again.

It was getting late in the day, and the light was beginning to fade when they finally smelled the smoke of wood fires and knew they were nearing Banbury. The woodland was becoming more open, showing signs of coppicing and little muddy paths ran here and there through the undergrowth. Adam was weary after so much time in the saddle and his twisted foot ached unceasingly.

Randulf spoke. "We'd better get moving. We need to be in town before long, or we will never find our way in this light. And besides, there will be a curfew after dark." He dug his spurs into Henry's flanks and the horse broke into a canter. Adam followed, moving as fast as Beatrix was able. She had walked further today than in many a month, and both rider and horse were near exhaustion.

The path was muddy and at times slippery, and the river ran close by. The trees gradually gave way completely to open land where stunted crops grew in thin furlongs of earth, and Adam could at last make out the candlelit windows of houses, the dark silhouette of the castle, and just ahead, the great stone bridge over the river. As Randulf raced on ahead, the gap between them widened, leaving Adam alone and desperate to catch up. He looked cautiously around him and nudged Beatrix on.

The light was almost gone and the bank had become hard to see. In the gathering gloom Beatrix slipped and slithered on a patch of mud. Her hooves skidded as she tried to control herself and keep upright, then one leg twisted beneath her and she went over. Adam was jolted out of the saddle and he lurched to one side pulling desperately on the reigns in attempt to stay mounted, but he could not turn her. Beatrix whinnied in fear and both horse and rider slid into the freezing river.

The river, swollen with rain from the previous day, was flowing fast at this point and the icy water made him gasp. He tumbled and felt panic rising inside hm. Not knowing which way was up, he thrashed about with his arms and legs. Then, after what seemed like an eternity, his head came out of the water and he took a huge gulp of air. His heart thumped within him as the cold and fear set in. He tried to cry out, but only took in a mouthful of water. He turned his head wildly about him and caught site of Beatrix clambering out of the water and into the shallows, shaking water from her head, the white diamond on her forehead flashing like a beacon. At least she was safe. He cried out again, and this time heard his voice come in a mighty roar. "Help! Randulf Help!" Then he went under again.

Randulf was by now two hundred yards away, a small shape in the darkness close to the bridge. Adam rose to the surface coughing and spluttering as the current carried him away. "Help me!" he shouted, before sinking below the water once again. As he rose to the surface for the third time he caught sight of a broken bough in the water, and grabbed it as he was swept past. The water gurgled round him and over him, and he struggled to cling on with his arms stretched out and his hands twisted around the gnarled branches, his energy sapped by the cold.

Randulf reached the bridge and turned in his saddle to find that he was alone. "Adam, where are you?" he called. There was no response. He waited a minute or two and then trotted back along the riverbank, calling Adam's name all the while. He could hardly see anything, just the odd glint of moonlight on the water and the white patches of froth in the eddies.

Adam cried out again, a sound that should have pierced the darkness but came more as a frozen moan of fear.

Randulf paused and searched the surface of the water.

Adam mustered his strength and cried again, "Randulf, please help me!" He unlocked one hand from the branch and waved his arm in the air.

Randulf saw his shadowy shape in the ever-darkening water. "Oh, by God's blood!" he swore, then shouted, "Hang on, I'll go and get a branch from the wood," and he raced off into the dark.

Adam tried to cry out after him, but no sound came. He realised that he was beginning to lose the feeling in his limbs. His fingers were unable to grip, so he hooked his numbed arm over the bough and tried to kick with his feet against the racing current. He searched the riverbank, desperately hoping for his friend to come back. Then all at once his energy drained from him like the fast flowing river and his lids grew heavy. He tried to force them open, but he had no control over them. Water gurgled into his mouth and nose.

"Adam! Catch this!"

Adam jolted awake at the sound of Randulf's voice. He had reappeared waving a long willowy branch in his hand and now dismounted and felt his way gingerly to the water's edge, trying not to get wet and to muddy his fine hose. He pushed the branch out towards the frozen body of his companion.

"Here, grab this branch!"

Adam tried to reach out, but his frozen fingers would not work, and he slid away from the bough and into the flow of the river. His body rolled face down and the deep water swelled around him and carried him away.

+

They buried Richard in a shallow grave, in earth softened by the rain. There were few there to see him go; Isabel and Agneta and two other friends, a few from the village who were prepared to stand with them, and the Black Friar who intoned in Latin. The cold sun shone mockingly as tears trickled down their cheeks, and the white shrouded body was lowered into the ground. Isabel wrung her hands in desperation. There was no hope now. Her mind was numb and emptied of all save the image fixed there of her dead son, and her heart ached as if torn in two.

"Let me take you home." The voice was sweet and gentle, and Isabel felt a hand in hers. She turned to see Agneta whose youthful beauty was tarnished by grief, her pale face streaked with tears and her eyes strained and red.

"What will I do?" Isabel's voice was no more than a whisper. "I have lost both my sons in one day…"

Agneta reached over to wipe a tear from Isabel's face, but the older woman brushed her hand away. "Go now," she said abruptly. "Leave me alone with my grief."

Agneta held a small posy of spring flowers in her hand, picked from the roadside, and tied with string. She knelt a moment by the grave and then tipped the posy onto the mud-stained shroud. She wiped away a tear and rose to find Isabel watching her.

+

Randulf paused a moment longer before giving in. Whatever else was to happen, he could not let Adam drown. He had orders. He followed his body downstream and then, at a point where the bank gave way to a shallow beach, he pulled off his boots and dived into the water. He swam strongly towards him, fighting the current and gasping at air, and catching hold, he dragged Adam's limp body coughing and choking back to the water's edge. He hauled him out onto the bank and crawled alongside, both men spluttering and shivering in the soggy mud.

"That's my clothes done for!" said Randulf with an attempt at a smile. Adam closed his eyes.

"We have to get into the town and into the warm before we freeze to death." said Randulf through chattering teeth. "Stay here." He ran after the horses and after a few minutes returned with both mounts. Once he had helped Adam to get back in the saddle they made their way as quickly as they could to the bridge and then crossed over to the gatehouse that guarded the eastern side of the town.

The night watchman was unsure of letting two young strangers in after dark, but seeing that they would not make it through the night without a warm fire and a change of clothes, he pointed them in the direction of the Red Lion Inn in the Beastmarket just down the road. The boy stabled their horses and as soon as they were shown the dormitory they peeled off their sodden clothes, wrapped themselves in blankets, put their clothes to dry on chairs, and settled down near the fire.

It took a long while for Adam to stop shivering, but the flames eventually warmed him as he dried. "Thank you for saving me," he coughed. "I cannot swim and was in fear of my life. The water was so cold! I thought I was a dead man."

"I know," replied Randulf, "I nearly froze myself."

"I'm sorry you got so wet."

"I did try not to. But I needed to save you from drowning and you are more valuable than all my spoilt clothes. They will dry and you will live, so no harm has been done."

Adam smiled at his friend. "Thank you all the same. I am forever in your debt, and will repay your goodness and friendship as soon as I have the opportunity."

Randulf pointed to Adam's chest. "What is that key hanging around your neck?"

Adam clutched it in the palm of his hand. It was an involuntary movement that sought to hide the key, but of course it was too late. "I ... I don't really know," he stammered. "My father gave it to me when I was young."

"So what does it open?"

"I told you, I don't know. All I know is that it is important and one day it will be made plain what it is for." Adam pulled the blanket higher over his bare chest to conceal the key from Randulf's gaze.

Sleep came quickly upon them and, as the inn was almost empty, they had the luxury of a bed each. They pulled the mattresses nearer to the fire and settled down for the night, scratching as the fleas began to bite. It was just after midnight when Randulf crawled out of bed and searched through Adam's still damp clothes. He quickly found what he was looking for and opened the vellum roll with care. The words had partially dissolved into an inky stain, but there was enough still left for him to read the poem. He smiled knowingly, reassuring himself that all was well, and then pulled on his own clammy garments. He hunched his shoulders against the cold, tip-toed through the dirty rushes on the floor and, after checking that Adam was still fast asleep, silently crept out into the night.

Dawn was still an hour away when he returned. He crept into the room, silently cursing as he tripped over one of Adam's boots, but Adam did not stir as he slept the deep sleep of the innocent.

Chapter 8 - The Nail in the Shoe

The man in the crow-black gown stretched and rolled over in the hollow he had made in the bracken. The day was just dawning and the faint light that had woken him from a disturbed sleep was already causing him to squint. With the thin fingers of his pale hand he tugged down his hood to shield his sensitive pink eyes. He looked about him, furtively checking that no-one was near. He cocked his head to one side and listened for approaching sounds. But all he heard was the song of blackbirds and the creaking of the massive wooden gates to the town as they opened to mark the end of curfew. He rose, stretched his aching limbs again and crawled out of the thicket.

He knelt at the edge of the river just below the old stone bridge and, cupping his hand in the icy water, he drank. He splashed some on his almond white face and shook his head to waken himself, the droplets of water spraying in the clear morning air. Above him he could hear the rumbling of cart wheels and the call of drovers as they trundled across the bridge. He knelt to pray, offering himself once again to the service of God, and asking for favour to accomplish his task, his voice intoning in Latin the psalms he had learnt as a child.

He rose from his devotions and walked back to the cover of the wood, where his horse was tethered. From here he could see the bridge and the townsfolk coming in and out of the town gates, and from here he would wait for his prey. He pulled himself onto the fallen trunk of an ancient oak tree and sat motionless in the shadow of the great wood. It would not be long. He knew they still had far to journey and that they would need to start early in the morning. He had little patience and chewed at a fingernail. But he did not have to wait long.

It was only a little while later that he saw them; two young men on horseback trotting out of town across the bridge and heading up the road, following the river to the north. He recognised the horses first, the white palfrey and the tired nag - the figures were harder to make out, being cloaked and covered. He mounted his own horse, a jet-black rouncy, and patted her gently on the neck.

"Come now Nightshade, let's see what today brings."

And what the day did bring was a long ride, firstly following the river through sparse woodland of oak and elm and ash; the path well-trodden and easy to find. He kept his distance from his quarry and for much of the morning he could not see them, but he knew that they had passed before him by the sharp-edged hoof prints in the wet mud, one set smaller than the other. Now and again he came across a recently broken branch, the torn wood green and still damp with sap, and, more often, the sight and smell of fresh horse dung.

At one point he heard voices up ahead, clearer and closer than before, and he pulled Nightshade to a halt to listen. But he could not make out the words, simply the tone of friendly chatter punctuated with laughter. He dismounted and waited in the shadows until the voices ceased and then led his horse around the bend in the river to the place where they had stopped. The shallows were muddied here where the horses had stood in the water drinking and the rough grass of the clearing had been pressed down where two bodies had sat and relaxed.

Eventually the river met a well-used road and the tracks ceased. They were right on target and headed for Daventre.

He allowed a smile to crease his face, his thin lips curling into something more resembling a snarl.

"Our Master will be pleased with us." He spoke to Nightshade and patted her on her neck. "Not long to go now, my dear, not long."

The road was badly rutted from the recent rain and the heavy carts that used it for market, and during that afternoon he saw a number of travellers upon it, complaining as they were jolted along. He could see Randulf and Adam a way ahead, but they never looked back, and even if they had, he felt protected by the cloak and hood that hid his face and disguised his shape.

The day wore on and he kept his distance from them. He spoke often to Nightshade in quiet tones, telling her of this and that; stories from his youth and wishes for the days to come. He confided in her and trusted her with things he would tell no man, only God. They had taken many a lonely road together and she had become his only true friend. Now and again she shook her mane as though in agreement or understanding and he took this to be a sign of her devotion to him.

And finally, as dusk approached, he reached Daventre. Randulf and Adam had already entered through the archway in the wooden palisade by the time he drew near, and he looked for a place to spend the night outside of the town. These towns were not for him. He slotted carefully into London, because there he was known and his position as servant to the Master gave him full protection. But in any strange town he was not welcome. His skin marked him out as different, and although many were disfigured through accidents, or deformed by birth, he had always been seen as a complete outcast, one who was not human. His pink eyes gave him away. Better to keep to himself and stay away from the mobs.

He rode past the gateway and headed back towards the wood. Suddenly Nightshade whinnied and reared up, almost unseating him. She came to rest on three legs, lifting the forth off the ground and pawing the air with her hoof. She shook her mane and nickered. The Albino jumped off and tenderly inspected her foot. There in the sole behind the iron shoe was the head of a nail, the rest of the shaft buried in the soft flesh. He closed his eyes and thought for a while, cursing this turn of events, then came to the decision he hated but could not avoid.

"Ssshh," he soothed, "let's find the smithy."

Taking the reins he entered the town and led her limping through the streets. A passer-by looked strangely at him but gave him directions to the blacksmith. He turned this way and that down narrow streets and before long he heard the dull clang of hammer on molten iron, and he smelt the hot coals and acrid smoke from the furnace.

As he entered the barn the blacksmith looked up. He was a strong round fellow with a pleasant face and a beaming smile.

"Looks like you've got a job for me," he said, casting a professional eye over the limping horse.

The Albino said nothing.

"My name is Walter. And you, kind Sir?" The smithy was trying not to look at the white face.

The Albino said nothing. He looked cautiously about him, taking everything in.

"And what is the name of your horse, Sir?"

Finally he spoke. "Nightshade. Take good care of her."

The smithy grunted and lifted her leg, steadying it between his knees. "The nail is not large, Sir, and will come out easily I suspect."

He fetched his pliers and deftly removed the iron point. Nightshade whinnied and tried to pull away, but the Albino held her reins tightly and whispered to her all the while.

"There, sir," the blacksmith smiled. "All well and done. She will be fine now; a little sore for a day or two, but nothing more. I would suggest you don´t ride her for at least two days."

Suddenly there was a commotion behind them, and a voice shouted, "Hey you! White-face!"

The albino turned to see three youths blocking the doorway

"Yes, you. What'ya doing here?" said a smug-faced one with missing front teeth.

"Yeah!" repeated his smaller sidekick, a boy of about seventeen with a beak nose and close-set eyes. "What are you doing here?"

The albino stood motionless and said nothing. But he felt the hair rise on his nape and his pulse pound on his brow.

"What. Can't you speak?" said the gap-toothed boy who was obviously the leader of the gang. "He can't talk, he's dumb as well as white!" His two friends laughed, a mocking snigger that the Albino had heard many times before.

"You need to go, white-face," added the third, a solidly built youngster with an angry red scar across his cheek. "We don't want your kind around here."

We don't want your kind around here. The words cut him deeply, just like the first time he heard them. Through a numb haze he remembered the children mocking and felt the sting of the flying stones as they bruised his tender face and legs. He remembered falling down; almost fainting with fear.

He remembered the beating they had given him, kicking him as he lay tormented on the ground.

"Are you deaf as well as dumb?" The ringleader was heading towards him, his fists clenched in frustration. "Let's see if you answer to this." He threw a punch at the Albino's face.

The Albino reacted faster than any of them could have anticipated. He drew his sword from under his cloak, and wielding it in both hands, sliced at the gap-toothed boy. The sword tore into his upraised arm, cutting the flesh and scraping the bone. He shouted in agony and backed away, clutching at his bleeding bicep, but his two comrades had by this time entered the fray. The scar-faced one charged at the albino, his sword held in front of him. The Albino circled his blade and metal clashed on metal. He forced his opponent's blade onto the anvil, holding it trapped there.

The other youth ran in from behind, a dagger in hand. The Albino sensed him coming and kicked out backwards. His boot landed firmly in the young man's groin and he grunted as he dropped the dagger and fell to his knees. The scar-faced swordsman regained his weapon from the anvil and struck again and again, raining down a frenzy of blows. He was strong and muscular and the Albino began to buckle under the attack, falling to the floor, his arms tiring from holding the heavy sword above his head. With a final clash of steel he felt his blade wrenched from his grip and heard it clank across the stone floor.

"Kill him!" shouted the gap-toothed boy who had collapsed in a corner of the barn, nursing his bleeding arm.

Scar-face lifted his sword to wield the fatal blow, but Nightshade, who all along had been jumping on her tether, kicked out and turned over a tall metal bucket that crashed to the floor spilling iron tongs and hammers across the cobbles.

In this moment of distraction the Albino moved like lightening. He rolled across the floor towards the brazier and, jumping to his feet, pulled a poker from the fire. He swung the white-hot tip around, forcing the scar-faced boy to jump backwards. The youth with the dagger had crawled over to the ringleader by the door, clutching his groin and trying to catch his breath.

"I am neither deaf nor dumb." The Albino spoke slowly with a strength that belied his thin physique. "Now leave before I send you all to hell."

The blacksmith, who had watched the fight from a safe place behind his bench, now stepped forward and in an attempt to bring peace laid his hand on the Albino's shoulder. Startled and tense, the Albino spun round and in blind instinct plunged the glowing poker into the fat belly of the man. There was a hiss of burning flesh and the blacksmith silently opened and closed his mouth like a gasping fish before crumpling to the floor.

In the still moment of shock that followed, the Albino reached down and picked up his sword. Scar-face turned to his companions, his face drained of blood and his hands trembling. The gap-toothed ringleader was already inching out of the door and suddenly the three assailants turned and ran out of the barn in panic.

The Albino soothed Nightshade with quiet words, then unhitched her and calmly walked her out into the daylight. He did not look back at the chaos he had caused or the dead man on the floor. He jerked at her reins and she tenderly walked beside him down the street. Behind him he heard the sound of people running and shouting as they discovered the dead blacksmith, but he fixed his eyes straight ahead, covered his face with his hood and walked out of town.

At the smithy the hue and cry had now been raised. Walter, the blacksmith, was the friend of all and somewhat of a hero in Daventre, for he not only shoed the horses, but made gates, nails, buckets and swords. Many of the metal pots and pans that were used by the housewives came from his forge, and he was known to have fathered a number of the children by these same women. Rumours soon started of a ghost that had floated into the barn and killed the smithy, a pale apparition that would appear out of nowhere from now on and destroy the townsfolk one by one.

"I saw his face." said the man who had pointed him towards the blacksmiths. "He was not of this world."

The Constable took a different view and ordered that the culprit be found and hanged. The first shouts of those who found the blacksmith dead soon multiplied. Before long a mob of men armed with swords, blades, shovels or pitchforks had gathered by the barn and, under the supervision of the Constable, they began to search the surrounding streets. A few rode horses and these he sent on ahead, scouring the outskirts of the town for strangers. The rest ran behind, streaming through the narrow streets and out through the two gates that lead North and South.

The Albino cursed aloud and headed for the woods. He knew that Nightshade could not travel far with her sore foot, so he would need to find a place to hide up for the night. As soon as it was dark he would be safe, but until then he needed to be on his guard. He pushed deeper into the tangle of trees, eventually finding a small clearing where they could rest. Now and again he tensed as he heard the sound of voices nearby, shouting and swearing as their clothes caught on brambles and as they tripped over branches in the failing light. He gently stroked Nightshade to calm her and keep her quiet, and whispered in her ears. And at long last night fell and the voices stopped and he knew he was safe until daylight.

+

Adam and Randulf heard the hue and cry and looked nervously at each other. They instinctively knew they were in deep trouble. They were strangers in this small town where everyone knew everyone else, and most were related, and by the simple fact of being strangers they were open to suspicion. This crime would not have been committed by anyone who lived in such a close community. Only a stranger would do such a thing. Whatever had happened they were now in immediate danger of being caught and lynched. They were the outsiders and therefore not to be trusted. The cry of the mob came ever closer.

"We need to get out fast," said Adam, his heart thumping in his chest.

Randulf looked about him quickly. "Down this alley," he said, and they squeezed into a narrow lane between two houses, coaxing their edgy horses to follow. The lane was dark with shadow and the edge of night, and as they moved down it they melted into the darkness. Behind them they heard the noise of the mob rushing past the end of the lane with excited voices, clanking swords and boots squelching in the mud and refuse of the main street. Then all went quiet. Adam and Randulf held their breath and waited a while longer.

"I think we should go now," whispered Adam. Randulf nodded, and the two led their horses farther down the alley until they met the town wall.

"Which way?" asked Adam. Randulf pointed to the left. "I think the North gate may be this way. If we get there fast we can get out before it is barred."

They sprinted towards it, tugging at their horses and keeping close to the mud rampart topped with its timber fence. After a few hundred yards they reached the gate, only to find that it had been closed fast after the mob had run through it. A heavy beam lay across two brackets, holding the two gates in place and locked together. A boy stood guard, a shiny new sword in one hand. He tapped his free hand against his leg and looking around nervously.

"I'll take him," said Randulf, and launched himself out of the shadows. The boy neither saw him coming nor felt the blow that felled him. Between them, Adam and Randulf dragged the unconscious body out of the way, removed the beam and slid out of the town and into freedom.

Chapter 9 Dreams and Nightmares

The Albino slept fitfully. He dreamt of being hunted and as always his dream turned into nightmare. Gangs of children were chasing him and taunting him, calling out to him and shouting names and insults. Over and over he drew near to them to play but each time they pushed him away. They called him again and he ran towards them, desperate for friendship, but they turned and hit him and spat in his face. Their cruel laughter mocked him and his white skin and pink eyes. They began to throw sharp stones that cut his arms and legs. He squealed as a knife-edged rock sliced into his arm and he watched the blood pour out of a gaping wound. And then he was falling, falling and they kicked and punched him as he fell.

A hand grabbed him and pulled him away. He spun round to see who it was, but there was no-one there. There was never anyone there. In all the times he had had this dream it always ended the same way. Alone.

He woke with a start.

The dream was vivid and stayed with him, and as his racing heart settled down he remembered that this was not the way it really happened. The hand that grabbed him had belonged to the wealthy man who had hauled him to his mansion on the edge of London. Here he had grown up amongst the other misfits, cripples and outcasts that had been collected by the man they just called 'Master'. He had been given good food and warm clothing but no name. And he had been trained for such a time as this. He had learned how to track a man and how to fight. He had been taught how to live for the cause and how to pray. He knew how to kill. His master had taught him these things so that the purity of the church might be maintained, and so that England might be cleansed of the heretics. This was the cause that he would fight for, and his Master and saviour would be pleased with him. This man had rescued him and now at last he had the opportunity to show his gratitude. He would not fail at this task.

He crept out of the wood to a place where he could see the North gate of the town and waited. The day dawned under thick grey clouds, and he watched for the gate to open. Soon his prey would leave as they had the day before and his task of tracking them would continue. It was obvious that Randulf could not be fully trusted, which was why the Master had chosen him, the Albino, to follow and observe and step in if need be. The cause was too important for the mission to fail, and an example had to be made of the boy, Adam. His very public death would be what was needed to stop the rot, and if they could catch the others that he was involved with at the same time, then so much the better.

He waited, growing more impatient as the time went by. He chewed at a fingernail. Why was the gate not open? He watched as an ox-cart lumbered up to the solid wooden doors, creaking a heavy load along the muddy road, the pair of oxen straining to pull it across the ruts. The drover called out and banged his staff on the gate, then took a step back and waited. After a few moments he called again. One gate opened just enough for a slim man to pass through. A conversation followed and then the thin man went back inside and swung the gates open. Two men with unsheathed swords stepped into the road and the ox-cart was waved in between them, then the gates quickly closed behind.

"Well, well," muttered the albino. "We have a shut in. Nightshade, my dear, we will have to wait a while longer. I do believe our friends may be unable to leave today. What a fine mess we made of it yesterday!" Nightshade snorted as if in agreement. The Albino moved into the shadows, gathered his rosary from his belt and knelt down to pray. *"Pater noster, qui es in caelis, sanctificetur nomen tuum…"*

It was much later that morning when he heard the gate creak open once again, followed by a clamour of voices. He stirred from his position and looked out to see a large crowd gathering at the gate. Arms were waiving and voices were being raised. It was obvious to him that, although he could not make out the words, a heated argument was in full swing, but at least the great doors were now open and people were free to come and go. He just needed to wait some more and before long Randulf and Adam would appear. He shielded his eyes with his hand and watched intently for the two men. Time passed slowly. He waited and watched, but they did not appear. He chewed at the remains of his nail. Where were they? Perhaps they had left by the South gate, but that would make no sense as they were headed north. No, he needed to be patient.

It was well into the afternoon before he finally understood. Masters Payne and Wolvercot had already left. They must have crept out some way or another and already be on the road. They would be miles away by now. "By God's blood!" he shouted. "They have made a fool of me!" He jumped onto his horse and tried to canter up the road, but Nightshade whinnied and refused to move at more than a walk, trying to avoid using her sore and tender hoof.

The Albino called down curses and dismounted. He paced up and down, trying to think clearly through the mixture of fear and failure that clouded his mind. The only way to follow them would be to find a new horse, but that would mean going into the town to do so, and that would prove fatal. And besides, he could not leave his beloved Nightshade. He could wait a couple of days and then try to follow, but the trail would be long dry and he knew he would never find them in the forests and villages that lay ahead. He knew they were headed for Lutterworth, Randulf had told him so much two nights ago, but they would be in Lutterworth tonight and then would move on quickly, who knew where. No, he needed a better plan. He needed to save his own pale skin. His Master would be furious and his very own life would be put in danger if he failed.

A crackle in the dry winter undergrowth made him start, and he turned to see a short fat boy of perhaps ten or eleven staring at him, nervously holding a pitchfork in front of him. His ears stuck out and his wide face was smudged with dirt. The Albino pulled his hood down tight, hiding his face.

"Who are you?" enquired the boy in a voice that shook. "And what are you doing here?"

The Albino thought a moment, then seized his chance. "And can I ask the same of you."

The boy looked flustered. This was not the answer he was expecting. "I'm…I'm William, Sir," he stuttered. "William Foreman. I look after the pigs." His face reddened. This was not how it was meant to be.

"Ah, the pig boy. I thought I could smell pigs." The Albino stared uncomfortably at the boy William. "And what are you doing with that pitchfork?"

"It's…it's a weapon! Have you not heard about the murder last night? All the town are out looking for him what done it."

"And you too are hunting him down?"

"Yes, Sir!" exclaimed William, with a note of pride. "And my father says that when we get him we'll cut out his entrails and hang him up and cut off his head!"

"That would make a pretty sight," murmured the Albino.

"My father says I can earn a penny from catching the murderer."

"A whole penny?"

"Yes, Sir."

"Well how would you like to earn a whole shilling?"

William's eyes glistened. "A shilling!" he whispered as if he were being offered the world.

"I need you to do something for me." The Albino put his hand on the boy's shoulder. "And if you do it well I will pay you your shilling. Can you ride?"

"Yes, I can ride a little. My brother showed me how."

"Good."

"And do you have a horse?"

"No."

The Albino thought awhile. "There are stables just inside the main gate over there. I can see the horses even from here."

"Yes, Sir."

"And do you have courage, boy?"

William puffed up his chest. "Yes!"

"Then for your shilling…" and at this point the Albino pulled a silver coin from his purse and held it in front of William's face, "I want you to steal a horse. Do you think you can do that?"

William looked bemused. "Steal … a … horse," he repeated slowly.

"Is there a problem?" asked the Albino, growing frustrated.

"No, Sir. No problem. But why should I steal a horse when my father has got one!"

The Albino closed his eyes and breathed deeply to calm himself. He spoke slowly and deliberately, "Then go and fetch your father's horse and come back here. But tell no-one about me. This is our secret."

William looked at the shilling, and then tapped the side of his nose. "I won't tell no-one," he said conspiratorially, "and then the shilling will be all mine. Won't need to share it with no-one." He turned and ran back towards the town gate, the pitchfork swinging happily from his hand.

The Albino pulled a sheet of parchment from his saddlebag and a quill from his purse and sat down to write. A while later William returned, without his pitchfork and riding a pony.

"I have a letter here. You are to take it to a tavern called the Red Lion in Banbury. It is in the Beastmarket. Can you remember that?"

"Yes, Sir."

"There is often a man drinking in the tavern by the name of Guy de Beauchamp. Give this letter to him, and then return to me and I will give you your due. Do you know where Banbury is?"

"Oh, yes. We have been there to market before. We have bought and sold pigs there."

"Then go quickly before you are missed. I will wait for you here until the sun sets tomorrow, so you must ride fast." The Albino held out the shilling once more. "Remember your reward."

William took the letter and squinted at it, holding it upside down. "What does it say?"

The Albino smiled. His plan was safe with this dolt.

As William trotted off down the road the Albino turned and spoke once more to Nightshade. "Well, my dear, let's make a move. We need to be well away from here before the townsfolk find him missing as well as me." He flipped the coin in the air and then pocketed it safely before taking her reins and leading her slowly up the path that led deep into the forest.

+

Adam Wolvercot jumped from his horse and stared at the view in front of him. The town of Lutterworth had no walled boundary, not even a rickety wooden fence to keep out intruders or unwelcome guests. There were the usual smattering of single storey cottages along a main dirt road, and here and there a garden or yard growing vegetables, a stable holding a few restless horses, an inn and a trading stall. A cluster of two storey buildings over to his left indicated the market, its once open space now crowded with shops. And beside this stood the church, with its tower rising high above the thatched rooftops.   A few people were out and about; men about their work, some carrying bundles of food, others with barrows or leading a horse. Children played tag in the muddy road and old women scolded them as they ran past.

Adam nudged Randulf. "I think the church is where we should go. Let's take a careful look and then go back after dark."

He led the way, carefully stepping over the stinking gutter that ran down the middle of the street, and jumping over the greasy puddles that overflowed with offal and human waste. A wide rutted road led off to the left towards the market square, and soon the two were winding through the grimy alleyways between the overcrowded shops. Butchers, cloth merchants, leatherworkers and sword smiths all vied for business alongside stalls selling vegetables and cheese. The town was busy and the market full of the clamour of traders. No-one would take any notice of two more strangers.

They pushed through the jostling crowds until they broke through into an open space, and there in front of them, across the graveyard, stood the church. For a moment they stood still, transfixed. Inside was the book they were searching for, the book that held so many secrets.

+

A deathly silence descended on the drinkers in the Red Lion Tavern in Banbury as the giant bulk of Guy de Beauchamp stepped into the doorway. All eyes looked away as the scar-faced hunter strode into the room, his nose clearly broken many years ago and his great black beard hanging in greasy curls from his cheeks. He grunted something and a man carrying a full tankard darted out of his path, spilling ale as he went. Guy de Beauchamp motioned for a drink and as he sat down the other revellers began to murmur once again in hushed tones.

He spat on the floor and wiped his mouth on the sleeve of his worn leather cloak. His legs ached from the hunt and the blood of the deer had dried on his hands, staining brown the lines on his palms and coagulating under his torn nails. It had been a good day, but hard. The hart had been fit and young and had led him a long way into the woods, his dogs trailing the scent and slavering as they ran this way and that among the trees. His mastiff was a touch overweight and slow, but she could kill a stag or a wild boar with one rip at the throat. His bloodhound was fast and intelligent, a natural at following a scent, however he was getting old now. Between them they had hunted for many a year since Guy came back from the wars, and had kept him and some in the town with meat and profit.

He gulped down his ale and banged the tankard on the table for another. A good day's hunting made for a good night's drinking.

It was three hours later, a while after the bells for *none* had echoed from the church tower, that William the pig boy crept into the tavern. He looked pensively about him, wondering which of the drunks lying half asleep across the benches could be the man he was looking for. He sidled up to the landlord who was wiping a wooden mug with a dirty cloth. "Kind Sir," he began, "I am looking for Guy de Beauchamp. I have something for him."

The landlord smiled. "So you have something for de Beauchamp, aye? Let's hope it is something good, for your sake." He pointed to the sleeping mound of leather, alone in the corner. "Best wake him gently."

William leant over the slumbering figure, its hand still grasping an empty wooden mug, and coughed. There was no movement save the rise and fall of heavy breathing. He looked back at the landlord who nodded his head and winked in encouragement. William whispered, "Guy de Beauchamp, Sir, please wake up!" He tapped the shoulder with a finger, gently at first, then more heavily. Still nothing. "Wake up!" he shouted and prodded harder. Guy de Beauchamp grunted an oath, almost indiscernible in its crudity, and lifted his heavy head from the table. He focussed his eyes on the pig boy's face and tried to remember where he was. William thrust the letter at him and he took it with a shaky hand.

"Wha's this?" he mumbled.

"It's a letter from a man who said it was urgent," replied William, feeling a little bolder now.

"Wha man?"

"A man with a white face. He had pink eyes."

Guy de Beauchamp suddenly rallied. He sat up and stretched his hands across his face as if to wipe away the effects of the ale, then unfolded the letter. What was the Albino up to now? He had more cunning than any other man he knew, and was colder and deadlier too. He knew from past escapades that his orders were to be obeyed but there was also a reward to be gained by working with him. It was always good to be on his side rather than against him.

"You can leave now, boy," he said to William. "I will take care of this from now on."

"What about my shilling?" asked the boy. "He promised me a shilling."

"You will never see your shilling."

"But he promised!" William tried to snatch at the letter, but de Beauchamp pulled it away.

"Get out of here!" he yelled. "And make sure you never meet up with that man again! It will be your last day if you do!"

William's ruddy face blanched. "But my shilling..." he whimpered.

"Go home, boy, and live a quiet life. Do not get involved in the dark things of men. For your own sake, keep away from him. And do not come near me again either!

William ran for the door and disappeared into the street. Guy de Beauchamp raised himself slowly from the table and staggered out of the Inn, calling for his dogs who were asleep outside in the dark and cloudy night.

Chapter 10 - The Book of Books

Under cover of night, Adam and Randulf crept into the church, hoods up and cloaked. Once inside, they lit the candles they had bought at the market and shielded their guttering flames against the draft from the door as it swung shut behind them. The flickering glow lit their ghostly faces from below and formed arcs of pale gold in the pitch-black interior.

"Where do we start to look?" asked Randulf. He held his candle aloft and tried to make out his surroundings. The stone walls and flagged floor seemed cold and unforgiving, and there was no place there to hide anything, let alone a book. The niches around the walls were full of life-size statues of the Virgin, and Jesus on the cross, and two saints that he could not identify. Adam ran his hand behind the statues, but found nothing but dust. Meanwhile Randulf was crawling up and down the oak pews feeling beneath the seats for any sign of a hiding place. Adam went over to the north wall on which was a large mural. He could make out a depiction painted long ago showing two men and a woman, each dressed in rich robes and wearing crowns. The men held falcons on their hands and they looked contented and full of life. But alongside them stood three of the dead, one pointing with a skeletal finger of judgement at the living. Adam shuddered.

Randulf drew close and whispered coldly in Adam's ear, "That's a portent of what is to come!" As Adam rounded on him, he winked knowingly, then changing his tone declared, "There's nothing here."

"Then we must look elsewhere. My father wrote, 'at *Lutterworth Church is the book*` and so it must be here."

Adam looked around, "Look, there's a door over there. Let's see what's behind it."

The door creaked open and they entered the vestry. There was a small table and chair and a large cupboard against one wall, but apart from that nothing. They opened the cupboard and searched the contents, but only found vestments and the silver chalice and platter for the mass. Once again there was no hiding place for a book.

Adam's injured foot was beginning to ache and he sat down heavily on the chair and put his head in his hands, partly in despair and partly to think. Where, oh where could it be? He realised he had no idea what size of book they were looking for, or what it contained, or even why it was so important. It suddenly all seemed so ridiculous. Then slowly it dawned on him.

"I know why we can't find the book."

"Why?"

"Think about it. How long has the book been here?"

Randulf shrugged.

"Don't you see? The book has been hidden for years. My father knew of it before he disappeared and that was at least ten years ago. So it would be almost impossible for a book to be hidden for that long and never be found. Randulf, the book is no longer here. Someone must have found it in all that time."

"Or it has been well hidden. Why do you think you received the vellum roll with the poem leading you to this place if the book was no longer here?"

"Perhaps whoever it was that wrote the poem did not know that the book had vanished."

"No. It is here."

"How can you be so sure? What do you know about it?"

Randulf kicked out at the wooden panelling angrily. "I ... I just have a feeling."

Adam clambered to his feet. "A feeling! Is that all we have to go on? Tell me then, where do you think a book that is so important could be hidden for more than ten years in this church?"

"Well it must be somewhere that no-one has been to." Randulf looked around the room. "How about behind that cupboard?" he suggested in frustration.

Adam hobbled over to the cupboard. It was a heavy oak construction, taller than he and about ten feet wide and it filled most of the wall. A thick layer of dust covered the mouldings where it sat on the floor and matted cobwebs hung between it and the wall. It had not been moved in a long time, and not surprisingly because it must have weighed more than his horse.

You know, you could be right," he said.

Randulf joined him and the two of them pulled and heaved at the cupboard. It rocked a little but did not budge from the wall.

"Empty it!" cried Adam with a rise of renewed excitement.

They pulled the contents out and piled them on the floor, working as fast as they could but taking great care of the holy objects. Then they tried again. The cupboard creaked and shifted slightly. Randulf managed to get a hand between it and the wall and pulled. It scraped across the floor, an inch or two. They heaved again, and little by little made a gap through which they could crawl. Adam pushed in first. Randulf handed him a candle.

"What can you see?"

"Nothing just yet. Only more wooden panelling."

Randulf squeezed into the cramped space and began tapping at the wall with a knuckle.

"What are you doing?"

"Seeing if it is hollow." He tapped some more but the wooden panelling sounded solid.

He kicked out once more in anger, stubbing the toe of his boot against the skirting.

"What was that?" asked Adam. "Do that again."

Randulf kicked the wall. "That sounded hollow."

They knelt down and Adam tapped at the panel. He grinned at Randulf and began to pull and push at the wood. It slid quietly to one side and then fell away revealing a dark cavity. Inside was a small oaken box. Adam breathed deeply. He wedged his fingers into the opening and withdrew it.

He placed the box solemnly on the table and they both stood back to view it. It was obviously very old and weatherworn and was bound by two rusty iron straps held by a metal clasp. Adam picked it up and tried to prise open the lid, but, as he expected, it was locked fast.

"The key. Adam, you have a key." urged Randulf. Trembling a little, Adam pulled the key from under his tunic and hesitantly placed it in the lock. Was this the great moment his father had told him about? Was this what his life had been purposed for? The key grated on the aged metal then turned and with a loud click opened the lock.

Suddenly there was a sound of a heavy footstep behind them and they turned to see a large bear of a man blocking the doorway. He had the grizzled look of someone who had lived a long hard life. A thick woollen cap was pulled down to his eyes and a wiry grey beard hung from his chin. His face bore the scar of a blade wound and he was missing several teeth. In one hand he held a candle and in the other a long dagger, and this he waved in the direction of the box.

"Give it to me." he said in a voice made of gravel.

Randulf looked at Adam, weighing up if they would be able to take him down.

"Give me the box." He took a step forward. Adam drew his sword, dropping his candle in haste and it sputtered out, darkening the room around him. Randulf blew his out, plunging him also into darkness and, unseen, picked up his sword from the floor. There was a grating of metal on stone as he lifted the heavy weapon and the old man swung to face it. He made an easy target, lit up as he was and wielding only a dagger. Randulf lunged towards him, sword in hand, and pinned the man to the wall, his forearm across the old man's throat and his sword raised above his head. "Wait!" cried Adam. Randulf froze.

The old man simply raised the palm of his hand in surrender. "Let me go, young man. Killing me would be a big mistake." His voice was calm and forceful as if he were not frightened. "I am your friend," he coughed. "I have been watching you this past while and I could have killed you at any moment had I wanted to. Do you believe me?"

Randulf, let him go!" Adam placed a shaking hand on his friend's shoulder. "That's enough. Let him go."

Randulf stared deeply into the eyes of the man. "Just be careful, old man!" he said, and released his grip on his throat.

"Who are you?"

"I am a friend. Please, let me see the box." Adam relit his candle and nodded at Randulf who kept his sword ready in both hands. The old man drew close. Gently and with reverence he opened the lid. His eyes reddened and grew moist. "All these years, all these many years, and you have been laid here." His voice softened as he spoke. "And I have waited for this day, not knowing where you were or how you would be." He chuckled to himself. "And all that time you were so very close."

He tilted the box on one side and a small book fell out it into his hand. It was just larger than his palm, and as he opened it up Adam could see by the light of the dancing flame that it was quite the most beautiful thing he had ever seen. The cover was of soft worked leather, embossed with lettering and designs and coloured here and there with gold. The old man opened the pages to reveal neatly written pages in two black columns surrounded by pen work and decorations in red and blue. Adam drew closer and as he leaned over to read he unexpectedly recognised the power of the book. It was a Bible, but a Bible like no other that he had seen. For it was written not in the Latin ordained by the church. This one was written in English, the language of the people, and for that simple reason his heart pounded within him. This book carried a death sentence, and yet within it were the words of life.

The old man thumbed through the pages, reading a little here and there and mumbling to himself in quiet contentment. "*Forsooth God so loved the world, that he gave his one begotten Son, that each man that believeth in him perish not, but have everlasting life.*"

Randulf had drawn near, his eyes wide and yet hard. "We should take this now. It is ours." He reached out to snatch the book from the old man's hands, but Adam stopped him.

"No," he said, "Let him look a little longer."

The old man smiled at him with gratitude, and read some more, turning the pages slowly.   "*In the beginning God made of nought heaven and earth. Forsooth the earth was idle and void, and darknesses were on the face of the depth; and the Spirit of the Lord was borne on the waters.*"

Adam waited impatiently, then asked, "Who are you, and how do you know about the book?"

I cannot say my name; it is not for you to know. But know that as this book says, there is much darkness on the face of the earth and it truly is idle and void. But the Spirit of the Lord is about to move."

Randulf spat into the dark. The old man paused and then continued, "I was told to wait by your father, Jacob, if indeed he was your father and you are his son Adam Wolvercot." Adam nodded. "You do have his features," said the old man, holding up his candle and peering closely at Adam, "I can recognise him in you. He was not much older than you are. We were great friends, he and I. You remind me of him. He said you would come one day, so since then I have waited and I have watched. I knew there was one last Bible written by Master Wyclif, but I did not know it was here, so close. It was not my job to find it, so I did not look."

"Did you not want the Bible for yourself?" asked Randulf.

"Oh, I would love to have had it but it is too precious and too dangerous for me to keep," said the old man. "I know the joy it can bring and the misery too. No, my task was to wait for you and to speed you on your way. It is you who must take it to the one who needs it." He stared at Adam, his gaze piercing and searching and making Adam lower his eyes to the floor.

At length he continued. "I worked with your father many years ago, taking Bibles by dead of night to poor preachers who needed them. It was difficult and dangerous work; we were often hunted and chased, and yet we still got many through. Your father Jacob was a brave man. He and I suffered much." He pulled back his sleeve revealing the long-healed scars of deep knife wounds and the deep brown mark of a firebrand. He could just make out the interlinked letters OC burned permanently into the skin. Randulf's eyes widened at the sight and he took a step back.

"Yes, they caught us one time," he continued, seeing the shock on Adam's face. "The two of us together, and by any means they set about finding out what they could. But your father was a brave man. He withstood more than I." Once again his eyes moistened, and he pulled his hand across them to wipe away the tears. Adam began to say something but the old man cut in, "Let me finish, young Adam, for I have more to tell you and the time may be short."

He drew in closer, their heads almost touching, and continued. "We have been called by many names, those of us who truly believe that all men should have the Word of God in their own tongue. The Church of Rome has banned us and labelled us Lollards and mumblers. But there are still many in our community, friends hidden away for fear of their lives, holding illegal meetings where they share the Word and teach the truth. In years past we provided them with as many Bibles as we could copy; slow work, but it became our very lives. And as we did so, the net drew ever closer around us. We were watched night and day, unable to go about even our regular business, and it became harder and harder to carry our precious cargo. And then, seventeen years ago, in the winter of 1384, John Wyclif perished and with him the secret of the last Bible. We knew there was one last copy, but we did not know where it was hidden – he always kept that secret to himself. At that time it had become impossible for us to move the Bibles without endangering the men they were going to."

The old man sat down heavily in the chair and looked straight at Adam. "A few years later they caught your father. I don't know how or what happened to him, for I never heard from him again. I am sorry, but I believe he is dead – killed at the torture."

Adam again made to speak, but the old man lifted a finger to his lips. "Before he died he left a message hidden in a book in the library where he and Master Wyclif worked. He hid it well, but knew that one day you would be led to it. He had friends who could take you there when the time was right."

"I was contacted with a written message that helped me find it." interjected Adam. He reached into his bag and pulled out the vellum roll and handed it to the old man. "Here," he said, "read it."

The old man carefully unrolled the vellum and squinted at it. The letters had been all but washed away by the soaking it had had in the river, but he could just make out some of the words. Adam helped him read it as he had long since memorised the poem.

> *In Merton's find a book to see*
> *The secret opened with a key*
> *The plowman digs in furrows deep*
> *But canst thou now the treasure keep?*
> *A priest that's poor in misery*
> *He now awaits his gift from thee*
> *Give to this man and feed his sheep*
> *So raise your father from his sleep.*

"It certainly leads you to the college library and the correct book. Your father had a sense of humour – he knew that the book by Piers Plowman would cause a stir, and would be the perfect book to hide his message to you. No man of religion would willingly read that book, with all its railing against the church. And there is a poor priest who needs this Bible."

"Do you know who it is?" interjected Randulf as he pushed his way nearer to the old man. "Tell us and we will be on our way."

"Not so fast, Randulf," said Adam. "I want to know more. It says I can raise my father from his sleep. Surely he is not dead. Isn't that what it means?"

The old man closed his eyes and stood silently for a moment. Finally he whispered, "I do not know. I have always believed him to be dead."

"And the name of the poor preacher?" asked Randulf again. The old man stared at him through half closed eyes, as though trying to tell if he could be trusted. Randulf held his gaze, unblinking.

Adam cut in, "He is alright. You can trust him. He has already saved my life from the river and helped me find my way here. Randulf is my friend and is with us in the cause."

The old man continued staring at Randulf as he spoke in a slow, measured voice. "You can never be too careful. Our enemies have multiplied over the years and many would seek to have both this Bible and the one who carries it destroyed. We cannot trust anyone. By whom did this message come? Perhaps by friends. Perhaps not. We cannot know. I believe that your father was tortured beyond the point of endurance, and died of his wounds. How much did he tell before they crushed him? How much do they know? Is your quest genuine or are you being trapped like a fly in a web?" His words hung in the air, and a chill crept through Adam's bones.

"Listen well. Both of you." He looked searchingly at Randulf. "This book is mightier than any weapon, sharper than any sword. When illuminated by God it can reveal the true state of any man and it has the power to cut him to the quick. It is more precious than any jewel, than any weight of gold. It is more important than anything else on earth. It holds the very thoughts of God, and shows what he is like. Sometimes it is hard to understand, sometimes a challenge to the very soul of man. But it is always uplifting, always strengthening, always beautiful. This is why you must guard it with your very life. It is why so many have died for it. It is why it must go to every man in this land."

"But how can it be given to common men?" interjected Randulf. "It should not be cast before swine."

"And who taught you that, young man? Where did you hear such heresy?"

Randulf did not answer, but glowered at the old man and inwardly berated himself for his quick tongue. He glanced sideways at Adam but he had not seemed to notice.

The old man turned to Adam. "You have a great privilege, handed down to you from Jacob your father. This book must reach its destination. It was his will and it is mine. Do this for both of us. I will now tell you the name of the man and where he is. I will tell you both, in case one of you is captured along the way, but on your life tell it to no one else."

He beckoned them towards him and whispered, "He is a man by the name of Gelfridus Lyttle, an old acquaintance and brother in the Lord, a good man of God who now works as an apothecary in the town of Thetford. Now you know where to go and to whom. Keep this information safe, and deliver the book. Do not share this with anyone."

He motioned to Randulf, with a smile and a slight bow of the head. "My apologies, young man, if I seemed to be uncertain of you, but these things are too dangerous to be spread around. The fewer who know, the better."

Randulf nodded back, but his eyes hardened.

"Master Adam, I need to give you a little more private information. Come close."

Adam drew nearer the man who bent forward and whispered in his ear. Randulf tried to catch the words but could not make them out. Finally the old man straightened. "Come, I will show you the way."

The old man rose creakily to his feet and led them outside, carrying the Bible clutched to his heart. He drew an unbleached piece of cloth from the belt at his waist and carefully wrapped the book in it, then with a kiss, handed it to Adam. "Guard it well."

+

Guy de Beauchamp rode the lanes from Banbury to Daventre as fast as he could, the letter of summons from the Albino stuffed in his tunic. His dark bay destrier was familiar with these journeys. He was a fine Spanish stallion taken as spoils of battle, strong and fearless and dark-natured as night. Alongside him ran the dogs; the mastiff lumbering behind the bloodhound, trying to keep up. But fast as he could ride, the journey was slow, for the horse was heavy and cumbersome and the dogs tired after every few miles. He rested much, giving the animals the chance to regain their strength, and for him to think about the hunt. The Albino had written that this was no ordinary hunt for meat, but a manhunt of the greatest importance. Matters that would affect the stability of the whole country were at stake, and he, Guy de Beauchamp, would use his tracking skills to hunt down these men and so win both gratitude and financial reward from King Henry IV himself. Perhaps he would even become *Sir* Guy de Beauchamp.

But first he had to find his victims.

The albino was waiting for him, and saw him coming from afar – the huge dark horse pounding the earth under the weight of the large leather clad rider and the dogs close behind, slavering and rolling as they lurched along the rutted road. He had spent the previous day searching the track north from Daventre, following the route taken by Randulf and Adam. He had not seen any other riders head that way and he knew what he was looking for. There would be fresh horse dung and a fresh scent to follow. And now as Guy de Beauchamp came into view he allowed himself a smile, his thin red mouth curving like a knife wound on his parchment white face. Now he was back on track. Now the hunt would begin, and his own pale skin would be saved.

Chapter 11 - The Primrose Wood

The first flowers of spring were just starting to appear in the woodland that surrounded the village of Wolvercot. Sweet violets and bright yellow coltsfoot fought for a place in the sunlight and struggled to get their flowers open before the taller plants squeezed them out. The buds on the trees were beginning to burst and form a haze of pale green through which dappled sunshine speckled the woodland floor. And here the primroses grew and covered the woodland floor in a carpet of pale cream. Agneta had always loved the spring flowers, and especially these gentle and cheery primroses. They were a sign of hope, and that was so much needed after the events of the past few days. It was only four days since Richard was buried, and there was an ache in her heart, an emptiness that could not be quickly healed.

She had gone to the wood to collect the primroses to brighten her room. Her mother had stopped filling the cottage with flowers since the death from the pestilence of her father many years ago, but Agneta had always tried to put a few on the table in spring and summer, as a token of the past and as a hope for the future. They were so beautiful, and yet their delicate flowers reminded her of her own vulnerability. So now she bent down and began to fill the fold in her cloak with flowers, laying them carefully side by side, stalks all to one side, and flopping heads to the other. If she was quick they would last the short journey home and revive in a pot of water.

Agneta hummed a tune to herself as she picked the primroses, pinching them between thumb and forefinger to break the stems. She was lost in her thoughts when suddenly she heard someone cough behind her. She jumped, spilling some of her flowers, and turned to see the brutish form of Hugh Cooper standing close by, leaning on a tree and watching her intently.

"You startled me!"

Hugh Cooper was chewing a dried grass stalk, turning it over in the corner of his mouth. He said nothing.

"I did not know you were there," added Agneta, beginning to blush.

Hugh cooper straightened himself and took a step forward. He bowed low with a gesture that was intended to be courteous but seemed to her more like mockery, and spoke. "Mistress Agneta, did I frighten you? That was not my desire. I just wanted to watch you picking those flowers; flowers that are as lovely as you." He took a step forward, and Agneta stepped backwards.

"That is very kind of you," she murmured, trying not to catch his eye.

"You are all alone in these woods. Is it safe for you to be out here with no protection?"

"I am quite safe. I am only a few minutes from home." She wanted to sound brave but inside she was quaking. "And there are villagers all around, I am sure."

Hugh looked about him, pretending to search the woodland for others. "I see no-one here. Just you and me. I don't think that even if we shouted there would be anyone to hear us." He took another step forward. "I was sorry to hear about the death of your dear friend Richard. I hear that you were very close to him. You must be in such grief."

Agneta said nothing, but the sting in her eyes said more than words.

Hugh Cooper went on, "and I also hear that your lover has left you, and run away at dead of night." He studied her face. "Such a shame, that he would leave one so pretty. And who knows why he left, or if he will come back. I fear you may be alone forever."

Agneta clenched her fist at the threatening words and dropped her hold on the cloak. The primroses tumbled to the woodland floor.

"I think..." she said in a low voice, "I think you should leave now."

"Oh, come, come. We have just begun to make friends. No, let us get more acquainted. There is so much more I want to know about you." He looked her up and down.

Agneta tore her gaze from his face and glanced about her, looking for some stick or branch or anything to protect herself. But there was nothing nearby.

"Mistress Agneta, you seem distressed. May I help you?" Hugh cooper moved closer, his hand outstretched to touch her shoulder. Agneta flinched and jerked her shoulder away.

"I am not here to hurt you," soothed Cooper, "I just want to look after you, now that you have no-one left to take good care of you." His breath smelt sour, his body rancid. Agneta creased her nose against the stench that cut the air.

"Come with me and I will watch over you," he continued, "I have wanted you ever since I first saw you."

His fingers touched her neck and he ran his hand up the side of her cheek, cupping the back of her head in his palm. As he pulled her toward him Agneta twisted from his grip and ran. Hugh Cooper laughed and chased after her, crowing that she could not outrun him. Agneta sobbed and ran as fast as she could, clutching her skirts and lifting them clear of her legs, as her feet tripped and slid in the tangled undergrowth. Cooper followed after, swearing as his boots caught in briars, and as he landed awkwardly after jumping a fallen bough. He was strong enough to catch her easily, but he enjoyed the chase and was in no hurry to win his prize.

She was nearing the edge of the wood when he caught up with her, and grabbed her by the arm. He pulled her in close, and as he reached out to embrace her he heard a man shout and the whistle and thud of an arrow as it flew past him and embedded in a tree. He dropped his hold, and Agneta ran. The archer with the longbow was aiming again. "Leave her alone, or you will be a dead man!" he said, in a voice that was at once calm and menacing.

Hugh Cooper watched in disgust as Agneta ran to the man and hid behind him, wiping her face with a flower stained hand. Then slowly, Cooper turned and walked back into the wood as though nothing had happened. But just as he was about to disappear from view, he stopped and spun around, crying out in a loud voice, "I have not finished with you Agneta. You will be mine! I will have you!" And then he was gone.

Chapter 12 - Companions of the Night

The pale light of dawn was creeping over the horizon, pushing back the night and creating a warm glow on the pathway leading from the church. Adam and Randulf walked beside their horses, and were accompanied for a while by the old man. He led them through the dark streets, eastward towards the rising sun. At the edge of the town he stopped and bid them farewell and God-speed. Then he melted into the darkness, and they were left alone.

They mounted in silence and, as the daylight grew stronger, continued eastward on the well-trodden road. There was nobody about at this early hour and Adam felt safe as he listened to the steady clop of the horses' hooves on the path, taking them ever further from Lutterworth. He had stuffed the cloth-wrapped Bible between his shirt and his body to keep it safe and close to his heart. This book, this powerful book, gave him a fresh purpose in life, and he would make sure that he delivered it to the one who needed it, and so fulfil his destiny. He would make his father proud and finish his life's work. He felt invigorated and more alive than ever.

It was mid-afternoon before they stopped for a rest. Randulf had urged them on, saying that the longer they rode, the nearer they would get to their goal and the sooner he could go home. He seemed anxious and kept looking over his shoulder, yet when Adam questioned him about this he just said he was tired.

Beatrix was also tired, and they had covered a good many miles when Adam finally persuaded Randulf to stop and rest. He slipped gratefully from the saddle and limped to a grassy knoll, where he sank to the ground and leant his back against a tree. Before long, the weariness of travelling and the lack of any sleep the night before caught up with them both, and they began to doze.

The sound of voices laughing and shouting woke them and, as they rubbed their eyes, they saw that they were surrounded by a company of travellers. Adam bolted upright and reached for his sword, but one of the men stepped forward and held up his palm in a gesture of peace. By the cut of his fur-trimmed gown and the rings on his fingers, he seemed a very wealthy man.

"Put your sword down, young man! We are just travellers like you," he said. There was an air of pomposity about him, and he looked down his long nose at Adam, as though surveying him for some malady or disease.

"Let me introduce myself," he said. "I am Geoffrey de Florin, and I am a physician. I heal the sick," he added in case Adam did not know what a physician was. "And you are...?"

"I am Adam and this is Randulf." Adam did not venture their full names.

"Well, masters Adam and Randulf, will you travel with us? Two young men like you would be easy pickings on a road like this, and there is more safety from thieves if we ride together."

Adam studied the group. There were six in total, five men who had dismounted and now surrounded them, and one woman who was still sitting astride her horse. They appeared to be an unlikely company, a mixed bunch of travellers from all levels of society, and yet groups like these often travelled together for protection.

"Where are you headed?" asked Adam.

A man wearing a large cross stepped forward. He was dressed in only black and over his shoulder was a large bag. His hair was long and limp and the colour of flax and he spoke in a voice that was at once high-pitched like that of a woman, and slimy. "We are on pilgrimage to Ely where the water is blessed for healing by Saint Etheldreda. From there, we go to Walsyngham to see the house where the Annunciation took place and the very milk of the Virgin sealed in a glass jar. We seek to be blessed and to impart blessing." He stretched out a limp hand in greeting. "May I introduce myself? My name is Athelard Drake."

"And let me introduce you to the rest of our group," interrupted Geoffrey de Florin. "This is Edward Gregory," he motioned to a man with a face scarred by boils and large spots, standing beside him, "and our Lady companion is Mistress Matilda Webb." The lady, wearing a wide brimmed hat with so much rich cloth beneath it that her features were largely obscured, nodded.

Adam bowed to them. The scarred man nodded briefly and mumbled something in Latin. Mistress Webb inclined her head again, and as she looked back up Adam thought he saw her wink at him.

"And finally, Hubert Bigge and Simon Carter." The latter reached out a calloused hand in welcome.

Geoffrey de Florin spoke again. "And where are you two travelling, if I may make so bold?"

Adam hesitated, and Randulf jumped in. "Eastward. Nowhere in particular." De Florin looked at him. "To seek our fortune," added Randulf unconvincingly.

"Well, masters, I think we could all do with finding our fortunes!" said Athelard Drake, the merest hint of a smile crossing his face.

Mistress Webb spoke up. "So will you come with us?"

Adam thought a moment, but before he could make up his mind, Randulf had agreed. Matilda Webb looked delighted. Here were two strapping young men and she was very happy indeed to have them accompany her.

They mounted their horses and trotted up the road, chatting with their new found friends. Matilda Webb fought for position next to Adam, and Geoffrey de Florin talked haughtily with Randulf. The rest followed on behind with Athelard Drake alone at the very rear. There was something unseemly about him that affected the others, and Adam noticed that none of the company engaged him in conversation.

At length they drew near a town. As they approached a number of men came out to meet them and informed them that this was Ketteryng. The evening was closing in and Hubert Bigge asked where they might stay for the night. The townsfolk led them through the streets, past the market cross and towards a church with the highest spire any of them had seen. To one side of this stood the manor house, and just in front was an inn, a painted sign announcing that it was The Bell. The innkeeper showed them the rooms; two large dormitories, one for the men and another for women, and because it was not market day there was a bed for all.

Adam was aching all over and his damaged foot made him wince as he walked on it, and so after a quick supper he excused himself and made his way back to the dormitory. He lay on the straw-stuffed mattress rubbing his ankle to ease the pain and slowly drifted into a deep sleep.

Randulf however stayed up, drinking and telling stories with the rest of the company. And indeed, they had many extraordinary and strange tales to tell, of travels and riches, or pilgrimages and churches, of knights and tournaments, of thieves and priests, but Randulf excelled himself by capping them all. His stories were almost too fantastical to be true, but he gave them just enough authenticity to ensnare his listeners. His life had been wondrous, and what he had packed into his few years was nothing but miraculous.

As evening became night they began one by one to drift away to bed, until only the physician Geoffrey de Florin, the pock-faced Edward Gregory, and Athelard Drake were left. Randulf cast a questioning eye over the three.

"I know that you, sir, are a physician," said Randulf, pointing to Geoffrey de Florin, but what occupations do your companions have?"

Edward Gregory, his face scarred by white pustules, dribbled as he drank. He wiped his chin with a cloth and announced in a loud voice so that all could hear, "I am a Summoner." He paused for effect. "*Summonitoris.*" He paused again. "Do you know what that is?" He looked smugly around him, his rough Latin aimed to impress.

"Oh yes, "said Randulf, "only too well."

Edward Gregory continued as if holding court, "I bring heretics to account. That is if they do not *penitere* first under my questioning. But I expect you know nothing of these things. These matters are of high state, and not to be spread before *hominis humile*." He took another swig from his tankard, and warm beer trickled from the corner of his mouth. "I, young man, have the authority of the King." He looked around the room for admiration, but nobody was listening. He spoke louder, "I said...."

"You have said too much! And drunk too much!" Geoffrey de Florin cut in. "We all know who you are and what you do. Be careful, Sir!"

"In the name of the Almighty, I will, I will. I just wanted to establish my position." And with that the Summoner stood to his feet, bowed to the uninterested room, and left.

Drake had remained very quiet during the entire evening, sitting on the edge of the group, and finding himself cut out of the chatter whenever he tried to butt in. But now he seized his chance. He slid along the bench until his leg was touching Randulf's and studied him closely.

"Do you know my occupation?" he asked, his voice high pitched and trembling with excitement like that of a young goat. "Have a guess, won't you."

Randulf inched away, and said nothing.

"I am a Pardoner. Do you know what that is?"

"Oh, yes. I am very familiar with Pardoners," said Randulf.

"And do you have any sins to confess? I have authority from the Pope himself to absolve you of any sin." He crossed himself and then delved inside his large leather bag and pulled out a number of objects, placing them neatly on the table, and then dug out some crumpled papers from the bottom.

"Here, look at these! They are genuine and signed by Pope Boniface the Ninth himself. Now tell me of your sins and I will pardon you." His face was growing red and he lisped a little as he spoke.

Randulf looked away. Geoffrey de Florin broke the tension. "Now, now, Master Athelard, leave the young man alone. If he has sins, and I'm sure he does, he can confess them to you another time. I am sure that he wants to go to paradise, and will avail himself of your indulgences as and when."

"Ah, but the present moment is the most opportune time. Do not hesitate, young man, or you may be lost for eternity. Take your chance of deliverance now, while I am here offering it to you."

"I am well set for eternity." replied Randulf, and turned his face away. "I have no use for your Pardons."

Athelard Drake huffed and began to repack his bag. Then he tapped Randulf on the shoulder with a slender finger. "Do you know what I have here?" he asked. "These are very precious relics that can keep the devil from your soul, should you wish to … purchase them." He smiled at Randulf. "They will not however endow you with eternal life. Unlike the indulgences."

He picked up each item in his willowy hands and held them up to his face, turning them over in the dim candlelight.

"This jar contains the bones of Saint Andrew. Do you see the holes where the nails went in when they crucified him? Oh, so precious are these." He shoved the jar of pigs' bones towards Randulf, who veered away. "No, not interested?" the Pardoner lisped. He put them deep into the bag.

"And this cross is of gold, incorruptible as the heavenly soul. It costs a pretty penny, but then I would predict that you have many of those, for you wear a fine costume." He plucked at Randulf's braided tunic.

"And here we have blessed water from the well at Jerusalem." A sprinkling of this will cleanse the spirit and heal the soul. Would you try a little? It does not cost much."

"Leave the boy alone!" cut in the Physician, his voice irritable with displeasure.

"I have no need of your relics or your indulgences." said Randulf.

"So you are clean are you? Pure as the driven snow? Washed and ready for heaven. I do not think so young Master Randulf. You have blood on your hands!"

"You must not speak so!" cried the Physician.

"But what I say is true! Master Randulf has killed another! I know when a man needs forgiveness, I sense it, I smell it, I see it on his face; a certain look of the eyes. And I see it in our friend here. Randulf, what do you say?"

Randulf dropped his eyes and studied the floor.

"Aha!" said Athelard Drake. "Your face belies you! Tomorrow we will see what secrets you are holding. For now I will leave you. The privy awaits me and then bed. I bid you goodnight." He rose with a flourish, shouldered his bag of fakes and left the room. An awkward silence followed. Randulf drank from his wooden mug and belched.

"Ignore the poor fellow," said Geoffrey de Florin. "He drinks too much and forgets himself. I hope you have not been offended."

Randulf hesitated for some moments and then spoke very quietly, as if not sure he wanted anyone to hear the words. "I am guilty as he said."

The Physician looked at him with concern. "You have killed?"

"Yes." He looked de Florin in the eyes, "and it was quite intentional."

"May I ask the circumstances?"

Randulf pulled at his ale again. "He was but a boy. I poisoned him. Foxglove. I had to."

Geoffrey de Florin closed his eyes. "Foxglove," he murmured. "Sickness, vomiting, aches and shivers, the heart racing and the head pounding, and if enough essence is administered, a collapse of the humours and violent death. Not a good way to go." He considered a moment. "And are you certain he is dead?"

"I did not see him die, if that is what you mean." A flicker of hope crossed his face. "Could he still be alive?"

The physician drew a piece of velum from a pocket deep inside his cloak. He unrolled it and Randulf could see that it contained two circles, drawn one inside the other, with numbers written between the two, and scattered around the spheres were inscriptions and signs. "This is the Sphere of

Apuleius. Have you heard of it before? It can predict whether a man will live or die. Tell me, what was his name?"

"I cannot tell you."

"Do you not want to know if he lived or died?"

Randulf squirmed on the hard wooden bench and thought for a while, tussling with the fear of mentioning the name. But at last he gave in. He needed to know. He drew in close to the physician and whispered. "You must tell no-one, but his name was Richard. Richard Wolvercot."

"And why is his name such a secret?"

"He was the brother of my travelling companion."

Geoffrey de Florin looked deeply at him for a long while and then mouthed the name and counted the letters out on the chart, assigning each one a number. "And on which day of the week did he fall ill?"

"It was a Sunday," said Randulf, fascinated by what was to be revealed.

The physician looked at the inscription written in one of the corners of the sheet and then closed his eyes to make some calculations. Randulf realised his palms were damp with sweat.

Geoffrey de Florin pointed his finger to the spheres. "You see that they are divided in half, there being *vita* in the top half and *mors* at the bottom - life and death. His number is twenty-nine. Tell me, in which half does that number fall?"

Randulf looked closely, his heart beating fast. At first he could not see it, but then, in spidery writing he found the number. Twenty-nine. It was in the half labelled *mors*. He looked up at the physician.

"Yes, it means you killed him. He is dead." He stared long and hard at Randulf. "So we have a poisoner in our midst. I had better be careful of what I eat and drink." A sarcastic smile crossed his lips.

"I had to do it." Randulf said.

"And did you know the pain it would cause?" asked the Physician, "Not only to the boy but to his family. Yes, these are murderous times, and there is much death, but did you need to add to it?"

"There is more at stake. The boy was but a pawn. His death was necessary. And there will be more to follow before many days have passed. " Randulf spoke angrily, trying hard to control his voice. "I will speak no more of this." He pushed back the bench and stood up, swaying slightly under the influence of the ale. "Goodnight, Master Physician. I pray that you also will not speak of this."

Geoffrey de Florin caught him by the arm and forced him to sit down. "Let me tell you one last tale," he said, "It is a true story and I think it will help you."

"I once met a man," said the Physician, "who had a tree that wept tears. Imagine that! He told me that a friend of his, a woodcutter, had given him an oak sapling to plant. He had grown it from an acorn that he found hidden in a forgotten corner of the forest, and he had taken great care of it, watering it and shading it from the fiercest rays of the sun, and keeping it from the frost of winter, and he had done this because he wanted to give it as a gift to his best friend.

"Well, this friend took the tree home and carefully planted it in the soil. He nurtured it with love, and over the years it grew into a mighty oak the height of a house. People came from afar to admire it. It was indeed a proud tree. But then one day the woodcutter caught the pestilence and died of it, and on that very same day the tree wept tears. The wife of the man called him outside. 'Look, she said, the tree is weeping for the departed soul of your friend.' And sure enough there were great silver teardrops hanging from every branch of the tree. And the next day they had disappeared and they never returned. This tree never cried before or after that day, that fateful day when the woodcutter died."

"And how is that supposed to help me?" asked Randulf.

"Young man, there is no shame in weeping for someone you know who has died, even if you only weep for a day. This is especially true if we think we are strong."

Geoffrey de Florin had been holding Randulf's arm all the while, but Randulf now jerked it away and stood up. Without saying a word, not even 'goodnight', he wove his way between the empty tables and, clutching the wall, made his way upstairs to the dormitory.

He slept fitfully that night, in and out of dreams and wakefulness. He saw Richard leering at him and stumbling towards him, his handsome face now distorted and foaming at the mouth. Yet each time he came close he would fall to the ground and dissolve like snow. Randulf awoke with a start, sweat on his brow and heart thumping. He got up to relieve himself and in his half-awake state thought he heard the rustling of someone rifling through his saddle bag, but in the dark he could not be sure. He stumbled back to bed and by the morning he remembered it only as a dream.

+

After breakfast the company saddled their horses and set out for the journey. Matilda Webb rode close to Adam and chattered incessantly to him about this and that. She smiled often at him, her lips parting to show a dark gap between her front teeth. In a younger woman it would have been attractive, but in her seemed more of a fault. Adam was courteous but wary. He tried hard to think of Agneta.

As the morning drew on he noted a change in the company. He could see Geoffrey de Florin talking often to

Athelard Drake as they rode at the rear of the group. They spoke conspiratorially in hushed tones and now and again Edward Gregory, the Summoner, would join them. Adam felt uneasy. There was a crash in the trees above him as a dozen crows beat their wings and took off, speckling the sky and cawing and flapping noisily as they flew away. "A murder of crows," muttered Adam to himself. "That is a sure sign of trouble today."

The open land around Ketteryng gave way to thin woodland, and the path wound through the trees following streams here and there. The going was flat and easy and the company covered the miles quickly. The woodland around them grew slowly denser until eventually they found themselves closed in by trees and hidden from sight. Adam had not noticed until then that the group had divided into two, and that he and Randulf were now separated by quite a distance. Matilda Webb had kept close to Adam, still chatting away, and Hubert Bigge and Simon Carter followed closely on behind. But when Adam turned around he could not see Randulf or any of the rest of the company.

"Should we not wait for the others to catch up?" he asked.

Hubert Bigge spoke up, "You're not worried are you, young master? They are not far behind."

"No, I just thought it was safer to be in a large company, especially in such dense woodland."

"Well, perhaps we should stop for a rest anyway," said Matilda Webb. "I am sure that Adam would like to ease his foot." She winked at Bigge.

They dismounted and Adam gratefully sat down and rubbed his tender ankle.

"Here, let me help." Mistress Webb took his foot in her hands and began to massage it. Her movements were gentle and soothing, and Adam closed his eyes, feeling a little guilty. Then all of a sudden she wrenched his foot hard to one side. Adam cried out in agony as the pain shot through him and tried to pull away, but her grip was fierce and the searing fire in his foot disabled him. A pounding blow to the stomach winded him and he looked up through a haze of tears to see the large figure of Hubert Bigge above him, grinning as he kicked him again and again. Adam grunted as the large leather boot landed in his groin, and he curled into a ball, gasping for wind.

"Simon, grab his bag!" shouted Bigge, and the shipman wrenched it from Adam's shoulder. He ripped it open and dug through it, lifting out the few meagre possessions that Adam carried.

"Where is his money?" cried Bigge. "Search him! He must have money."

Adam sensed rough hands grasping him, pulling at his clothing and fumbling in his cloak. He tried to cross his arms over his chest to conceal the Bible, but it only took a moment for the dirty hands to find it and rip it from him.

"Got the money," yelled Simon Carter and waved the cloth-covered book above his head. He threw it to Bigge who struck Adam again and everything went black.

+

"Wake up, Adam, wake up!" Randulf was shaking him by the shoulder.

Adam could hear his voice through a bleary haze of pain, and though he knew it well he noticed that it was slurred and somehow oddly different. He forced his eyes open, and as he focussed on the face of his friend he hardly recognised him. There was a long knife cut on Randulf's forehead and the stream of blood that had flowed from this had dried in large smears on his cheeks. His face was swollen on one side and there was a red stain in the corner of his mouth. He held his hand up to his bruised face. "They stole everything."

Adam sat up and breathed deeply.

"They stole everything. All my money. Everything. They beat me." Randulf collapsed on the forest floor.

Adam reached inside his shirt and suddenly his blood grew cold and a shiver went down his spine. "The Bible! Randulf, they have the Bible!" His energy sapped away and he slumped back, his head in his hands. "They have the Bible..."

The two of them remained motionless for some time, regaining their strength and reliving the events in their minds. Finally Adam spoke, "Are you alright?"

"My head hurts, and my money is gone, but I will live."

"We have to get the book back. We must find it."

"They are headed for Ely. We will go there too. We will get them back for this." Randulf stretched and stood up. "Let me go and find my horse. I saw him flee when they attacked, but he will be nearby. I can see Beatrix over there by that thicket. She too must have run or they would have stolen her as well, but at least she had the sense to come back. You stay here." He wandered off into the wood, calling and cooing for Henry.

Adam watched his friend go, and a new respect arose in his heart for him. Randulf was good to have around. He knew what to do, even when things looked bleak. Together they would deliver this Bible. But first they had to recover it. Trust no-one. That is what his mother had said, and how true that had turned out to be. These companions, these fellow travellers, had turned on them and robbed them. How good it was that Randulf could be trusted! After all he had already saved his life when he was near to drowning.

The sound of hooves and footsteps brought him out of his thoughts and, as they made their way along the path and out of the wood, Adam smiled.   Yes, with Randulf on his side all would turn out well.

Chapter 13 - Fynchyngbroke Priory

It had been two days since Guy de Beauchamp let the bloodhound sniff the horse dung that the Albino had collected. The dog had easily picked up the scent of the horse and was quickly on the trail. They had followed it as it ran down the track to Lutterworth and then circled around the market and the street leading to the church. It paused by some trees near the graveyard and had barked at the church door before heading off on the road to Ketteryng. A large bear of a man in a thick woollen cap and with a wiry grey beard watched them come and go, and as they went he entered the church, knelt and prayed.

The Albino and de Beauchamp camped overnight in a glade some five miles to the east of Lutterworth and rested their horses and dogs. The next morning they mounted again and continued towards Ketteryng, the bloodhound becoming more excited as the scent became fresher and stronger, and the mastiff slavering with anticipation.

"See how the dogs have changed their mood?" said Guy de Beauchamp. "They have a fresh energy even though the day is growing old. We must be getting closer."

The bloodhound lead them into town, and to the stables of the Bell Inn. It slavered and pawed at the straw where Henry and Beatrix had been stalled and barked at the one bay mare that was tied to a hook on the wall. De Beauchamp glanced at the Albino. If the stalls were empty, then the horses had gone and with them the riders.

"Quick, search the Inn. We have no time to lose."

The Albino ran through the open door and accosted the Innkeeper. "Have you seen two young men? Are they staying here? They have an old nag and a white palfrey."

The Innkeeper wiped his hands on a cloth and laid it on the table. He was not in a hurry to reply.

"Come on man, I need an answer. Have you seen them?"

The Innkeeper spoke slowly and with a heavy accent. "I might have? What business is it of yours?"

"This, Sir, is my business," said the Albino and pulled a dagger from his belt. The Innkeeper blanched.

"Aaah, I think I do remember them now," he said as he waved a hand in the air. "They were with a larger company of pilgrims but they left this morning. I have no idea where they were going."

+

The candlelit windows of the priory church of Fynchyngbroke shone like a welcoming beacon in the darkness as Adam and Randulf rode across the flat open countryside. Both were sore and tired, and hunger gnawed at their empty stomachs. Neither spoke; their sombre mood reflected in the silence between them. Adam was brooding on the loss of the Bible. How could he have been so stupid as to lose it so easily? Why had he not seen through the friendly veneer of the company and not seen their wicked hearts? Now he was bleeding and bruised and empty and the cause seemed hopeless.

The low priory buildings surrounding the church slowly came into view; a collection of houses, stables, workrooms and a refectory. A high stone wall protected the priory from the outside world, and the pair walked their horses around it until they located the gateway. The door was locked but there was a small bell which rang out crisply when Adam pulled on the rope. A young female voice called out from behind the door, "Who is there?"

Adam answered and asked if there were a bed for the night. The gate opened to reveal a nun, no more than sixteen or seventeen years old, with the white woollen veil of a novice covering her wimple and contrasting sharply with her black Benedictine habit. She held a candle in her hand, and lifted it to see her guests more clearly. As she did so the light flickered on their injuries, and her mouth opened in horror and her free hand covered it quickly to stifle a cry.

"Oh!" she cried, "What a sight you are! What has happened to you? Come in, come in!"

She ushered them in and locked the gate behind. Suddenly, Adam felt an almighty wave of relief. He felt his legs weakening beneath him and he crumpled to the floor. The novice dropped to her knees beside him and cradled his head.

"O my Lord! You need food and a warm bed and rest."

"Sister Imelda!" A large nun had appeared in the porch. "Sister Imelda! Away from that boy! What do you think you are doing?"

"I was only trying to bring him some comfort."

"That is no way to comfort a young man! Put him down! You must leave the ways of the world behind you Sister!"

Sister Imelda blushed and stood up, dusting down her habit with her palms.

"Pick up your candle and lead our guests to the Prioress. You should be in time if you hurry. Compline will be starting soon. I will stable their mounts."

Randulf dragged Adam to his feet and they followed Sister Imelda as she led the way across the open courtyard. The tower of the little church rose above them, dominating the area and blocking out the moon. They followed the novice around the church and towards a two-storey house. Sister Imelda tapped at the door and opened it, and then stood aside to let them in. Adam rested his hand on Randulf's shoulder to steady himself as they ducked under the low doorway and entered the building. Behind a large desk sat a nun, her hands clasped in front of her in prayer. She looked up as they came in and made the sign of the cross. "Dear Lord," she whispered. "Look at you two."

Prioress Catharine Multon had been in charge of Fynchyngbroke for nine years, during which time she had seen the withdrawal of a number of benefactors and a considerable loss of income. The priory was now smaller than ever and poorer than most. The few cattle and sheep they possessed provided little revenue and the weather was rotting the vines, so in recent times they had resorted to allow paying guests to stay overnight. They were on the pilgrim route, well placed for such a venture, and little by little their fortunes were reversing.

The Prioress looked Adam and Randulf over, casting a discerning eye over them and assessing what they might be able to afford. She was about to be disappointed.
Randulf spoke up. "My Lady, we were robbed today, and sorely beaten. Can we please stay the night and have food and shelter? You have a fine Priory here," he added for good measure.

"You have no money?" she asked, already suspecting the answer.

"None."

The Prioress looked from one to the other and compassion rose in her from somewhere deep within. She had never been a mother, but the desire to mother was strong, and these two young men were in a bad way. Their bloodied and bruised faces tugged at her heart, and the hungry look in their eyes drew her in.

"We will make a bed for you tonight, so you can rest and find peace from your day."

A bell rang from somewhere outside and she stood up. "It is time for Divine Service. Would you accompany me, or would you prefer earthly food to spiritual food?"

"We have not eaten all day," said Randulf. "And we are near exhaustion. Would you excuse us Compline?"

"Very well. But tomorrow I would ask that you help us by attending to some chores to show gratitude to God for all you will receive here." She opened the door and called for Sister Imelda.

The next day was Sunday, and they were woken early by the clanging of the church bell. The room they were in had a small window high up on the wall and Randulf strained to look out, standing on the edge of the hard wooden bed.

"What can you see?" enquired Adam.

"Nuns!"

Randulf turned around, revealing a large black eye that had developed overnight. He grinned. "Lots of them!"

He jumped down from the bed and pulled on his hose and tunic. "I'm going out to see."

Adam hauled himself out of bed and followed. There before them were about twenty nuns walking in single file across the courtyard towards the church, black veils swirling in the morning breeze, and black habits flowing with each stride. At the rear was a nun with a white veil, the novice Imelda. She caught sight of Adam and Randulf from the corner of her eye and smiled. She had been sent to them the night before with a vegetable broth, bread and ale, and had also brought them a bowl of warm water for washing. She had said little, but she had not needed to.

The nuns filed into the church and before long the smooth sound of chanted psalms echoed across the yard. Randulf closed his eyes, and Adam wondered if he was in prayer. How much of God did Randulf know? How much did Adam himself know? So little really - and that little was from the meagre teaching of the church. Of course he believed in God, but then didn't everyone? It was a sin not to. But was it only two days ago when he saw the Bible and felt something strange and new touch his soul? Was that God? How could he tell? And would he be able to stand up to the authorities if he was ever caught holding this book? Would he survive torture if it came to that? Did he believe that much? So many questions raced through his mind. "Oh God, show me..." he said out loud, and Randulf woke with a start.

After Lauds had ended the nuns filed out of the church and then scattered to their various duties. Sister Imelda walked over to them, her head cocked on one side. "Good morning," she said. "I hope you slept well."

"Very well. Although the beds are hard."

"Yes, aren't they? They make them especially hard so that we remember the suffering of the Saviour." Sister Imelda scratched her neck and rolled her shoulders. "They have made me wear a hair shirt next to my skin to teach me to suffer for my sins. They say I need to give up all worldly passions, but I know that they themselves do not." She blushed. "I'm sorry, I should not be saying these things. Forgive me."

Adam looked at her. She was just a girl, and a pretty one at that. He knew that when she entered the Priory they would have shorn off all her hair and removed all her possessions. She would have vowed three things; never to leave the Priory, to be totally obedient to the Prioress, and to devote her life to the faith until death. But in spite of all these things, she was still a girl, with all her desires and dreams. Adam envied her for her strong faith, but he also pitied her. She was as captive as a bear for the baiting.

"Has the Prioress asked you to help with the chores?" she asked.

"Yes, but we do not know how we can help."

"Follow me and I'll show you. Can you collect eggs?"

They spent the hours between Terce and Sext feeding the chickens, cleaning the henhouse and collecting eggs. It was light work and yet the long hours made it onerous. The nuns filed into the chapel for a Chapter Meeting and again for a Mass, but Adam and Randulf kept working. Their innards growled with hunger, but it was not until the start of the afternoon that they were brought out a bowl of soup and some bread. Sister Imelda was sent to them to tell them to stop work for the rest of the day, it being the Lord's Day. They could sleep in the courtyard if they so wished, on the stone benches that supported the walls.

The friar arrived in the middle of the afternoon. He was a sturdy man of middle years with a red nose and a constant hacking cough. He smiled oddly as he dismounted from his pony and greeted the Prioress.

"My Lady Prioress, how good to see you again."

"Indeed, Friar Stephen. How was your journey?"

"Fair, considering the cold winds and the soreness of my saddle." He stretched to ease his back and rubbed his backside.

"You have come far this time?"

"Ah, yes. I should have been here a day earlier, but I got caught up with a travelling company who kept me waiting. They were somewhat drunk and in a state of great excitement, having recently come across a small fortune, and they insisted I join them to celebrate. I could not be persuaded not to." He coughed and the hiccupped loudly. "I am afraid I have already missed Sext and None but I assure you I will be ready to lead Vespers."

The Prioress looked him up and down, a grimace of distaste on her face, and offered up a silent prayer that God would grant her grace. Friar Stephen had arrived reeking of drink and in no fit state to preside, but she was duty bound to submit to his ministry. She had never understood why the church needed a friar or monk to minister the sacraments when it allowed a woman to preside over all the other services, but that was the way it had always been, and so she obeyed, albeit grudgingly.

"Well, Friar, come and eat, for you must be hungry." The Prioress led him to the refectory, while the novice Imelda wiped down his pony and stabled it.

Adam had been listening to the conversation from his position reclining on the cold bench. He nudged Randulf. "We need to talk to him. It sounds as though he has met our thieving company. He must know where the Bible is." He jumped up and strode after the friar, across the courtyard towards the refectory.

"Not now!" called Randulf. "You cannot barge into the refectory and speak during mealtime, you should know that."

"I know nothing about monasteries and nunneries and the workings of the religious," said Adam. "I have never been in such a place before. How should I know what to do?"

"Then keep close to me," replied Randulf, "and do as I say. We will talk to our friar after he has eaten and before he sobers up and tightens his tongue. Until then, we watch and wait."

They sat back down in the yard opposite the refectory door, until, after a while, the friar came out. He coughed noisily and wiped his mouth with a small cloth which he then tucked back into his belt. Adam and Randulf approached and he smiled at them and nodded his tonsured head.

"Friar Stephen, we must talk with you," said Adam.

"I will take your confession in the chapel."

"No, no, I have nothing to confess," blurted Adam.

The Friar looked at him strangely. "So you are sinless? Holy and righteous? Above all other men? Have you today not done an evil deed or said a bad word or thought of lust or greed? I think not, young Sir! I *will* hear your confession!" And with that he started to walk away.

Adam looked at Randulf, who just raised his eyebrows. "You should have let me lead. However this may turn out for the good. Let's meet him in the chapel and find out what he knows. But Adam, do not mention the Bible."

Adam knelt in the small booth and could hear the rasping cough of Friar Stephen through the curtain that separated them. "Tell me your sin, that I might pardon you."

"Friar, I have lost something of great value to me."

"That is not a sin. I want to hear how you have sinned!"

Adam persevered. "I was robbed and I think you may have met the company who did this to me."

He heard the curtain rustle as the Friar shifted position. "This is irregular for this is not a sin, but go on. Tell me, what did you lose?"

"They stole money."

"And anything else?" The question came in a tone of voice that suggested that the friar knew more. Adam hesitated.

"No, nothing else, just money."

"Ah, so you *do* have sins to confess. Let us start with your lying!"

"Lying, Friar? I have told the truth."

"I think not. The company I met spoke too freely when they were drinking and revelling in their fortune. One bragged about a stolen book. A book he took from a young man matching your description."

Adam felt the blood chill in his veins. So Friar Stephen knew about the Bible, and that Adam was implicated in it. He had the right to turn him over to the law if he so wished and watch him hang.

"I know nothing of a book."

Suddenly the curtain was whipped open between them. The Friar stared into Adam's eyes long and hard and slightly blearily. Adam stared back, trying not to blink and give himself away. He repeated, "They must be mistaken. I know nothing about a book."

Friar Stephen looked wearily around him. "I am tired of pretence," he said. "I know what book this was. An outlawed Bible in the language of the common people. And I know that it belonged to you, and that for this you could die." He let his words weigh heavily. Adam continued to stare unblinking, praying that this moment was not happening.

"And yet…and yet," continued Friar Stephen in a hushed voice, "I have some sympathy with you. For too long I have ministered in Latin to people who have no idea what I am saying. I stand and spout forth and look on simple men, their blank faces uncomprehending and their souls heading for hell. I want to help them and, even though I stand between them and God, I want them to also understand what He is like. They cannot do that in a strange tongue. I am growing tired of this deceit. I have kept my thoughts to myself for some years now, afraid of the storm they might unleash, but when I was in the company of men who had an English Bible in their possession, and was able to see it and to touch it, and read for the first time the words in the language I now speak

to you I began to sense that this was right…" He paused. "
Does that shock you?"

Adam did not know how to reply. He said nothing.

"I fear I have said too much. It is the wine. Please do me
the service of forgetting that I ever bared my soul." He
snorted. "I now am the one who has confessed."

"Friar, your secret is safe with me, as I hope mine is with
you."

"Nothing goes beyond the walls of confession. Besides, I
do not have much longer in this world." He coughed again.

"I need to know one thing more," said Adam. "Where are
the company now and in which direction are they headed? I
have to find the Bible."

"I heard them say that they were going to Ely and then on
to Walsyngham Abbey."

So they have not changed their plans, thought Adam.
That was stupid of them. "Thank you, Friar Stephen."

Stephen coughed again, and wiped green phlegm from his
mouth onto a dirty cloth. "The Fen Ague," he explained. It
gets all of us in time." Friar Stephen saw that Adam did not
understand. He laid a hand on his shoulder. "The fens that
surround the Isle of Ely are foul and produce an ague that
causes illness of many sorts. It is a place of marshes and
swamps and dead water, only fit for the eels that grow there
in abundance. And yet out of this watery wilderness rises the
Isle of Ely with the magnificence of heaven itself built upon it.
The great cathedral with the octagonal tower. What a
masterpiece! What glory goes to God from there!"

He turned his eyes heavenward and made the sign if the
cross.

Adam interrupted, "I look forward to seeing it, because I
must go to Ely and get the Bible again."

"Beware, young man, for Ely is a stronghold of the church and has a reputation for sniffing out heretics and Lollards. Be very careful how you go. Be very careful." His chest heaved in a spasm of coughing, and he leant back against the wall to rest.

"May God go with you. I suggest you leave as soon as you are able." Friar Stephen held out a hand and Adam shook it.

Once outside the chapel, Randulf grabbed Adam. "How did it go?"

"They are headed to Ely and then on to Walsyngham. They have not changed their plans," replied Adam.

"And what else did he say?"

"I cannot tell you," said Adam with a smile. "What happens in the confession is a secret."

Randulf slapped him on the back. "Well, my friend, you have done well. I will soon make a good Catholic of you!"

Prioress Catharine Multon was surrounded by paperwork and had her head in her hands.

"Enter," she called, when Adam and Randulf knocked on her study door. "How may I help you?"

"We have much enjoyed your hospitality," said Randulf, "but we are on an urgent mission and we need to take our leave. We have come to say goodbye."

"And where are you off to in such a hurry? I think your wounds are not yet healed."

"We must go to the Isle of Ely," said Adam.

The Prioress studied them. "And how do you propose to get there?" she asked.

"If we may unstable our horses we will ride today."

"You have not been to Ely before." This was a statement not a question, but Adam still answered it.

"No, My Lady, we have not."

"Then I must tell you that you have no need of horses. Does the name not tell you something? It is the Isle of Ely. Ely is an island surrounded by marshes and water. You will need to take a boat. There are some to be had on the river Ouse and there is a quay at Ely where you can disembark. But you may not take your horses."

This information was a shock. "So what will become of them?" asked Adam, thinking of Beatrix.

"You may leave them here. We will stable them and feed them for you until you return. For a small sum," she added.

Randulf looked at Adam who just shrugged. "Thank you," he said.

"There is a boat leaving tomorrow morning that you could catch. The boatman brings salted eels here in barrels, and he will be able to accommodate you I am sure. The journey takes a day, so you will be in Ely by tomorrow night. Farewell." She put her head back in her hands and studied her papers. The meeting was over.

Chapter 14 - Cat and Mouse

It was late in the morning when Osmund Clarke heard the clatter of hooves in the courtyard below, and peering out of his window, saw the entourage of the Archbishop. He swore under his breath, a curse upon the man that could stir up so much trouble. He straightened his clothing and sat down heavily on his chair behind the desk, assuming an attitude of work. There was a bang on the door and without waiting for reply, Thomas Arundel, Archbishop of Canterbury and loyal friend of King Henry IV, strode into the room. Sir Osmund hurriedly rose from his chair and bowed low. "Archbishop, you are most welcome," he said. "Please be seated." He motioned to the high-backed chair behind his desk, and fetched a stool for himself.

Thomas Arundel gathered his robes around him and settled into the chair. He looked tired and careworn, and the lines that had begun to develop on his face belied the fact that he was only forty-eight. His unshaven jaw was grey with fine stubble. And yet despite all this his eyes were as bright and cold as ever.

Osmund poured them both a glass of wine, and took a large sip. There was an uncomfortable silence, finally broken by the archbishop.

"Sir Osmund, the King enquires after your progress." Thomas Arundel spoke quietly; his voice was even, balanced, powerful, menacing. He picked up a small knife from the table and absentmindedly played with it, rolling it around between his fingers. "I assume you *are* making progress." It was more of a statement than an enquiry.

"Yes, all things are in hand." Sir Osmund tried hard to control the nervous tremor in his voice.

"Tell me."

"Well, we have the boy, Adam Wolvercot, under our watch. My men are following him and he has responded well to our game so far. It will not be long now." He tried to sound convincing.

The archbishop was unimpressed. "And why do you leave such matters to a mere youth? He is but twenty-three and a farmer. Is there not a great risk here? Why did you not find and destroy the Bible yourself before it fell into the wrong hands? You have known for many years where it might be." Thomas Arundel looked accusingly at Osmund Clarke, his eyes narrowed and piercing.

"My Lord, I swear I did not know the whole story. I knew that the whereabouts of the Bible had been written down by the boy's father in a book when he worked at the great library in Merton College along with those other Lollard heretics. He was already frightened and was sensing that his time had come, so he wrote it down in case he was not able to deliver it himself. Perhaps his heretic son would deliver the book in the future. We should have destroyed them all in '95 when we cleansed the college of them and tried to remove their teachings. But in that cleansing, Jacob de Wolvercot was interrogated and told us much. Under the branding of the hot iron he named the book in which he had written the location of the Bible. It was written in a book called *Piers Plowman*, a hateful poem that attacks the holy church and should itself be destroyed. And from the moment of his confession I planned my revenge. It has taken many years, but now it is about to happen."

"You did not see fit to find this book and hunt down the Bible yourself?" asked the archbishop.

"My Lord, that would have been too simple, and I could have been so easily implicated. No, I had a greater plan. We did not kill Jacob de Wolvercot in the torture but allowed him to live so that he could see the downfall of his own son and so be put to more pain than ever we could force upon him. And afterwards we will put him to the stake as well. He has done us a great service, and by his confession now we can catch his son and the Bible together."

"It seems a complicated process."

"Ah, yes, but the rewards are so much greater! Besides, I enjoy toying with their lives. It makes my mundane existence so much more... pleasurable. I am like a cat with a mouse. The joy of the game is in the playing."

Thomas Arundel grunted. He disliked Osmund Clarke, but was forced to work with him by King Henry, who enjoyed his strange ways.

"The boy Adam has the Bible now?" asked the Archbishop.

"And as we speak, he is on his way to deliver it." Osmund Clarke smiled. He hoped that the questioning would soon stop.

"Do we know who the recipient is? Some 'Poor Preacher', I suppose?"

"No. But we are confident that Adam Wolvercot will lead us to him. As I said we are on his trail, and he now knows the whereabouts of this Lollard. We will catch them both together.

"And why now? Why have you not acted before?"

"Because of the new law that will soon be in place. The *De Hæretico Comburendum*. I have long awaited this piece of legislation. I am a patient man, my Lord Archbishop, and I am now about to see just how much more can be gained by waiting. I can now catch a handful of rats in the trap and crush them lawfully."

The Archbishop grunted again. "So you plan to catch this preacher and also Adam Wolvercot, along with the heretical Bible, and in one fell swoop do away with the lot of them? That will be a worthy prize. If you can do it."

"I have two of my men following the boy. We will not let him slip the net. And then we will catch them both together, and make an example of them by destroying them publicly. The people will see how powerful we are and how we stamp upon the heresies that could undermine this nation. Three rats caught in a trap for the price of one!"

"You say you have two men following him. Who are they?"

"One has no name. He is an unfortunate creature, an albino. But he is trustworthy and he will do anything for me."

"And the other?"

"He is Master Randulf Payne. I have known him a long time."

"Of course you have." The Archbishop put his hands in an attitude of prayer and rested his chin on his fingers. "After all, he is your son."

Sir Osmund Clarke recoiled.

"Come, come, Sir Osmund. We know all about you. It is a part of our duty to the realm. We know that Master Payne is your illegitimate son, born of some whore. Did you think that this was your secret alone?"

"The boy does not know."

"And that is how you keep him under your control. He does your bidding because he is grateful to you for rescuing him from life on the streets. Or so you have led him to believe. If he knew he was your son he would surely have rebelled by now."

Sir Osmund Clarke sipped clumsily from his goblet, spilling a trickle of red wine down his beard. He wiped it away with the back of his hand.

The Archbishop continued. "No matter. Your secret is safe with me. Not even the king knows of this. I do not tell him everything."

And therein lies your power, thought Sir Osmund.

There was silence for a moment. The Archbishop stood up and paced the room. Osmund Clarke stood as well, not sure what to do, whether to walk or stand still. He fumbled with a large ring on his finger.

At last Thomas Arundel broke the silence. "I have a man in London who I have been questioning, a priest who has turned to Lollardy. Perhaps you have heard his name, one William Sawtrey. Three days ago I questioned him for many hours, but he would not recant. He will not worship the cross, or angels, and believes that the bread and wine of the Eucharist do not become the body and blood of our Lord, and refused to say otherwise even after three hours of... interrogation. I do not think he will ever change his views, though in the past few months we have given him many opportunities to come back into the fold. He is a black sheep, and a dangerous one at that.

"In two days' time, on the 23rd, I am due to question Sawtrey again and I will give him one last chance to embrace the truth of the holy Catholic Church. And if then, as I suspect, he still refuses to give up his ridiculous beliefs, I will arrange for the King to pass a decree against him and have him degraded through the seven steps from priest to doorkeeper, and then hand him over to the civil authorities to be burned at the stake. This will be a trial to see how the people react. If there is horror and revulsion as the common man witnesses this scene, then I will recommend that the

King quickly enacts the law. Then your young man Adam Wolvercot will have the honour of being the first man in England to *legally* burn for his heresy. I believe you have had a hand in the writing of the new law, the *De Hæretico Comburendum*. May I congratulate you."

The Archbishop walked to the door and placed his hand on the doorknob. The interview was over. As he left the room he stopped and turned. "Oh, and by the way, send your son Randulf to watch the burning of Sawtrey. It will be an education for him."

Chapter 15 - The Safe House

The boatman offloaded the barrels of salted eels from his cart at Fynchyngbroke Priory, rolling them down a plank to the ground and spilling briny water from the loosely fitting lids. He wiped his wet hands on his hose and held out a rough palm as the Prioress introduced him to Adam and Randulf.

"They are to go with my blessing to Ely. You will be recompensed on your return," she said, and turning to Adam and Randulf added, "And you will pay me for the stabling of your horses when you collect them. I cannot afford charity."

The boatman beckoned them and they climbed aboard the empty cart for the journey back to the river. The novice Sister Imelda waved them off, biting her lip as she watched the cart trundle down the lane.

The boat was a type of barge, shallow-keeled and able to manoeuvre the channel of the river that wound its way through the scrubby woodland near the Priory. Then, as the day dragged on, the landscape slowly changed and the river banks melted into a watery plain of marsh, bog and reed bed. A scattered line of willow trees clung to the edges of the river bank marking its path; but apart from them Adam could see no way of telling where river banks ended and marshland began. All was under a layer of water. Now and again eels and catfish would jump and splash on the surface, creating ever widening ripples in the otherwise stagnant lake. It seemed to Adam that he was lost in another world, one without edge or form, and in the far grey distance the lake became the sky. The barge slid onwards to the steady rhythm of the boatman. Only the slop and splash of his oars broke the silence.

Late in the afternoon the boatman shook Adam awake and pointed towards the horizon. There, surrounded by trees and bushes, rose the shadowy form of an island, crested by the soft brown rooftops of the town. From there rose two vast towers, glowing like gold in the pale light and pointing like great fingers into the silvering sky. Adam gulped. Even from this distance the sight was awe inspiring. He wondered how it was ever possible for man to build something quite as beautiful and grand as this, and in such a desolate place.

A few hours later they moored at the quayside and climbed the low incline to the market square. In the distance they could hear a great commotion and as they topped the hill they saw a large crowd ahead of them, shouting and jeering. Randulf grabbed Adam by the arm and pushed his way through the crowd, wanting him to see what was going on. There in the centre a man was being paraded around. He was bareheaded and barefooted and was carrying a wand and some strange wooden plates covered in mystical signs. Onlookers spat at him and shouted abuse. One or two hit him as he was pushed past. Adam leant over to a man standing next to him. "Is he a witch or a magician or some such?" he asked.

"No, son, he's a Lollard, but it amounts to the same thing. They all talk the same evil nonsense and are up to no good."

"Ay, parading's not enough for them. Hang them all!" shouted another, and the cry went up, "Hang him! Hang him! Hang the Lollard!"

Adam turned away, a nauseous feeling rising up in his stomach. He tried to catch Randulf's eye, to slip away silently from the baying crowd, but Randulf was transfixed. He had a look of hatred in his eyes.

"Let's go!" Adam pulled out of the crowd and headed for the cathedral. He wanted to see the beautiful eight sided tower that rose high above the nave, the most extraordinary sight in all of England and a feat of incredible engineering. He wanted to get away from the crowd and closer to God.

Randulf found him there, staring up at the building that towered above him. Never had Adam seen such a sight, and he felt overwhelmed. Randulf punched him on the arm.

"Come on, we've work to do."

He led him down the lane in front of the church and followed the stone wall that protected the monastery. "I've made a few enquiries while you were gawping at the cathedral, and it seems that our book has already left the town."

Adam stopped in his tracks. "What?" he cried.

"They have already left, and are headed for Walsyngham. They left early this morning so we are not too far behind. We can catch them if we hurry. They caught a river boat."

They ran to the quay. Randulf ran about, asking this person and that, but it was now late in the day and no boatman would venture out towards dark. Finally he came back to Adam who was sitting on the ground thinking.

"We cannot sail today, and we have no money anyway to pay a boatman, let alone to feed ourselves or find lodging for the night."

Randulf too slumped to the floor and scratched his head. "So what do we do?" For once he was lost.

"The old man at Lutterworth told me of a man who lives in Prickwillow, a good Christian and one who can help us. He has money waiting for us and food and a bed for the night. He hides in secret, but the old man told me how to find him."

Randulf looked amazed. "Adam Wolvercot, you have just saved our souls!"

"Prickwillow is joined to Ely by a causeway, and is only an hour's walk away."

"Then what are we waiting for?" asked Randulf, and he leapt to his feet.

The poor and sleepy hamlet of Prickwillow lay just four miles east of the Isle of Ely. Between the two lay the wide river crossed by a small rickety wooden bridge, surrounded by green and foul-smelling marshland. The two young men clattered over the bridge and found themselves on a narrow path of mud and stones that had been laboriously laid across the marsh connecting the hamlet to the town, so parishioners could walk safely to mass and back each Sunday, or go to market, carrying their goods on their backs or tied securely to donkeys. But it had seen better days and in places the causeway was now crumbling into the wet bog on either side, leaving just a narrow footpath. It looked unused in recent times, and was slowly sinking back into the marsh. Adam could see the low dwellings of the hamlet away in the distance amidst a small copse of trees. The land was flat and marshy for as far as the eye could see, and the massive sky above grew dark with storm clouds. There was a rumble of thunder in the distance.

Adam shivered a little but knew that a safe house and a warm welcome were waiting for them. The old man at Lutterworth had told him of these houses; places where men sympathetic to the cause would put them up and feed them and encourage them. Many were known as Poor Preachers, forever hiding from the law, and were themselves in danger. And here in Prickwillow was one such man, a man by the name of John Brevetour who they could trust. He would have food for them and a bag of money to help them on their way. He would know what to do next.

"There's a strange quietness here," said Randulf as they drew near the first of the cottages. "There is no smoke from the rooftops, or anyone about."

"Is it a trap?" asked Adam.

"Be careful, my friend, it may be."

Adam crept up to one of the houses, keeping close in to the wall and peered in through the window. Through the darkness he could just about make out a room long deserted. Rats had begun to nest there, making use of the straw bed for material, and the place smelt heavily of their stale urine. The rest of the meagre furniture was covered in a deep layer of brown grey dust. Large cobwebs hung from the thatch of the roof and joined the table to the chair. It was as if the owners had left in a hurry. All was silent.

Randulf tried the door and it swung open. He nodded his head at Adam and then stepped inside. Adam held his breath. Suddenly there was an almighty screech and the noise of beating wings and a great black bird flapped frantically out of the door above his head. He ducked low and Randulf tumbled out of the darkness, looking white and shaken.

The next cottage was much the same, and the next, and the truth began to dawn on them. This hamlet had been emptied by the pestilence that still ravaged around the countryside, not as in former days where it swept through the whole nation, but in pockets that sprung up and decimated communities such as these.

"It must have been a few years ago," said Randulf quietly. "And no-one has ever come back. There is a curse upon this place. We should leave before it kills us."

"No, we will find the house of Master Brevetour, because there may still be something for us there. He will have left something behind. Come on, let's search the other cottages and see if we can find his. He may even still be here." Adam did not really believe his own words but was becoming desperate. If this Poor Preacher was not here they would surely soon starve. Hunger was already gnawing at them as they had not eaten since leaving the Priory. They had no food and not a penny left to buy any. They could steal from the townsfolk of Ely, but that would risk losing a hand to the axe, or worse. No, this man had still to be here.

"You are crazy. There is nothing here but bones and disease." Randulf seemed quite shaken and frightened. Adam had never seen him like this before; he was usually so calm and in control.

"Well, you can wait here, but I am going to search the houses," said Adam, unsheathing his sword.

He kicked open the door of the next dwelling and found nothing but more dust and cobwebs. Adam began to worry. What was it the old man had said? The cottage of John Brevetour was the last in the hamlet, standing next to the well. Adam looked about him for the well but could not see it. He ran up the street and down alleys, cursing his twisted ankle for slowing him up. And then at last he found it, a two story cottage standing a little apart from the others and guarding a broken-down well. Adam hobbled up to it and drew up the bucket and drank deeply from the cool fresh water. Then he opened the latch and bringing his shoulder hard against the door, forced it open. It creaked heavily and grated in the dirt floor. A rat scurried away as he stepped in.

"Master Brevetour?" he called out, his voice shaky with fear. "John Brevetour? Are you here?"

Silence greeted him. He made his way to the old wooden staircase and placed his good foot upon it, testing its strength. The wooden step creaked a little under his weight but held firm. He breathed in deeply and trod on the second step. A rustling from the floor above made him stop for an instant, his heart pounding loudly in his chest, but he recognised the common enough sound of rats scratching on wooden boards, and continued slowly up the stairs. There were two doorways, leading to two rooms. One was pitch black as though the shutters were closed, but a pale beam of evening light poured into the other. He entered the room. In the dim light of the one small window he could see a figure with its back to him, bent over a desk in an attitude of writing, a hood covering his head. He wore a gown of stained brown that fell to the floor. Nothing moved. Adam approached cautiously. "Master Brevetour? Is that you?"

There was a scratching from the desk and for a brief moment Adam thought the man was writing, but as he crept slowly closer he realised it was only a twig scraping on the wooden window ledge as the wind blew outside. He realised he had not drawn breath and now gulped in air.

Adam held his breath again and reached out a trembling hand. He was about to tap Master Brevetour on the arm as if to waken him, but the sudden sound of a rat squealing made him jump and instead he let his hand fall heavily upon the cloaked shoulder. There was a hollow crash and the figure twisted to face him and then collapsed before his eyes. A huge pall of dust rose with the stench of decayed flesh, and a skull rolled across the floor.

Adam jumped back with a screech and flew down the stairs. There in the darkness another figure blocked the doorway. Adam unsheathed his sword and lashed out with it. The figure ducked. "You madman!" it shouted. "It's me, Randulf!"

"Get out!" cried Adam. "We are done for! He is dead!" and he pushed past his friend and ran out into the fresh air, panting deeply.

Randulf ran after him. "And is there any money?" he asked.

"Is there any money? Is that all you care about? I have been scared witless and you ask about money!"

"Well, is there?"

"I did not look."

"So there may be. Come on, it's only a dead body, and we've all seen plenty of those. We need to search the house. You go downstairs and I'll go up as I can see that you are too scared to do that!"

They crept back inside the house and began to search. Randulf went upstairs and kicked at the dry bones now lying in a heap and covered by their woollen gown. The bones rattled as they moved. He withdrew his sword and flipped the worn gown this way and that, looking for a purse or some bag or container for money. But there was none. He checked the cupboard that stood against one wall and the drawer in the desk, but again nothing. "This damned Lollard," he muttered under his breath.

By the time he had come downstairs again Adam was already waiting outside. "Did you find anything?" asked Randulf.

"Just this." Adam held a dusty longbow in his hand and was checking it over with a trained eye. It was a good war bow, made of Mediterranean yew and capped with fine ram's horn, the cord made of hemp and human hair twisted finely together. The bow was painted to keep the moisture in and the wood flexible. But this was no ordinary dull paint. This bow had been decorated exquisitely with symbols and signs of heraldry. This was a bow that had seen action in the wars and had been greatly loved.

He smiled at Randulf. "There may be no money here, but with this bow and my aim we can eat well tomorrow."

The bloodhound sniffed at the stone-arched gateway at Fynchyngbroke priory then cocked his leg against the door. Guy de Beauchamp drew his sword and hammered on the gate with the pommel. "Let me in!" he shouted. "I am on the king's business."

The Albino smirked. Whatever business this was it was not directly from the king, but if it opened doors, then they would make themselves ambassadors of God himself if necessary.

The bolt drew back and the novice Imelda peered through a tiny gap in the gates. Guy de Beauchamp pulled on his reigns and forced his mighty destrier against the door barging it open. Imelda let out a cry and was thrown to the floor as the heavy oak timbers swung against her, and as she tried to pick herself up again she was brushed aside by the horse as de Beauchamp rode in. The bull mastiff lunged at her and growled until de Beauchamp called him to order. The Albino trotted in on Nightshade, and he smiled thinly at her.

"Take us to the Prioress," he demanded.

Sister Imelda nodded, too afraid to speak, and ran across the courtyard towards the church. She could hear the clatter of the hooves close behind, but did not dare to turn around until she reached the safety of the Prioress's house. The door was slightly ajar and she flew through it and into the protective arms of Prioress Catharine Multon.

"My child, what is this?" asked the Prioress as she disentangled herself from the clutch of the young girl. "Whatever has frightened you so?"

In answer the door crashed open and de Beauchamp stormed in followed by the Albino.

"Who on earth…" began the Prioress, but her sentence was cut short as the Albino removed his hood and she saw his white ghostly face.

"I am looking for two men," said he. "I believe they may be here."

The prioress composed herself. "And what makes you think that?" she enquired.

Guy de Beauchamp cut in. "My dogs are following them. They are here. I want to know where."

Catharine Multon thought quickly. Whoever the two young men were that she had helped to leave that morning, and whatever they were mixed up in, they were infinitely more deserving of her assistance than these two bullies who stood menacingly in her study. She decided to call their bluff and not for the first time in her life, to lie. "I do not recall two young men being here."

"They are here. Now tell us where."

"I think I would know if there were two men here. We are a convent after all!" The Prioress tried to sound confident, but she found herself wringing her fingers behind her back.

The sound of barking came from across the courtyard near the stables, first the bloodhound and then the deeper growl of the mastiff. Guy de Beauchamp turned on his heel and strode out of the room. "Watch her!" he commanded the Albino.

He ran over to the stables where the two dogs were jumping and pawing excitedly at the enclosure. Inside were a pure white palfrey and an old nag with a distinctive white diamond on her forehead. The bloodhound howled and tried desperately to scramble into the stable.

Guy de Beauchamp headed back to the study. He spoke first to the Albino. "They are here. Their horses are here. "Then he turned to the Prioress. "Thank you for your help. We will wait outside the gates for them to leave. Do not tell them we were here, or there will be consequences for you, your Priory and your lovely nuns. Do you understand me?"

The Prioress spoke quietly. "Clearly enough." She bowed her head and allowed herself a tiny smile as they stormed out of the study.

They left the Priory and hid in the woodland that surrounded it, tying their horses and dogs to the branch of an old beech tree. Then they settled down to wait. It would only be a matter of time before Adam and Randulf would leave the Priory and then they would follow, stealing after them in secrecy. The Albino felt good again for the first time in days; he was now out of trouble and his Master need never know that he had lost his prey in the first place. His plan had worked and de Beauchamp had proved his worth as a tracker. Now all would be well. He untied his rosary and began to pray.

A little while later they heard the priory gates open and Novice Imelda appeared with a basket in her hands, heading towards them down the footpath. Every now and again she stopped to pull up a wild plant by the roots or pick a few leaves from a bush or tree and drop them into the basket. As part of her training as a novice she was expected to supply the medicines for the elderly nuns and this required a regular trip to the woods. She drew ever closer. The Albino looked at de Beauchamp, who motioned for silence. Then Nightshade whinnied. The girl looked up and peered into the shadowy woodland. The mastiff growled. Imelda went white and she dropped her basket and started to run back to the Priory, her frightened hands flapping like broken wings.

"Damn it!" cried the Albino and chased after her, easily catching up with her as she stumbled on panicky legs that caught in her long habit. He pulled her to the ground and lay on top of her to hold her down. She cried out and he clasped his hand over her mouth. "Shut up," he said. "I will not hurt you."

Novice Imelda blinked back her tears and stared at him in horror, and it dawned on him just how beautiful her eyes were. He slowly removed his hand and studied her pretty face. It had been a long time since he had been this close to a pretty girl.

He whispered gently to her, trying to calm her nerves. "Go back to the Priory and forget that you have seen us. We do not exist. We will not hurt you if you say nothing. But I will know if you speak about us, and then…" He narrowed his pink eyes and stared at her. Neither moved. "I cannot say what will happen if you tell that we are here. Do you understand?"
Imelda nodded her head.

"Now tell me. When are the two young men due to leave?"

Novice Imelda held back a sob. Her voice when she spoke was high pitched and squeaky. "My Lord, they have already left."

"What do you mean, 'they have already left'. Do not lie to me – I have seen their horses in your stable. They cannot have already left."

"But, Sir, they left by boat this morning."

"By boat! Where have they gone?"

Imelda realised that she had already said too much. "I do not know," she ventured. The Albino slapped her across the face, reddening her cheek but immediately he regretted causing the welt and felt his first ever pang of guilt. "I... I am sorry," he murmured, surprising himself with his own softness. "Just tell me where they have gone, and I will not hurt you anymore."

Imelda held a hand to her stinging cheek. "They have gone to the Isle of Ely."

Chapter 16 - The Hunter and the Hunted

Adam carefully looked the longbow over, turning it in his hands and checking the bow in case it had warped. He looped the string over the notches and pulled gently on it and felt its tension. It was good. He now searched the house again and found a quiver of long English arrows, each tipped with a good head, and he fired one to see if it flew true. It struck the wooden shutter two hundred yards away and stuck fast. Adam looked at Randulf. "I think we can have meat tomorrow! Let's go hunting!"

"And what would we catch? There may be the odd rabbit, but all I have seen are eels!"

Adam's shoulders slumped.

"We could sell the bow at market. It must be worth a pretty penny," suggested Randulf. "That would be easier than hunting, and I could get a good deal on it."

Adam looked at the bow with sadness. It was a quality weapon that he would have liked to have owned, but it certainly would fetch a good price. He acquiesced, "You are right. After all there is not much to hunt around here. It is all marshland, and unless we want to be eating frogs…"

"Talking of which, do we have anything at all to eat?" asked Randulf. "Is there nothing here in this god-forsaken place that we can make a meal of?" He looked about him in despair at the long empty hovels and sighed. "I am so hungry."

They bedded down for the night in a one-roomed hovel on the edge of the hamlet and the next morning they decided to make the return journey to Ely along the crumbling mud causeway that crossed the bleak wet landscape. Adam caressed the longbow as they walked, stroking it gently with one hand and wondering how John Brevetour would have felt about them selling what would have been his prized possession. But he would not care now that he was in Paradise.

Adam suddenly realised just how much he missed his own bow and began to remember the good times he had had with it, shooting rabbits for practice or competing in the contests. His thoughts turned to home and he wondered how his brother Richard was. By now he should be fit and well again because it had been … how many days? Was it eight or nine? He counted the days on his fingers marking them by the places they had stopped. No, it was now the tenth day since leaving home. Richard should be back at work now and providing for his mother.

Then his mind wandered to Agneta. Oh, how he missed her. He pictured her smiling at him and taking his hand. Surely this journey had to end soon so he could see her once again. But it had all begun to go horribly wrong. They had no food or money, the Bible had been stolen and they only knew it was on its way to Walsyngham. What should he do now? In order to find his father he would have to retrieve the Bible and somehow get it to Gelfridus Lyttle. But how long would that take? And in the meantime he longed for home.

+

The Albino and Guy de Beauchamp left Ely on the path to Prickwillow, and were not far into the thin strip of woodland surrounding the town when they heard the voices. They stopped and waited in silence, craning their necks to hear better. The Albino nodded. Yes, this was them. Finally they had caught up.

"Let's have some sport!" murmured de Beauchamp, smiling grimly at the Albino, and he released the dogs. The bloodhound howled as it raced towards the prey it had been chasing for the past four days, the scent now stronger and fresher than ever. Adam saw it first, bounding up the causeway towards him, growing ever closer. He saw its eyes fixed on him and the teeth that dripped with spit and his heart pounded in his chest as panic flooded his brain.

And then behind the bloodhound he saw the bull mastiff. Terror now overwhelmed him as he recalled the mastiff in the village tearing into his ankle, and he froze. He tried to run but his legs would not move, and with every passing second the dogs came closer. He tried to cry out but no sound came, and he felt as though his whole body was paralysed. The dogs were just a few feet away now. Tears ran down his face. Everything inside him screamed 'No!'

Suddenly Randulf was beside him. He swung his sword and knocked the bloodhound soundly across the head. It whimpered and tumbled headlong into the marsh alongside the path, its legs trembling. The mastiff hesitated a moment and then snarled and leapt at Adam.

"Shoot! Adam shoot!" shouted Randulf and suddenly Adam came to as if from a slow-motion dream. He shook his head and automatically lifted the bow, aimed it at the mastiff and fired. The arrow hit the dog in the foreleg and it yelped and crashed to the ground. Adam loaded again and fired, wiping tears from his eyes that blurred his vision. The arrow missed the mastiff by inches and shot into the distance behind. There was a mighty agonising cry and Guy de Beauchamp clutched at his chest, his hand grasping the arrow shaft. He looked up in disbelief at the panicked face of the young archer ahead of him and he tried to say something. Blood trickled from the corner of his mouth, his lips were stained red. Then he slumped to the ground and slid into the marsh face down.

The Albino had watched all this from a distance, his features impassive, as if untouched by the death of his ally. He felt no pain at the loss of his friend. He was simply a casualty of war. And this was war; not the type that causes thousands to die on the battlefield, but the sort that could cause thousands to die in hell if these Lollard heretics had their way. And in war, soldiers die. Guy de Beauchamp had just added himself to their number, and for that he would receive a rich welcome in heaven. So there was no feeling, no loss.

But he was saddened by the sound of the dogs yelping in pain and scrabbling to get back onto the dry path as the marsh slowly dragged them under. He wanted to help them escape, to nurture them back to health, but he knew he had to keep hidden. He could not be implicated in this murder. He needed to be invisible. He pulled his hood closer over his eyes.

Suddenly a voice behind him called out, "He killed that man! Did you see that? That young lad murdered him!" The Albino turned to see four woodsmen standing in line on the path, white with shock. "Get him!" they cried and pushed past the Albino, running along the path. "There's money in this if we catch him!"

Adam heard their cries and spun round to run. His foot felt as though there was a knife twisting in it sending flames of searing pain up his leg. His head swam. He limped away as best he could, dragging his torn foot behind him. Randulf looked about him and quickly assessed the situation. If he stayed he too would be caught and accused of murder. There was nothing he could do for Adam now. But if he ran they might just catch him too. There were four woodsmen, and all fit from working outdoors. He had no chance of outrunning them and there was little cover here and nowhere to hide. All of a sudden he knew what he had to do. There was only one course of action.

He grabbed Adam by the arm and twisted it behind his back, lifting it high until it hurt. Adam was forced to the ground, kneeling in the wet mud on the path. He was still in shock from the fear of the dogs and the way he had killed a man. His thoughts were slurred as was his speech. "Randulf, what...?"

"I have your man! The murderer! Quickly help me!" cried Randulf to the woodsmen who now ran faster, spurred on by the fact that the culprit had been caught and there would be no fight. Together they held Adam down.

"Were you not with him?" asked one of the woodsmen.

"I was walking with him, but I do not know him," lied Randulf.

Adam twisted his head to stare at him in disbelief. How could his friend say that? Someone jerked him to his feet and a rope was tied about him binding his arms to his body. He felt a sharp jolt as a woodsman pulled him by the rope and another pushed him from behind. He called out "Randulf!" and a piece of cloth was rammed into his mouth. "No more words from you until you speak to the sheriff," laughed one of his captors.

And so they led him back towards Ely, bound and stumbling like a trophy of war in the middle of the group, and they laughed and jested at the thought of the reward they would get for the capture of a murderer. Randulf slowed his pace and fell behind them, his mind racing, and the Albino dissolved into the darkness of the thin strip of woodland surrounding the town.

They dragged Adam down through Brays Lane to the Market Place. A crowd began to gather as word went out that a man had been caught for murder, and as the word spread the stories were embellished until latecomers believed they were to see a boy who had killed three men and a bear. They were disappointed when they saw young Adam, thin and muddied; his boyish face pale with fear as he knelt on the ground, his arms bound with rope and his mouth stuffed with cloth. His captors stood around him, showing off their prize and regaling the onlookers with stories of their bravery in catching him.

"Hang him now!" came a cry from a man in the crowd, and a murmur of approval spread around.

"Flog him first!" called out another.

Adam glanced around in panic. He was searching for Randulf, still hoping that his only friend had not really deserted him, but fearing with a heavy heart that he had. He was now alone and at the mercy of a baying mob.

One of the woodsmen lifted the longbow belonging to Master Brevetour and waved it above his head to silence the crowd. "We cannot take this matter into our own hands. There is a reward to be had! And we four are to claim it." He pointed to his fellow woodsmen, who bowed mockingly as the onlookers whistled and clapped. This was fine entertainment and the woodsmen were making the most of their moment of glory.

"No," continued the ringleader, "we will take him to the gaol and see what the law has to say." He paused for greater effect. "Then we will hang him!" The crowd hooted with laughter, and the woodsman, grasping his moment, yanked Adam to his feet as if to show him off. He pulled the rope and, as if leading a mule, walked through the crowd, his head held high, and followed by his fellow captors.

+

   The Albino stepped out from behind a tree and blocked the path just in front of Randulf. Randulf jumped then relaxed. "You startled me, old friend," he said.

   "I saw what happened." The Albino looked deeply into Randulf's eyes. He was a couple of years older than Randulf, and six inches taller, and he had always thought of him as a younger brother. Of all the misfits in Sir Osmund Clarke's menagerie, these two were the most normal. In fact, the Albino had no idea why Randulf was included in the collection at all. He had no obvious physical defect, no pale skin or lack of limbs and he was handsome and well built. Rumours had of course abounded about Randulf Payne, the Perfect One, the Apple of their Master's Eye. They had grown up together and the Albino had observed what he could only imagine was a sort of tenderness shown to Randulf Payne by Sir Osmund, a favouritism that none of the others received. There were times when Sir Osmund would take a trencher of bread from a boy he was punishing and give it quite openly to Randulf. There were times when Randulf avoided being beaten or whipped for some misdemeanour when any other boy would have been black and blue from the birch. Certainly he did seem to have God on his side and angels watching over him. Although it seemed that right now they had turned away and were playing dice with someone else.

   "What chaos you have made of this," said the Albino. "The Bible is lost and Adam Wolvercot is to be locked up. It looks like both may be left to rot before we have had a chance to make an example of them. Caught for murder! God's blood, Randulf! Can't you get anything right?"

"It wasn't my fault! What was I supposed to do?" retorted Randulf, his face flushing.

"You were supposed to be looking after him, taking care of him, getting him and the heretic Bible to the Poor Preacher and ensnaring them all! That is what you were supposed to be doing!"

Randulf stared unblinking into those strange angry pink eyes. "And *you* were supposed to be helping me do it!" he said finally.

The Albino felt as though he had been winded. He knew this was true and he could not lay all the blame at Randulf's feet. Events were spiralling rapidly out of his control and he was powerless to do anything about it. A violent blend of anger and fear welled up from deep inside, needing an outlet. He drew his sword and lunged at Randulf, stopping the tip of the blade just before his throat. Then he cursed and lowered the sword and kicked at the dirty ground beneath his feet.

"We are in deep trouble." He spoke quietly as if not wanting to admit his part in it.

Randulf sat down and began toying with a twig, scratching mindlessly in the dust. He had to think hard and to think straight. He had to rescue Adam before they hanged him for murder, and he had to get the Bible back. And he needed to do this soon before Sir Osmund Clarke found out that all was lost. But how on earth could he accomplish all this?

"We must dispose of the body first and that will delay the trial. They cannot hang him for murder if there is no proof that a murder has happened." It was as if the Albino had read his thoughts.

Randulf tossed the twig away. Of course! That would give him time to try and recover the Bible. If there was no body, then there was no murder, and Adam could not be hanged.

"Quick. Let's do it," he said.

"But first, tell me the name of the Poor Preacher who is to receive the Bible. It is … safer if we both know who he is." said the Albino.

"You do not trust me?" asked Randulf, though he already knew the answer.

The Albino simply stared back at him with those watery pale eyes. "The name, and where he is to be found." he said.

Randulf had no option but to tell. He spoke slowly and with a degree of hesitation, as though by speaking the name it would somehow break a spell and cause disaster to befall him. "He is a man called Gelfridus Lyttle. He is an apothecary in Thetford. That is about a day's ride from here. To the east." he added.

The Albino closed his eyes and made a mental note of this. "Thank you." he whispered. "Now let us dispose of a body."

They heard the whimper of the bull mastiff as it lay licking the wound in its leg. The bloodhound was nowhere to be seen, perhaps it had recovered from the blow to the head and run off. Randulf knelt down beside the splayed form of Guy de Beauchamp.

"What can we do with him?" he asked, looking to his mentor for ideas. The Albino said nothing, but surveyed the open flat landscape for onlookers, and seeing none, bent down and heaved the limp body into the marsh. The wet land opened to receive the leather clad figure and then closed back over him with barely a sound. His body would not be found for a thousand years.

The mob dragged Adam as far as the newly built Ely Porta, the southern gateway for the monastery and the building which housed the prison which came under the auspices of the Prior, a man named Poucher. He was already waiting at the high arched carriageway that lead through to the monastery beyond, his staff in hand and a concerned expression on his fat round face. His black Benedictine habit, tied by a belt around his waist, strained to contain the belly of a man who had indulged in too much excess, and his red cheeks told of a love of fine wine. Beside him stood a mean, large man in the garb of a gaoler.

Prior Poucher had been warned by a runner of the arrival of a captured murderer but on seeing the pathetic sight of Adam, he rubbed his hands in relief. He would be no trouble, this thin youth.

"Take him within," said the Prior, motioning to the dark archway. The woodsmen bowed and jostled Adam into the building. There was a door on the left under the arch, and the gaoler now made a great fuss of opening this with a large iron key. Adam was pushed through, and into an antechamber. There was a small door on the opposite wall, and the gaoler pushed Adam's head down, making him stoop low to go through it. He released Adam from his ropes and then the door slammed shut behind him and for a moment all went black.

Adam stood for a moment, trying to gather his thoughts and waiting until his eyes adjusted to the gloom. One small window, set high in the room, brought a shaft of soft daylight in from the outside world, and motes of dust floated in the beam. Slowly the room came into view. It was small, no more than five paces across, and bare. There was clean straw on the flagstones and a wooden pail in one corner filled with water, but nothing else. No bed, no chair, nothing. The shaft of light fell on the wooden door and Adam could just make out something scratched there. He hobbled over, and then his blood froze. Someone had carved a design into the hardened oak of the door that separated him from freedom. It was the image of a man hanging from the gallows.

Chapter 17 - The Petition

Saturday February 26th 1401

Randulf was sore from riding. Since leaving Ely the day
after Adam was imprisoned he had travelled far. First he
blagged a passage on a boat heading for the priory at
Fynchyngbroke and collected Henry, his horse, and then
followed the paths that skirted the fenland, heading east and
then north. He stopped many times to ask the way, and stole
or begged food from those who let him in for the night.

Finally on the third day of his journey, the paths became
wider and easier and he began to be joined by pilgrims
heading for Walsyngham. Many wore the distinctive long
grey gown so common among those on pilgrimage, and
covered their heads with cowls and broad hats to keep off
both rain and sun, and they carried few possessions, perhaps
just a staff, or a small pouch and a drinking bottle. Some had
travelled for many months, crossing the country from one
holy site to another; others were going to Walsyngham first
and then on to Canterbury. They were devout, hoping to gain
reward and hoping for heaven. They laughed and cajoled one
another, yet walked on blistered feet, with half-starved
children hanging on to their gowns stained with mud.

Randulf rode past many a group of pilgrims as they all
made for Walsyngham and the Shrine of Our Lady. He
remembered the story, how long, long ago the widow of the
lord of the manor had three visions of the Virgin Mary, each
one the same. In the vision Mary took her to Nazareth where
she showed her the place where the Angel Gabriel had
appeared to her. Mary told the widow to remember the
measurements of the house where the annunciation
happened and build a copy of it in Walsyngham. So the

widow instructed carpenters to build the house but was not sure where it should be erected.

One night there was a heavy fall of dew but next morning in a meadow close by there were two dry spaces where all else was wet. The widow took this as a sign and chose one of the plots close behind a pair of wells. The workmen tried to build there, but were not able to. When the widow found out about this she spent all night in prayer.

The next morning a miracle had happened. The chapel was found fully constructed and standing on the other dry spot. Everybody knew that Our Lady had moved the Holy House to the place she herself had chosen. And since that time pilgrims had travelled from across Europe to see this shrine – an exact copy of the very place where the Angel Gabriel had spoken to Mary.

As they approached Walsyngham, with its mighty Priory rising over the shrine, the pilgrims stopped at the Slipper Chapel and removed their shoes to walk the last mile barefoot. Randulf rode past. His pilgrimage was of a different sort, and while he believed in the story of the Virgin's house, he was at Walsyngham for a very different reason. Somewhere here were the company who had robbed him, and if he was not too late, he would be able to find them and get his revenge.

He crossed the little packhorse bridge over the shallow brown river that slid gracefully through the wood, and trotted into the town. Randulf was amazed as he had never seen a town quite like it. Walsyngham had been built solely for the pilgrims who were now thronging the streets and so almost all of the buildings were inns or taverns, just places to sleep and eat and all laid out on a grid pattern of streets. He quickly familiarised himself with the layout of the town and spent the day criss-crossing it looking for the company.

And then at last he saw him, the tall man dressed in black, his limp flaxen hair falling over his shoulders and his bag of relics slung on his back. There was no mistaking him, or the way he walked as though he were a woman: the Pardoner, Athelard Drake. Randulf squinted and searched for the others, but could not see them. The Pardoner was alone among the throng of pilgrims. Randulf watched him from a distance and eventually saw him sit down on a low step and begin to arrange his relics around him, placing each one gently on the ground for all to see. One by one people would approach him and fall into deep discussion, others would kneel humbly as the Pardoner placed his forgiving hands on their heads. Most left with a signed paper and little money.

Randulf waited and watched. A couple of peasants came near to the Pardoner, their feet bare and their clothing in rags. They held out their hands in a gesture of begging, only to be at first ignored and then later shoved away by Drake. For all his supposed piety he was not concerned with those who had nothing to offer. Randulf watched them hobble away and then he cautiously approached. The Pardoner was rifling through his bag of treasures.

"Athelard Drake, you have something of mine!" said Randulf loudly. The Pardoner looked up.

"And who might you be to address me in this manner?"

Randulf pulled back his hood to reveal his bruised and beaten face. "I think you will remember these wounds!"

"Ah, yes. So it is the poisoner come back for revenge! Master Payne isn't it? What are you doing here, so far from home? I would have thought that one beating would have been enough." Drake's voice was slimy and arrogant.

"You have my money!" cried Randulf. "You and the others!"

"What others?"

"The rest of your companions who robbed me!"

"Ah, they are all gone, all gone. They left yesterday, having seen the shrine. They are so shallow, one glimpse was all it took for them and then they were on their way."

"And where is my money?"

"*Your* money? I believe it is now *my* money."

"In the fires of hell it is! Where is it?"

"I only had a small part of it. We divided it among us as we had need. You will not see it again." His high voice cracked in a shrill of laughter. "I have spent my portion, dear boy, there is no more."

"And the book?"

"Oh, the book. Such an exquisite thing, but oh so dangerous." Athelard Drake looked intently at Randulf. "Now where did such a pretty thing like you get such a book?"

Randulf ignored his comment. "Where is it?" he repeated.

"That is precious information. I do not give it away lightly. I wonder, what will you give me for it? Let us see how much you want that perilous, beautiful book!" Drake was enjoying himself, he loved toying with this young man Randulf. He waited for a moment and then added, "But I see that this is unfair, for you have nothing left to give me. You have no money, I made sure of that, and you have nothing else I need. Unless...unless..." he looked Randulf slowly up and down. Randulf recoiled under his gaze.

"No, you are not ready yet. Come back when you are. Until then stay out of my sight!"

Randulf stood his ground for a moment longer, then turned on his heel and walked away. He found the Pardoner disgusting, and yet he would have to meet with him again if he was to get the Bible back. It was true he had no money, but he did have his sword and his wits and if he could only get the Pardoner alone he would get the book.

His chance came sooner than he expected. He had followed Drake for the rest of the day, seeing where he went and who he met, watching him ply his trade of relics and indulgences in the busy streets among pilgrims hungry for his pardon. Then, late in the day, he saw him head out of town alone, and he knew this was his opportunity. He casually walked after him, letting Drake know that he was being followed. The Pardoner walked a little faster, and Randulf matched him, step for step, pace for pace. Randulf could tell by his gait that Drake was getting anxious now, he was almost running, and he kept looking back over his shoulder. Finally, as he crossed the pack bridge he broke into a run, his limp arms flapping by his sides. Randulf chased after and soon caught up with him. The Pardoner was gasping for breath as Randulf drew his sword, his face taut with panic as he looked this way and that for escape.

"Please, I beg you, do not harm me! I was but being foolish earlier today!"

"Yes, you were foolish," replied Randulf. "And even more foolish now!" He waved the sword above his head and the pardoner ducked and whimpered. "I want the book!" he shouted.

"I cannot give it to you," squeaked the Pardoner.

Randulf swung his sword in a large arc to one side of the Pardoner and then to the other, making him weave like a slippery fish as he dodged the blade. Drake dropped his bag and fumbled in his belt, pulling out a small gilt dagger with a jewel-encrusted handle. He held it shakily in front of him in a useless gesture of self-defense. Randulf laughed.

"You threaten me with that!" he crowed, and flicked the dagger out of his trembling hands with the tip of his sword. The Pardoner fell to his knees.

"You are not so brave now you are alone," said Randulf as he picked up the dagger and tucked it into his belt. "Now tell me where the book is and I will be on my way."

"I do not know!" cried Drake.

Randulf pressed his blade against the Pardoner's throat. "I have no time for this," he said, "Where is it?"

"Please, Master Payne, I do not know. I ... I sold it. It was worth so much money, a book of that quality and..." he gulped as Randulf pressed harder with the sword. "I only know that it was a merchant who bought it from me."

" A merchant? What was he like?"

"He was a man of means, well-dressed and not wearing the gown of a pilgrim. He was not one of the faithful."

"What else? How else will I recognize him?"

"He had a forked beard. His hair was red."

"And where is this merchant now?"

"I do not know. But I fear you will not find him now. It is too late. He told me he is leaving Walsyngham tomorrow at dawn."

+

Thomas Arundel, Archbishop of Canterbury, approached King Henry IV, bowing low. He was a trusted adviser and friend of the king and he knew well his position and the unspoken protocols that, if carefully applied, would enhance his standing with the most powerful man in the realm. He carried with him a rolled parchment, tied with a red ribbon.

Henry spoke. "Thomas, I hear you have a petition for me."

"I do, my Lord. It is signed by myself and a goodly number of my bishops, and concerns a heretic by the name of Sawtrey." He held out the parchment for the King, who unrolled it and carefully read the statement. Finally he laid it down and tapped his desk with a finger.

"It is a death warrant?"

"It is, my Lord."

"Tell me why I should sign this death warrant."

"My Lord, William Sawtrey is a man who seeks to undermine the power of the church. Your power. His teachings go against what is holy and he will turn many from the way."

"And what exactly is he preaching?"

"Sawtrey preaches all the Lollard beliefs; he rejects the Catholic saints and the sacrament of the Eucharist. Indeed he teaches that after the priest consecrates the host it remains just bread and does not become the body of our Lord. This is most heretical. He also does not believe in venerating images or embarking on pilgrimages. And much else besides. All his teachings go against the church and many are beginning to follow him. I … we… fear for the future of the holy church if we allow such teachings to be broadcast."

"And you fear that the very rule of the land will also be shaken?"

"Yes, my Lord. If these lies spread, then we will all be in trouble. You remember the Revolt of 1381?"

Henry remembered it well. He had been fourteen at the time and had witnessed the fires burning and the ten thousand or so men who had rampaged and burnt and killed on their way from all corners of the south-east to converge on London. Many had carried longbows with which they had fought in France, and they were formidable. They believed that they were the greatest force in the realm and came to

London to demand the overthrow of the nobility. And all because they felt they were being overtaxed and the money was being wasted on the rich.

Henry had been taken to safety in the Tower of London. And as the young King Richard II refused to give in to the rabble's demand for the heads of certain noblemen including the Archbishop of Canterbury and Henry's own father, the Duke of Lancaster, the destruction and burning began. The rebels, drunk on wine and heady with blood, invaded Henry's home, the Savoy Palace, and tore apart the tapestries and furniture, ripping the paintings and smashing everything in sight. They threw gold and silver vessels into the Thames. They used a padded jacket belonging to the duke for target practice. And when they had finished destroying the furniture and family belongings, they set the Palace ablaze. Oh yes, Henry remembered it well.

"We cannot afford another revolt." Henry spoke slowly. "I will sign the warrant for the death of William Sawtrey." He snapped his fingers and a servant brought him a quill and parchment.

Thomas Arundel interjected, "I do not think this should be a normal execution. If we simply remove his head it will be soon forgotten. Do you not think it would be better to make a display of him? Something for the crowds to remember and fear?"

"And how might we do that?"

"Burn him, my Lord. If he burns it will show that we mean business. I understand you have already drafted a law to this effect. Why not use Sawtrey as a test of how effective the law will be when it comes into force? Let us see what the Lollards will do when one of their number is publicly burnt at the stake."

The King thought it over for a while, then remembered once again the way the rebels had burnt his father's house. This was a fitting way that he could challenge these new revolutionaries, these Lollards. Fire for fire. It had a pleasing harmony to it.

"And where is this William Sawtrey now?"

"He is in the custody of the Sherriff of London, my Lord."

Henry dipped his quill in the inkpot and wrote:

The decree of our Sovereign Lord the King and his council in the parliament, against a certain newly sprung up heretic.

To the Mayor and Sheriff of London.

He scratched away with his pen, pausing now and again to think of the correct wording. He explained how the Archbishop of Canterbury and his bishops had investigated the claims about William Sawtrey and had found them true. They had proved him to be a heretic, and because they were zealous for religion and lovers of the Catholic faith they had a great desire to defend the holy church by plucking up by the roots the heresies and errors that were now occurring.

He then wrote:

We therefore do command you as strictly as we can, firmly enjoining you, that you cause the aforesaid William, being in your custody, in some public and open place within the liberties of the city aforesaid, to be committed to the fire, and him in the same fire really to be burned, for detestation of his crime, and the manifest example of other Christians and hereof ye are not to fail, upon the peril that will fall thereupon.

Teste Rege, apud Westm. 26th Feb.. An. regni sui 2,

William Sawtrey was to burn in four days' time.

+

It was not hard for Randulf to find the merchant. He just
needed to sit in the square and wait and before long he saw
him, parading down the street in all his finery. A shock of red
hair marked him out and the forked beard confirmed that this
was Randulf's man. He followed him for a little while,
watching him as he meandered along the streets, stopping to
go into a shop or to drink ale. Finally, as darkness fell and the
street emptied of pilgrims, the man entered a tavern and
closed the door behind him. Randulf waited a short while
and then followed him in.

The tavern was lit with tallow candles that gave off more
acrid smoke than light, but there was just enough to see by.
The room he found himself in was not large and housed a half
dozen gaming tables, where men were noisily playing at dice
or cards. Over in the far corner sat the merchant, throwing
two bone dice as he began a game of hazard. His opponent, a
yeoman by trade, began to take great delight in winning, and
during the time it took Randulf to down two pints of ale, had
stripped the merchant of most of his money. Randulf crossed
the room and stood by the table, watching the match. The
merchant had but a few coins in a pile by his hand and as the
game wore on, these disappeared one by one until there
were none left.

"So, you are ruined!" cried the yeoman with delight. "I
think you cannot play again. So I bid you goodnight and
thank you Sir for your generosity!" He stood up and with a
flourish picked up his dice and left the tavern.

Randulf seized his opportunity and sat down on the still-
warm seat. "You have had a run of bad luck, Sir. I sympathise

with you," he said. "Would you like to try your hand at winning something back?"

The merchant looked up from the table. "I can still play," he said, "but not with that rascal."

"But you could play against me," said Randulf. "I am not sure if you have any money or possessions left, but I am willing to take my chance."

"My money is gone but I still have possessions. And what do you have?"

"I too have no money, but I have this." He pulled the Pardoner's bejeweled dagger from his belt and laid it on the table. The merchant's eyes widened as he looked at it. "May I?" he asked. Randulf nodded and the merchant picked up the weapon and turned it over in his hands. The jewels glittered in the lamplight. "This is a fine and handsome dagger. I will play you for this."

"And what can I play you for?" asked Randulf. The merchant thought for a moment.

"I have this." He reached into his bag and drew out the Bible.

"A book!" Randulf feigned ignorance.

"Yes, but a very expensive book. Take a look inside."

Randulf opened the pages and tried to look unconcerned. "It is well made," he ventured, "and must be worth something, I suppose."

"It is worth a great deal. More than you can know. This book is much sought after and will fetch as much as this dagger in the right hands. So will you play?"

"I will. I have dice and can play raffle well." Randulf place three dice on the table and smiled. These weighted dice had never let him down yet.

The game went well for the merchant at first as Randulf let him win by making silly mistakes. But then, as the ale flowed and he saw that the time was ripe, he began to sharpen up. This was a good way to have fun, and he had spent many hours in taverns playing the people as much as the game. It was all about the timing. To win every throw from the beginning would give him away, so he needed to win some and lose some in order to keep his opponent in the dark.

But there always came a time when he would begin to tire of the sport and just wanted to finish it quickly. And now was the time. He began to win each throw. Each and every time. The merchant began to sweat in the fusty air of the tavern, and beads of moisture appeared on his temple. He called for more ale, not knowing how he would pay for it. His hands began to shake as he tumbled the dice from them, and the knowledge that he had lost became a reality. Finally he could take no more.

"Enough!" he cried and launched himself from the table. "Enough! Have the damned book!" And with that he stormed out of the tavern, overturning chairs as he went.

Randulf slid the Bible towards him and hid it in his cloak. He tucked the dagger away in his belt and, throwing what few coins he had garnered during the day at the Innkeeper, left the smoke-filled room for the fresh air of the night. It was only when he could no longer be seen that he knelt on the ground and crossed himself, saying a prayer of gratitude to the Virgin Mary.

Suddenly he felt a hand heavy on his shoulder, and a gravelly voice spoke in his ear. "You are a hard man to find. But it is good to see you at your devotions."

Randulf recognized the voice immediately, even in the dark of the unlit street.

"Simon!" he said, "Simon, what are you doing here?"

"I have come to accompany you to London. There is something Sir Osmund wishes you to see. A man is to be burned at the stake for heresy and you are to be present to witness it."

Chapter 18 - A Woman Scorned

Long before he approached the barn Hugh Cooper could hear the chattering of the women and the clatter of the foot treadle and the rhythmic whisper and clank of the loom as they wove their handpicked wool into cloth. He caught their laughter as they talked about their neighbours in Wolvercot and what they had been up to the day before. He recognised the sounds; a young girl giggling, an old woman with a croak, another cursing in a high-pitched voice as her threads caught, and yet there was one voice he was listening intently for. He knew it well because it had inflamed his thoughts for many a night. Was she there? He waited outside the half-closed door, his ear cocked. And then he heard it – the sweetest sound he could imagine.

"I have some chores to do later, so I can't stay long. I want to pick some flowers for Richard's grave." It was Agneta. The lovely, beautiful, sensual Agneta.

He carefully positioned himself so he could peek through the gap between the barn doors and peered through the dusty room, searching for her. Ah yes, there she was, sitting with her back to him and the light from the open window falling on her hair. Someone in the barn coughed and he jumped backwards to hide himself.

Cooper drank once more from his flagon of ale. He had been drinking for some hours now to gain courage, and was almost ready to act. Almost. But he needed it to be darker. He slunk across the street and sat down heavily on the road, hiding as best he could behind two trees. He had travelled that afternoon from his own village a few miles away, on foot and with a heart full of lust. He had been planning this for some time now. Agneta had to be his now that her lover Adam had left. He knew she did not like him, but what did that matter? He was infatuated by her, and would make her his. He wiped his lips to remove a cake of dry spittle and pulled his fingers through his greasy hair. Oh yes, she would be his! He swigged a large mouthful of ale.

After what seemed a long wait, and as the light was beginning to fade, he saw the barn door swing gently open, and Agneta came out, wrapped in her cloak and carrying a small basket. She waved back at her friends inside and trotted up the road towards the wood. Hugh Cooper crept after her, trying as best he could to walk silently, but now and again he stumbled on loose stones that grated noisily or sloshed in a puddle. He drunkenly put a finger to his lips. "Sssshhhh!" he commanded his feet.

Agneta was not aware of him. She was lost in her own thoughts concerning Richard and Adam. She had lost a good friend in Richard and she did not know when, or if, she would ever see Adam again. He had disappeared so suddenly, and though she knew that this was for her own protection, as well as that of his family, she wished he had not had to leave. Suddenly she felt a hand clutch at her arm and squeeze it hard. She spun round and straight into the leering face of Hugh Cooper.

"Well here I am!" he said, rather too loudly. "I am yours."

Agneta was flummoxed and was not sure how to respond. Hugh Cooper swayed gently before her like a vain weed in the breeze. She decided not to respond.

"Don't you want me? You must want me. Now that your man has left you, I can be your man." He began to realise that he was talking nonsense and stopped, pulling himself upright and lifting his heavy head high. Agneta giggled nervously.

"I made you laugh!" he slurred.

Agneta blushed. This was not going well.

"So I think that means that you love me. My mother always told me that a woman loves a man if he can make her laugh. And you laughed, so that means you love me." He attempted to throw an arm around her, but Agneta was quick on her feet and sidestepped his advance. He stumbled groggily and then dropped his ale.

"Dammit!" He kicked hopelessly at the damp earth at his feet. "Look what you've made me do, you stupid … " He searched for the right word, but not finding it, stopped cursing.

Agneta looked about her for help and saw Isabel heading in her direction down the street. She was bound to get a ticking off from her now as well, as she had been found talking to Hugh. Isabel came closer and Agneta held her breath, waiting for the shouted accusations. But none came. Instead Isabel quickened her pace and put a finger to her mouth to signal secrecy. Hugh Cooper only had eyes for Agneta and was totally unaware of Isabel behind him until she whacked him across a shoulder with her stick.

"Get off her, you drunken lout! Get away home before I beat you some more!" she yelled.

"Ouch!" cried Cooper, massaging his shoulder, "what d'you do that for?"

"Can`t you see she doesn't want you, you foul animal? She loves another. She loves my son." Isabel suddenly realised she had finally admitted it. Agneta loved Adam, and it had taken a confrontation with this drunken suitor to bring the truth to her lips. She had never wanted to allow herself to believe this; she had always been so protective of her son. But somehow this girl had won his heart and had become a part of this triangle of love, and she had now said it out loud, making it real.

Hugh Cooper acted as if he had been stung by a wasp. He flinched at her words and opened his mouth to speak. But, not knowing what to say, he just stood there gaping like a fish and rubbing his shoulder.

"Oh, run away home won't you," said Isabel, almost kindly. "Don't waste your time chasing after what you can't have."

Hugh Cooper pulled himself up to his full height and tried to recover his dignity. "Farewell then mistresses," he slurred, then circled on his heel and swayed off into the distance.

Agneta watched him go for a moment then turned to thank Isabel, but she had already melted into the dusk.

Chapter 19 - The Chained Man
Wednesday March 2nd 1401

Randulf found himself in the middle of a jostling crowd, hungry to see the burning. Like them he had read the notices pinned to tavern doors and to the beams of the market stalls, and he had joined the masses walking through the gateway in the great north wall of London and over the River Fleet to the open grassland of Smooth Field. Here there was plenty of good grazing and for this reason the livestock market had been held here each week for the past eight hundred years.

And today was market day. The various wooden-fenced pens were now full of bleating sheep, cattle, goats, ducks and geese. Steam rose from the reeking bodies of the bellowing cows and the geese ran about honking at each other. Crowds were everywhere; buying, selling, gambling, looking. The lanes that separated the pens were nearly ankle deep in foul-smelling filth and everyone was getting covered. A swine herd called out as a sow with five piglets pushed past him, and Randulf swore as he brushed down his clothes, now mired in mud.

He took his eyes off the muddy path for a moment and saw in the distance the chapel of New Church Haw and alongside that the graveyard and pit for victims of the Pestilence that had killed a large part of the population just over half a century before. Smooth Field really was a place for life and death. And today it would witness a manner of death never before seen in England.

Randulf pressed his way through the silent crowd to see for himself the place where William Sawtrey was to be burned. There was little to see apart from a large wooden stake planted firmly upright in the ground, and beside that a neat pile of kindling and alongside that some larger branches and timbers. It was all quite unimpressive.

He had been ordered by Sir Osmund Clarke to watch this spectacle and to report back how the crowds reacted, but he wished he was as far from here as possible. He had had to travel for several days to get to London from Walsyngham, in the amiable company of Simon, but he was becoming tired of all this riding.

Suddenly there was a murmuring in the crowd and people pushed forward to see what was happening. Voices were raised and curses called out and fists punched the air. A small group of men in clerical vestments came into view leading a man who was bound around his waist in heavy metal chains. His hands and feet were linked by other chains so that he was barely able to shuffle as they moved him ever closer to the stake. He looked about him at the jeering crowds and Randulf could see from his face that he was in a pitiable state. His once shaven jaw and the tonsure that marked him as a man of God were now both smudged with short dark hair and his clothes were matted with dirt.

He looked furtively about him with eyes that were fearful and yet at one and the same time composed, as if some inner peace was keeping him sane. Now and again the short chain around his ankles tripped him and he stumbled forward, only to be pushed back by his guards. Behind him walked several priests, their hands clasped together in reverent prayer, and behind them the Archbishop of Canterbury, Thomas Arundel. And at the end of the procession a lone drummer boy beat a funeral march. The crowd fell silent.

William Sawtrey was stripped and then covered with a shirt smeared with sulphur. They took his chains and bound him tightly to the wooden post, and kindling was laid in a circle around him. Then they took some of the smaller branches and finally the stouter pieces of wood and placed these carefully on top, making a chest-high barricade of timber. Straw was pressed into any empty spaces, until he was covered. Someone brought a burning torch.

The Archbishop spoke to the crowd. "This man, William Sawtrey, has been found guilty of heresy and of being one of the group of heretics they call the Lollards. He has failed to recant, though he has been given many opportunities. His teachings go against the traditions of the Church and will lead men to the pit of hell. This is why we are to burn him at the stake. It will remind us all of the flames that await heretics in hell. We do this, in the name of the King, to protect all England from such heresies. This is the task of the Holy Church."

There was a small ripple of applause.

The Archbishop continued, "What you are about to witness is a warning to all who would walk the same path. Do not be lead astray by the Lollards or you too will meet the same fate." Then Archbishop Thomas Arundel called out to Sawtrey in a voice that was almost pleading. "William, do you renounce your beliefs? Will you turn back to God and receive His salvation? Will you come back into the fold of the Holy Catholic Church and receive forgiveness? "

William Sawtrey opened his mouth as if preparing to speak, then said nothing. A murmur went through the crowd.

The Archbishop spoke again. "My friend, this is your last chance, but I will give you one more opportunity to turn from the devil you are about to face and come back to the teachings of the Holy Church. Repent, I plead with you, and go free!"

All eyes were on Sawtrey, but he said nothing. The Archbishop began a prayer in Latin and motioned for the man holding the torch to come forward. As he pronounced the

Amen, he motioned once again, pointing to the base of the bonfire. The torch bearer stepped forward, and then hesitated as William Sawtrey finally spoke. His voice was strong, but there was a tremble of fear within it.

"I am not afraid of this fire, but only of the fire of hell." He forced himself to look at the crowd and continued, "and yet that is not where I am going. I have but preached the truth, and my God will save me. Today I will be in Paradise. But all of you, seek for yourselves the truth. Turn from the lies of this church and find for yourselves your salvation in Christ…"

"Silence!" shrieked the Archbishop, "you have said enough!" He turned to the torchbearer. "Burn the heretic!"

The flames played around the small twigs and dry moss that made up the kindling, sending out small wisps of grey-blue smoke into the thick atmosphere of the market. The torchbearer moved around the bonfire, lighting more kindling as he went. This now began to catch quickly and little yellow flames were soon licking at the larger branches. The crowd were absolutely silent as they now began to understand the horror of what they were about to witness. This was no quick hanging at the gallows. This was no instant slicing off of a head with the executioner's axe. This was something different. Something inhumane. One or two turned and pushed their way out of the mob. A mother covered the eyes of her young daughter.

The flames were now growing so large and hot that the closest bystanders had to edge their way backward, forcing the crowd to create a wide ring around the stake. William Sawtrey made no sound, but Randulf could see his lips moving as he prayed. Then the flames rose higher, obscuring his face as the acrid smell of burning flesh began to penetrate the air. Randulf felt his head begin to swim and tried to turn and run as the nauseous smell welled up in his nostrils, but the crowd were too thick around him. His legs felt weak and then he felt his stomach heave and he threw up violently, spattering his already soiled clothes with stinking vomit. He pushed a path through the crowd and ran as fast as his feeble legs would carry him, as far from this scene as he could get. He slipped on the slimy path and fell over, then crawled to his feet once more and ran. He had never felt so dirty in all his life. What had he become a party to? It was his own master, Sir Osmund Clarke, who was central in ordaining this inhumanity. And he, Randulf, was a part of it. He sat down in the mud and sobbed.

Chapter 20 - Proclaim the Law!
Thursday March 3rd 1401

Randulf Payne ran for his life. He quickly arrived back at the manor, changed his clothes, gathered up his few possessions and made sure that the Bible was well concealed in his bag. He then crept into Sir Osmund Clarke's study and opened the small drawer below his desk. It had been many years ago that, as a small boy, he had discovered the drawer and its contents. The bag of coins was still there, topped up as always and easy to steal. Usually he would just take a half dozen or so coins which were never missed, but this time he picked up the whole cloth bag, testing its weight in his hand. He smiled grimly as he hid the coins under the Bible and slid out of the room unseen.

And then Randulf Payne rode out of London avoiding the main roads that were guarded and constantly watched. He knew how far reaching the eyes and ears of Osmund Clarke were – after all he had been a part of them. He had scouted and informed and lied for Osmund. He had crossed the country and cheated his way into many a so-called friendship in order only later to betray those who were the kindest to him. He had killed. And for what? To become less human than his enemies? Is that what the church stood for? His mind raced back to the burning and his stomach churned again.

Randulf patted the neck of his fine white palfrey. He had called his horse Henry after the king, but that name was now tainted. The whole of his life seemed to be tainted.

He headed out of town on a small track and set his course towards Wolvercot.

+

King Henry IV listened intently as the Archbishop of Canterbury described the burning of William Sawtrey. He explained how the onlookers had gathered in their hundreds, or perhaps even a thousand or two, and how their initial festive mood had quickly turned to shock and silence. He had witnessed their appalled faces as they walked quietly away, back to their homes and neighbours to spread the news. He knew that in every tavern and in every hovel that night, there would be tales told of the burning of this heretic.

"And so our plan has worked, Thomas?"

"Yes, my Lord, I believe it has."

"The people will turn against Lollardy?"

"I believe they will."

The King thought for a moment. "And will we need to burn others?"

"If the Lollards will not turn from their preaching, then yes. We must rout this land of such men and their lies – they are a danger to us all."

Henry rose from his chair and walked to the window. He peered through at the gardens below where a servant was sweeping a path, clearing away leaves and debris and creating a neat and tidy order to the natural world. He pondered as he watched the man tidying and sorting. All things if left to themselves return to disorder and disarray, he thought. Leaves left to rot would soon cover the pathways, and the bricks and tiles, laid to such a careful design by man, would disappear forever beneath them. This was the law of the world, the world of which he, at least in part, was ruler. And so he needed to rule, for a king who did nothing was merely a servant of nature, and that nature, the result of the Fall, would soon rise up to bring chaos and disorder. It had to be tamed, like the garden. Henry made up his mind.

"Thomas, I will today proclaim the *de Hæretico Comburendo* and make it law in all England. I will make it law that any heretic can be burned at the stake if he does not renounce his beliefs and turn from his ways. And I shall also make it unlawful in the same way to carry, own or preach from a Bible in the language of the common man, in English. We must stamp out this heresy before it spreads any further."

"Very well, my Lord." Thomas Arundel looked very pleased with himself.

"That is all, Thomas. You may go."

The Archbishop was ushered to the door, and as he reached it he heard the king speak once more.

"Thomas!"

"Yes, my Lord."

"Give word of this to Sir Osmund Clarke. He will be well pleased."

+

Randulf reached Wolvercot three days later. He stopped briefly at The Angel tavern to pay for a room for the night and then set out to find Adam's house and his mother, Isabel. He had ridden here almost without thinking; it just seemed the right place to hide away for a while. Adam was in prison, he had the Bible, and he needed time to think. His whole world that had seemed so safe had been torn apart by the simple act of burning a man to death. He needed to go back to the beginning and start over, and Isabel and The Angel were the beginning.

He soon found the house and tapped at the door. Isabel opened it and gasped as she recognised his face. She looked behind him for Adam, but he was nowhere to be seen.

"Mistress de Wolvercot..." he began, but could say no more. Suddenly he felt like a small boy again, in need of the mother he never knew. Isabel sensed his confusion and simply clutched him to her breast. Randulf tried to hold back the tears, but they still slid in a warm stream down his cheek.

"Come in, come in," said Isabel, "and tell me your news." She poured him a drink and sat him down and then looked deep into his eyes, desperate for news of Adam. "My son...?" she asked.

Randulf looked her straight in the eyes. "He is safe," he lied. Isabel sighed in relief. "And where is he? You are alone."

Randulf paused. "He is in a safe place, but I cannot tell you where."

"But he is alive?"

"Yes, he is alive." Randulf suddenly realised that he did not know this for sure. It had been over a month since he last saw him. But the Albino was there to watch over him, and he surely would have heard news if Adam had been sent to the gallows. Wouldn't he?

"Thank the Lord for that!" said Isabel. "Now you look as though you need some rest and a good meal. Take the bed over there and I will wake you later with food. Then we will talk."

She led him to the pallet in the corner where Richard used to sleep and he lay down without an argument. Sleep began to flood over his whole being, and the last he remembered was Isabel pulling a blanket over him for warmth.

He stayed for many days. She would often see him sitting alone and reading, but whenever she drew close he would snap the book shut and place it where she could not see it. Of course she knew what it was, but it was never spoken about. This was both the cause of the trouble and the key to peace.

Randulf helped with the chores and carrying the water. He helped to plough the strip of land they had for planting, and picked the vegetables that struggled in the poor soil. He went with Isabel as she took flowers to Richard's grave, and stood in silence with her, head bared and eyes closed as she recited a psalm. He was becoming like a son to her. She asked often about Adam, but Randulf always lied or changed the subject.

As the days passed he began to leave the house more and more, walking by himself or riding Henry to the point of exhaustion. His frustration surfaced time and again, revealing itself in angry outbursts or a flow of tears. And often he found himself at Richard's graveside, just sitting and thinking.

And then one day, as he was sitting by the grave under a leaden sky he heard a voice behind him. "Did you know him?"

He jumped up and came face to face with a girl just a few years younger than himself. She was the prettiest girl he had seen; her green eyes sparkled below a parting of shoulder length brown hair and she carried a small bunch of flowers in one hand. "I'm sorry I startled you."

Randulf reddened. "Oh, no. I was just sitting here..."

"So did you know him?" The girl was not to be diverted from her question.

"He was the brother of a friend of mine," he replied cautiously. At this the girl cried out, "You mean Adam! Adam was his only brother! Oh, tell me, where is he? Where is Adam? Is he here?"

"He is not here."

"But he is safe?"

Randulf said nothing more. He could no longer lie about his safety. He was becoming tired of lies.

"And what is he to you?" asked Randulf. At this the girl blushed.

"Aaah, now I see," said Randulf. "Of course! You are Agneta! Adam told me about you."

"How is he?" she asked. "It has been so long and all of us had hoped he would be home by now. We are sure that something must have happened to him. Have you seen him recently? You did not answer me before. Is he safe?"

Randulf tried to think of an answer that would not be a complete lie. Finally he stammered, "He … he…"

Suddenly Agneta dropped her flowers and clutched at her belly. Her face screwed into a grimace of pain and she held out an arm for him. Randulf caught her and steadied her. "Are you alright?" he asked.

"I'm fine. It's just …"

Randulf looked her up and down, her face was pale and tired and her eyes were frightened. She squeezed her belly with her hands, willing the pain to go. This must be three months now and everyone knew how dangerous a time that was.

"Is it his?" asked Randulf. She nodded.

"Please," she whispered, "tell no-one. It will bring shame on my family and on his. I could not bear that."

The pain was abating and some colour came back to her cheeks. She looked Randulf in the eyes. "I love him so much," she said, "tell him I love him. If you know where he is then please tell him." Agneta grasped Randulf's sleeves and bunched the cloth in her fists, clinging on to him and imploring him with her eyes. "Bring him back to me. Please bring him back. He is all that I have…"

+

Monday March 28th 1401

King Henry IV ordered the writing of five hundred copies of the *De Hæretico Comburendo* and sent them with riders across the kingdom to all the major towns and cities. They rode into town, nailing the Law to church doors and other public places, then set out for the next town, and the next. And so the Law spread throughout the land, from London to Oxford and on to the north, and eventually, after two weeks, to the Isle of Ely, where Adam languished in his prison at the Porta of the monastery.

Chapter 21 - The Prior's Prison

Adam knew nothing of this. The notices were pinned in the market place, down at the quayside and in the town square. There was even one inside the cathedral, nailed to the great West door where all the worshippers could not miss it. It became a subject of debate and discussion in all the taverns and before long was the talk of the town. The good people of Ely were already well known for their hatred of Lollardy and this edict just strengthened their resolve to stamp it out. The days and weeks passed and the deadline of the forty days within which a man could repent was drawing close.

By May 7th Adam had been locked in his cell for seventy-four days. He knew this because each day he had picked up a jagged stone that he kept hidden under the straw in the corner and had scratched a small vertical mark on the door. He had sharpened the stone by scraping it on the flagged floor until it cut easily into the wood, leaving a thin pale line. And as the days passed the column of lines grew.

Each day he had watched the beam of light from the high window crawl across first one wall and then another, starting high and then curving low in a shallow arc as it reflected the rising and falling of the sun. It had become a source of comfort, this moving light, a friend who dropped by most days. The square of light was crossed with the shadows of the iron bars that barred the window, and Adam saw in this cross a hope of salvation. Some days the light shone bright, and the cross was distinct and strong and he felt close to his Maker, but on others when thick clouds obscured the sun it was pale and watery and Adam felt his soul darkening with it.

He used the days to pace the cell, walking first one way around and then the other, counting his paces and strengthening his crooked foot. When the pain came he would try to walk through it, but each time it would at some point defeat him and he would crumple to the straw-coated floor in agony.

And during each of those long days he saw no-one apart from the gaoler and his mate. He could often hear voices outside and would shout hoarsely, but nobody would answer him, save to throw abuse. The window was too high for him to see out of and so he was left having to imagine the people on the other side walking the streets in freedom. He imagined merchants carrying their wares, children skipping alongside their mothers as they went to market, drinkers in the taverns. He sometimes caught fleeting words from the monks, whisperings of worship and snatches of song. Dogs barked and made him shiver, and at night the lonely owls haunted him.

Night time. That time of utter blackness that put fear in his heart. The time of dreams and the time of nightmares. Now and again when there was a near full moon the cell was bathed in a cold light, and Adam would stay awake for as long as he could, dreaming of home. But most nights were pitch black, and he could do nothing but listen to the hoot of those owls as he drifted to sleep.

Soon after waking each day he would wait for the footsteps of the gaoler. He knew the sound exactly, as the gaoler trod the same path each and every day, his stride always the same and with a particular slap of his leather soles on the flagged path. And then he would hear the scrape of the bolts being dragged across, and the low door would creak open and the gaoler would come in. He was a large man who had to stoop to half his height to get through the doorway, and frequently banged his head doing so. He would say nothing, but would pour the water into the pail in the corner of the cell and leave the plate on the floor, and then he would leave.

During the first few days Adam had tried to engage him in conversation, but the gaoler had just grunted back, and before long Adam realised that he was mute. This was a clever decision of the Prior, to employ a man who had no means of communicating with the prisoners. There was no way that information could be brought in from outside; he could not be bought or otherwise coerced into helping an inmate. And yet he was not without compassion and would sometimes look on Adam with pity. Once a week the gaoler would shovel out the soiled straw and replace it with fresh. But the stench in the cell never lessened.

Adam had tried to escape once, and once only. It had happened a few days after he was thrown into the cell and he had decided that he could overpower the gaoler and rush the door. He waited for the man to put the plate of food on the floor, and as he bent over, Adam shoved him so that he stumbled heavily, and then Adam ran for the door. But the door was closed and by the time he had wrenched it open the gaoler was upon him and beating him with his fists. Adam, weakened by the meagre rations of gritty food, had been no match for him, and hunched himself in the corner of the cell as the blows rained down. It was a clumsy attempt and he had not tried again, knowing that as the days passed he was growing weaker and weaker. He knew that if he were to escape it would need cunning and not force. And as the days passed a plan came to him.

+

The sheriff was coming to town. He needed to summon the jury. He had been advised of the murder of Guy de Beauchamp, and now headed up a small retinue of clerks and administrators who would oversee the legal process of trying the prisoner. He was met at the quayside by Prior Poucher and six of his monks, who sweated as they carried the heavy bags up the incline to the monastery and through the Almonry that lead to the Prior's house. The Prior had laid on a large banquet, and as they sat and ate quail, lamb, goose, and the local eels soaked in vinegar, the sheriff began to question him.

"So tell me what you know of this murder."

"There is not much to tell. The poor deceased was simply walking his dogs on the causeway to Prickwillow when he was brutally shot in the chest. The arrow lodged in his heart and he died in agony. Some noble-minded townspeople captured the murderer red-handed and he is now locked in our new prison cell."

"And that is all you know?"

"That is enough."

"I will need to interview the townspeople who captured him."

"That will be no trouble. I have their names written down here." Prior Poucher reached into a pocket in his habit and pulled out a hastily scribbled note. The sheriff glanced at it, then handed it back.

"Has the culprit confessed?"

"We have not asked him if he is guilty, because it is obvious that he is. He was caught at the scene."

"My dear Prior," said the sheriff, "that may not be enough to hang a man. I will question him later. And I will need to see the body."

The Prior blanched. "My Lord Sheriff," he said quietly, "We do not have a body."

"There is no body? What do you mean, you do not have a body?"

"As I say. We have not been able to locate the body of the murdered man. We have searched the area, but it is all marsh and he cannot be found."

The sheriff thought for a while, his hands clasped below his chin. Finally he spoke.

"And do you know who he was?"

"We do not know that either." There was another long pause and the Prior was becoming uncomfortable.

"So," said the sheriff, "we have a possible murder but no body. And without a body, we have no murder. I cannot try a case where we have no proof of a crime. I fear I have wasted my time coming here."

Prior Poucher mopped his brow with a cloth. This was not going as he had planned. He had recently completed the building which housed the prison cell and already, within a few months he had not just a prisoner in the cell, but a murderer. This was good news for him and his standing in the town. He was now the law enforcer in Ely, and this prisoner was quite a coup. But it looked as if his world was now about to fall down around him. His hands flustered as he spoke. "My Lord Sheriff, we will continue the search for the body and we will see this boy hanged. I will supervise the search myself."

The sheriff scowled. "Then see to it, Prior Poucher, see to it. And do not ask me back here until you have proof that a murder has indeed taken place. I cannot try a case on the stories of a few woodsmen. Keep the boy in prison for as long as you need, but find that body."

Adam had his plan. All he needed was the presence of a priest at night-time and some sort of weapon. The weapon had been the problem. He had spent days working on a way to steal a knife or even a sword, but this was not going to be easy. But then the solution came to him.

For days now Adam had been scratching away at a loose lump of rock in the wall of the cell. He had picked at the soft mortar and chiselled it and scraped it until the rock came free. It was perfect. It was heavy. It fitted neatly into his palm and was rough enough not to slip out of his grasp.

He called the gaoler. "I need to make confession and I need to be pardoned before I die. Can you send a priest to see me?" The gaoler grunted some obscenity and marched off to see the Prior.

+

Randulf arrived on the Isle of Ely, having stabled Henry at Thetford with an innkeeper. He disembarked from the skiff and made his way cautiously across the quayside. He was sure he would not be recognised, but he still hugged the shadows and turned his head from passers-by just in case. For what he was about to do he wanted to be invisible, a phantom unseen and unremarked. For several days he had been hatching a plan to rescue Adam and as he had made his way from Wolvercot to Ely, his plan had grown. It was simple really. He would steal a monk's robe, and dressed in this disguise he would be able to gain entrance to the prison and rescue Adam. And he needed to do this at night because the monks were well known to the gaoler and he would only be able to pass if his face were not seen. Now all he needed was a habit.

As evening came he crept into the courtyard of the great cathedral. Somewhere overhead a bat fluttered past, catching insects in the cool breeze. The sound of monks chanting came from deep within the cathedral walls, a hollow echoing sound that rose and fell with the wind. Randulf waited patiently for the mass to end. He huddled beneath a large yew tree, out of sight and shaded by his deep blue cloak. A full moon slowly ascended above the wall surrounding the monastery, marking the time as the service continued.

Then as the great bells rang out midnight Randulf made his move. He slunk in through the great west door and pressed himself tightly against a wall, holding his breath and freezing as a line of weary monks snaked from their stalls in the choir under the high octagonal tower and filed out of the Prior's door to bed in the cloisters. Prior Poucher followed behind them, holding a candle in one plump hand and a heavy psalter tucked under his arm. The door closed behind him on well-oiled hinges, and Randulf heard the rasp and clunk of the latch falling.

He blew out his breath and quickly ran down the nave to the door. He twisted a large wrought iron ring and lifted the latch. The door opened as silently as it had closed and he squeezed through. The monks were now talking and murmuring as they turned off to the left through the cloister and on to their dormitory. One solitary figure continued straight ahead. Prior Poucher was headed for his own house a little further down the lane, but first he needed to replace the psalter in his private chapel. He stopped at a small door and bent his head a little as he opened it and started to climb the narrow stone spiral staircase. Randulf watched him disappear and then ran to the door, slipped inside and closed it behind him.

The Prior had now reached the chapel and gently placed the book into its niche. He nodded respectfully at the altar and then let his eyes fall to the stone tiled mosaic floor beneath it. In the flickering light of the candle he could just make out the images of Adam and Eve being tempted by the serpent, but this snake had the head of a man. He had often wondered why this should be. Had his predecessor Prior Crauden designed it this way for a purpose when the chapel was built three generations before? Was he saying that evil was in the shape of a man? Was that his message? He was musing on these things when the blow fell and all went black.

Randulf sheathed his sword after checking that the hilt was undamaged where it had struck the bald pate of the Prior. "Forgive me, Lord," he muttered and crossed himself. "There are greater things at stake here. And now forgive me Prior as well for what I am about to do."

He rolled the unconscious man over and untied his belt, and then, with much grunting and heaving managed to roll him over several times more and divest him of his black habit. He wrapped it around him and secured it with the belt. Then, he checked that the Bible was still inside his tunic, pulled up the hood to shield his face, and left the chapel, locking the door behind him with a large iron key.

Adam heard the murmur of low voices on the other side of the door. He jumped to his feet and picked up the rock. He felt its weight in his palm and squeezed it lightly between his fingers, holding it fast. He hid beside the door.

The bolts drew back, first one at the top, then the bottom and finally the third in the centre. He held his breath as the handle turned. A man spoke. "I have the Prior here to see you."

A figure dressed in a black habit and hooded, crouched low to enter the cell. The door slammed behind him and the bolts slid back and before he could straighten up Adam smashed the rock into his head. The Prior crumpled to the straw-covered floor with a low groan.

Adam knew what to do. He would exchange clothes with the Prior, lean his body in the dark against the wall as if he were asleep, and after a few minutes would call for the gaoler to let him out, absolution being accomplished. He would walk out in disguise. This was his plan. It was so simple, so easy.

He turned the man over, pulled back his hood and started in surprise. There in the dark and bolted cell, he could just make out the unconscious face of his friend. Randulf's eyes were shut and a trickle of blood meandered down his cheek.

Chapter 22 - Sanctuary

Adam swore and then panicked. Had he killed his friend? He hoarsely whispered his name, "Randulf! Randulf, wake up!" There was no movement. He slapped his face, once, twice, but Randulf didn't stir. Adam looked wildly around him, searching for something, anything to wake him up. Water. The pale of water. He dragged it across the floor and splashed some on his friend's face. Still Randulf did not move. Adam prayed and in desperation picked up the heavy pale and tipped the cold water over him. Randulf bolted upright, coughing and spluttering and shaking his head.

"What happened?" he asked in a voice that slipped and slurred. "Where am I?"

"You are locked in prison with me. What in hell's name are you doing here?"

Randulf rubbed his head and tried to marshal his thoughts. "Rescuing you," he said finally.

"Rescuing me! Now we are both trapped inside here. What sort of rescue is that!"

Randulf stared at Adam, taking in his drawn, pale and haggard face, his beard that now clung in greasy strands from his sunken cheeks, his eyes now dulled and set in dark hollow pits, and he cursed himself that he had taken so long to return to Ely.

"Agneta is with child." He had not meant to say it so abruptly, but it just came out. Adam recoiled on hearing her name but at first did not seem able to take in the meaning of what Randulf had said. He stared straight ahead. And then it sunk in.

"With child?" His lips hardly moved as he spoke the words. "She is carrying my child?"

Randulf nodded, and then added, "Well, I suppose it is yours."

"What do you mean?"

"Agneta told me that Hugh Cooper has been after her."

"Then we must get out of here fast. I must go to her."

"And what about rescuing your father?" asked Randulf.

Adam had risen to his feet, but now he sat down again and pressed his palms against his forehead, his mind in turmoil. "What do I do?" he murmured, "I cannot save both of them."

"Agneta can wait," said Randulf abruptly, "there is nothing you can do to help her right now, so let's concentrate on getting the Bible to Gelfridus Lyttle and rescuing your father."

"Do you have the Bible?" asked Adam, "I thought it was stolen."

"My friend, you underestimate me," laughed Randulf, "of course I have the Bible. I have risked life and limb for you to get it back, but I have done it, and the book is safely in my possession."

"Show me," said Adam. "I need to see it."

"It is safe. I have it hidden. We can fetch it when we get out of here," lied Randulf.

"And how in the name of the Almighty are we going to do that now?" cried Adam. "I had one plan – a good plan – and you have wrecked it." He looked about him, searching the dark cell for an answer.

"Randulf, do you have a weapon on you, something metal?"

"I have a dagger and a sword."

Adam crawled to the middle of the room and scraped at the straw until he had formed a pile. Then he tore a piece from his already tattered cloak and pulled at the threads forming them into a light ball of wool. He tucked this into the straw.

"Give me your dagger."

Randulf handed him the jewel encrusted dagger he had taken from the Pardoner. Adam held it up in the shaft of silver moonlight that shone in through the window and whistled. He looked at Randulf but asked no questions. He would do that later. He picked up his sharpened stone and struck it against the blade of the dagger. A few sparks flew into the air and fizzled out. He struck again and again, aiming the shooting sparks at the wad of wool.

"Come on," he urged, and struck again. A cluster of sparks caught on the fibres and Adam blew gently on them. They glowed orange and gold. He blew again and the wool caught. Tiny flames began to flicker and he carefully fed them with more woollen strands until a flame the size of his little finger glimmered in the dark. The tinder-dry straw scorched and then burst into flame, quickly spreading from stalk to stalk until the pile began to smoke and grow red.

Randulf looked around him at the barred room. "Are you mad?" he asked. "We are locked in here, and you start a fire!"

"Shout for help." answered Adam, and began yelling at the top of his voice. "Fire! Fire! Save us please! The cell is on fire!"

Randulf now understood. He started to shout as well and pounded on the door with the handle of his sword. "Let us out before we burn!"

The flames were soon well and truly out of control as they spread across the floor, consuming the straw and filling the cell with a pall of ash-speckled smoke. Adam began to choke and cough as the sharp fumes swirled around them and the flames grew closer. Randulf rounded on him. "You stupid

fool. We are going to die in here. There is no-one outside..."
He stamped at some burning strands close to his boots.

Adam wheezed and rubbed his watering eyes. He knelt
down and tried to sweep the flaming straw away with his
hand, now desperately aware that his plan was flawed.
"Help!" he cried again, "please, someone help!" The acrid
smoke stung his eyes and he tried as best he could to cover
them with his sleeve. His voice became hoarse as he shouted,
and he coughed with every gasping breath. His head grew
heavy and he knelt on the floor, wheezing and shaken.

And then, as if by a miracle, he heard the rough grating of
bolts being withdrawn and felt a rush of cool clear air sweep
over him as the door flew open. The guard waved his arms at
the thick smoke and stumbled into the room. Randulf barged
into him, knocking him to the floor as he raced for the door.
Adam clambered to his feet and chased after. He squeezed
through the low doorway and drank in the fresh night air,
filling his lungs with freedom. Tears fell from his stinging eyes
and trickled down his smoke-greyed face. Through a watery
veil he could just make out Randulf running towards the
cathedral, and he stumbled after him.

The full moon lit the way with a ghostly glow. It was just a
matter of a few hundred paces between the prison cell and
the cathedral, but in the short time it took to limp there he
sensed that he was being followed. He turned and in the
moonlight saw a band of sluggish monks running awkwardly
after him. Their thin sandals slapped on the stony path and
they panted breathlessly as they gave chase. Adam ran
faster, his twisted ankle shooting pain with each jolting step.

Randulf opened the Prior's door and ran into the
cathedral then helped bundle Adam through into the dark
and slammed the door shut. He pulled the bolt across, barring
the entrance. They could hear the monks fast approaching

then hammering on the gate before muttering amongst themselves and heading off towards the great West door.

"Quick," said Randulf, "we don't have much time. Can you make it up the aisle to the door before they get there from outside?"

"I ... I don't know. I don't think so. My ... my foot..."

"Hell's blood. This is a mess. We need to find somewhere to hide."

There was the unmistakable sound of large metal hinges creaking and the great West door swung open. In the moonlight they could see the monks creeping into the nave.

Randulf pointed to the choir stalls, silhouetted beneath the canopy of the octagonal tower, and he and Adam slipped across. It only took a few steps, but was enough to alert the monks to their presence.

"Give yourselves up," shouted one of the monks in a voice nervous with tension. "There is no escape, so please, in the name of our Mother Mary, give yourselves up."

Adam squinted around the cathedral. The light of the moon flooded in through tall stained glass windows high above him at the top of the tower, illuminating the beautifully painted celestial ceiling. Motes of dust floated downwards, glimmering in the pale light that made the bright painted stonework glisten as though still wet with the painter's brush. A few yards away he saw a small door that surely must lead to the outside. He nudged Randulf and pointed to it. The monks were warily walking closer.

"Run!" shouted Adam and he and Randulf raced across to the door. It opened easily. "Hell's teeth," exclaimed Randulf. The door did not open to the courtyard outside and instead they found themselves trapped in a narrow corridor with a tightly twisting spiral staircase, leading upwards. Adam looked back. The monks were racing towards them. "Go!

Go!" he yelled and pushed Randulf from behind so that he staggered up the stairs, the Prior's black habit scraping the walls as he went. They emerged onto a balcony that ran the entire length of the nave, just a few feet wide and divided into areas for private prayer.

"They are in the *triforium*," called a voice from below. "They cannot escape, so take care brothers. Do not rush. We have them now."

"What do we do?" asked Adam.

"Keep going up – it's all we can do."

Across the nave was another door and they pulled it open to find another spiral staircase. Adam put his hand behind his knee and heaved his crippled foot upwards with each painful step. At the top they found themselves outside on a narrow gunnel at the base of a leaded roof. They were now high above the ground, shielded only by a low balustrade to their left. The wind had died down and they could hear the sound of the monks puffing and calling out behind them.

They crossed the roof and squeezed through a very thin doorway and climbed yet another narrow flight of stairs. As they fell through an arched door they realised they were now inside the top of the octagonal tower. Huge wooden beams were bolted and woven together to create an extraordinary feat of construction, and Adam saw that they were on a circular walkway that encompassed the centre of the tower. They had walls to the outside and walls to the inside and no means of escape.

"The monks are right. There is no way out from up here," he cried.

"There must be." Randulf ran around the circular walkway searching for another door. "Here," he shouted.

Adam limped around but before he reached Randulf he tripped and fell against one of the painted wooden panels that opened out into the centre of the tower. The panel flew open and Adam peered through. What met his eyes was fantastic. A hundred feet below lay the choir stalls and the altar, looking like children's playthings on the heavily decorated stone floor. The light of the moon filtered through the stained glass above his head and a myriad of colours radiated downwards, growing ever dimmer. It was as if the panel had opened a doorway into heaven. He marvelled at the beauty of it all.

"Randulf, look at this."

The crashing of a door jerked him back from his thoughts.

Adam spun around to see one of the monks barging through the doorway that lead from the stairs below, brandishing a stout stick in his hand.

On impulse Adam grabbed Randulf and threw the hood of the Prior's cloak over his head, turning him in the half dark from friend to Prior. In one swift movement he twisted an arm behind Randulf's back and pulled his knife to his throat.

"Take one step further and the Prior dies," he shouted at the monk in the doorway.

The monk looked at the staff in his hand and reflected for a moment and then took one cautious step into the room. "Now, my son, do not do anything rash. Remember that this is the House of God. Drop your knife and let the Prior go for the sake of your soul." He took one more slow step towards Adam.

Adam pushed Randulf halfway through the open window, holding him in an iron grip and suspending him above the drop below. Adam held him tight yet Randulf could feel the tremor in his clasp that meant that he was straining hard to keep him there. All Randulf could see was the hard stone floor so far below him, and he flailed around with his arms to find something, anything, to hold on to. His hand brushed against Adam's cloak and he clutched at it. He cried out and the monk stopped in his tracks.

"Get out now or I will drop him," said Adam. The monk dithered and then lowered his staff and stepped backwards through the open doorway. "Do not do that, I beg of you. I will leave, but please let Prior Poucher go. But know this, you will not escape from here. And if you do, then know that you will not escape the wrath of God. Be warned, your soul will be in hell for what you have done." He melted into the darkness of the stone stairwell.

Randulf was pale with fear and drops of sweat fell from his brow and disappeared into the void below him. "Let me up," he whispered hoarsely.

Adam hesitated for what seemed like an eternity, then peered down at him, and knew that finally he had his chance. "Let me ask you a few questions first. And do not lie to me or I shall drop you."

"Adam! What...?"

"Who are you? Who are you really?"

"What do you mean?"

"You pushed your way into my life just as this whole thing was beginning. You took my brother Richard's place and lead me much of the way here as if you knew where we were going from the outset. You have too much money for a merchant, and expensive clothes and a fine horse besides. Where did you get all that? Whose pay are you in? And now you have stolen the Bible from me and hidden it..."

"I have the Bible! Don't be so stupid, Adam. Did I not save your life when you were drowning in the river? Have I not been a good friend to you?"

"Where is the Bible. Let me see it." Adam was growing red in the face from the exertion of holding Randulf. Randulf pointed to his belly, where Adam could see the sharp corners of a book protruding through his shirt. He thought for a moment, then slowly dragged Randulf back through the opening.

"Never do that again," hissed Randulf as he brushed himself down and straightened his clothing. Adam muttered a sort of apology.

"And what now?" asked Randulf, after he had regained his composure. "There is only one way out and that is through the door I found. Come on let's go!"

The door creaked open and they clambered through it and out onto the roof. Adam peered over the edge of the rampart and his head swam as he looked down. The courtyard was a long way below and the ground seemed to be swaying in the pale moonlight. There really was no way out.

"What do we do now?" asked Randulf. "Think, Adam, think. We have to get away."

"Sanctuary," said Adam. "We can claim sanctuary. We are in the cathedral, in the House of God, and so we are protected by God and cannot be removed. So let us claim sanctuary. "

"Are you mad? They will just wait for us to starve."

"We are half-starved already. What is there to lose? And even if we have just one more day here it will give us time to plan an escape," said Adam, his eyes alight with hope.

Randulf nodded slowly in agreement. "It might just work," he said.

+

Prior Poucher woke in his chapel to the sound of the commotion outside. He rubbed his sore head with a fat hand and looked at the stain of blood on his palm. He could not remember how he had ended up lying on the floor, disrobed and bleeding, and he took his time to sit up and pull himself together. It was obvious that he had been attacked, but by whom?

He crawled to the altar and used the heavy table to pull himself to his feet. The room swam and he clutched the wall to steady himself. His head thumped and he felt sick, but somehow he staggered to the stairs and carefully made his way down the spiral staircase, step by slow step. He reached the bottom, panting with the exertion and red in the face, and pulled at the door. It didn't move. He pulled again and again, before finally realising that he was locked in. He shouted, but by now there was nobody outside. This was going to be a long, cold and lonely night. He sat on the second step and held his head in his hands, and swore by Almighty God that he would catch the perpetrator.

+

Adam and Randulf made their way cautiously back down the stairwells to the *triforium* and crept silently out onto the balustraded corridor than ran the entire length of the cathedral. Below them they could hear the agitated voices of the monks, chattering and talking over each other as they debated what to do. Who were these men? Where was the Prior? Had they captured him? What were they to do now? Adam nodded at Randulf, then shouted down, "Sanctuary! We claim sanctuary in this House of God. You cannot arrest us in this holy place. We claim our rights to sanctuary!"

The monks fell instantly silent as each one raised his tonsured head to look up. Then they began to murmur amongst themselves, wondering whether this was true and what they would have to do. Finally a tall, thin monk waved his hand in a gesture of command and called up into the darkness. "We are duty bound to accept your request. We will post a guard outside the doors of the cathedral day and night to keep you from leaving until the sheriff can be recalled. He is not many days from here, so your time is short."

Another monk tapped his arm and whispered something, then the thin monk continued, "You must stay within these walls apart from the need to relieve yourselves, for which you may use the courtyard outside. This too will be guarded."

"By the law we demand to be fed and watered," said Randulf. There was more murmuring amongst the monks. The thin one spoke again, "As you have chosen to imprison yourselves here, then we choose not to help you. It is your choice whether to live or die of starvation. Give yourselves up and leave the cathedral and you will be given food and water. Stay within these walls and starve or die of thirst. The choice is yours. Goodnight gentlemen." And with that he led the monks in single file from the cathedral.

Chapter 23 - The Love of a Mother

Agneta stared in disbelief at her mother. "Please, please, no! You cannot do that to me!"

Her mother whipped around and slapped her across the face. "You have brought shame on this household. How can you hold your head high?"

Agneta winced and held a hand to her reddening cheek. "Mother, no!"

"You have let us all down. How dare you do that! How could you have done what you have done?"

"It was a mistake..."

"A mistake! How on earth can sleeping with a man be a mistake?"

"I loved him."

"Oh, and I suppose that explains it. You loved him. And what about all the other girls here who love a man? Do they get with child? For the sake of the Almighty could you not have married him first?"

Agneta lowered her eyes. "I made a mistake." She repeated.

"You surely did. And not only once, so I am told. How many times? How many times did you lie with him? Tell me, or have you lost count!" Agneta blushed, but her mother continued, "I am now the laughing stock of this village. The mother who could not control her daughter. We have been put to shame!"

"I am so sorry. I do not know what to say. I wish I could turn back the days and change it all but it is done now, and I am carrying his baby. Surely you can find love in your heart for us both?"

"Love! What do you know of love? Do you know how hard I have worked to raise you and your brothers and sisters? Do you know the endless days and nights of toil and labour to provide food for you to eat and clothes for your back? Do you know the tears I have shed as I nursed you back to health? This, this is love! Do not tell me that a night in the hay is love!"

"How can I make amends?"

"It is too late for that."

"I could hide here in the house, away from prying eyes."

"And how do you propose to hide that? Just look at you. Look at your belly! You cannot hide a child…"

Agneta watched as her mother turned her back on her.

"For all our sakes you must leave."

"But I am your daughter."

The words cut like ice. "You are no daughter of mine. You are a disgrace. You have no love for me. Now leave, you and your child."

As Agneta stepped into the street the door slammed behind her. Instinctively she clutched at her belly and then ran up the road.

It was Isabel who found her hunched up and weeping in the corner by the barn. Her first instinct was to walk on by, but something tugged at her heart. She stopped.

"What's wrong?" she asked

Agneta looked up with a tear-stained face, her eyes red.

"I said, what's the matter?"

"Nothing," whispered Agneta.

"Nothing! How can this be nothing? Dear child, something has caused you to be sitting here all huddled up against the cold in a corner of the street. Are you unwell?"

"No."

"Then what is it? You have been crying." Isabel paused. "Aah, I see. It is because of the child. Am I right?"

Agneta nodded.

"You were a fool."

Agneta nodded again.

"But then so was my son. This is as much his doing as it is yours. More so I expect. You led him astray and he could not say no."

"It was not like that."

"Oh, so how was it?"

"Adam was … is … a good man. He is honourable and he loved me. We were planning to wed, but…."

"But what?"

"But for your dislike of me. He said you would not allow it."

"And so you got with child? And tried to hide it from me?"

"I did not know what to do. Adam had left before I knew I was with child, and now that he is gone I do not know what to do. And now even my mother has abandoned me. I cannot go home."

Isabel sighed. Agneta looked so small and childlike herself, sitting there hunched on the dirt road, wrapped in a thin cloak and shivering with fear and cold. She looked at her tear-stained face, and compassion welled up within. She herself had lost three babies before they were weaned, and had now also lost both of the two sons she had managed to raise. She was now as alone and helpless as this poor girl huddled at her feet.

"Come child, I will take you in. The house is so empty with Richard dead and Adam gone. The babe within is my grandchild after all, and someone will need to care for him and for you. Come and stay until Adam gets back, and then we shall see… we shall see."

Chapter 24 - Judas

It was the day after Adam and Randulf had claimed sanctuary. Randulf was starving and his belly ached and he curled up on a bench in the north aisle of the nave and pulled the Bible out from a pocket in his cloak. He eased it open and began to read.

He found that he was being drawn to read it more and more, to explore its mysteries. What was so important about this book? he wondered. What made it so priceless? Whenever he stopped for rest he opened it up at random and read whatever passage was there, guiltily at first, like a small child stealing a toy, then later with more fascination. There was something in the beauty of the words that pulled him in, enveloping him in a world beyond this one, and yet so connected with it. He knew the Latin versions of some scriptures by heart as he had been brought up to recite them daily, but they were cold words and meaningless. It was not a language that was used apart from in the mass. But this book was different, and the words in English were alive. They reached out and spoke to his soul, as Spirit speaking to spirit. He felt at peace when he read them, yet at the same time strangely confused.

There was a very liyt, which liytneth ech man that cometh in to this world.
He was in the world, and the world was maad bi hym, and the world knew hym not.
He cam in to his owne thingis, and hise resseyueden hym not.
But hou many euer resseyueden hym, he yaf to hem power to be maad the sones of God, to hem that bileueden in his

name; the whiche not of bloodis, nether of the wille of
fleische, nether of the wille of man, but ben borun of God.
And the word was maad man, and dwellyde among vs,
and we han seyn the glorie of hym, as the glorie of the `oon
bigetun sone of the fadir, ful of grace and of treuthe.

"What are you reading?" asked Adam as he came and sat down beside him.

"I do not know. All I do know is this is not what I have been taught to believe. Here is grace and salvation not by my own good deeds or by attending mass or by my confession. This is grace given freely. Heaven awaits me if I just believe... But how can that be?"

The sudden swing of the great doors and the hurried crunch of footsteps broke through his confusion. Randulf looked up to see the irritated face of Athelard Drake, the Pardoner, leading a group of six armed men in through the archway under the west tower. His eyes bulged with glee.

Randulf slammed the Bible shut and threw it to Adam who hid it behind his back.

"Arrest him!" screamed the Pardoner, pointing a limp finger at Randulf. "Here is the thief who stole from me." The Pardoner's voice was slimy and squeaking with the excitement of victory.

"You cannot arrest us," shouted Randulf. "We have claimed sanctuary."

The Pardoner laughed. "Sanctuary?" he said, "Sanctuary? I know of no such word. And see, I have the guards with me. They have come to arrest you, a common thief, under my orders. You have no right to sanctuary!" He turned to the guards. "Arrest him now. He has stolen from me."

One of the armed officers pushed past him and strode purposefully towards Randulf.

"I do not know what you are talking about," said Randulf. "What have I stolen from you?"

"A fine dagger. Or do you not remember?"

"I stole no dagger from you."

The officer hesitated and looked to the Pardoner for direction.

"Don't listen to him! I am employing you to make an arrest. This man stole my dagger – a jewel-encrusted thing of beauty and great value. Now arrest him!"

"I do not have it. Search me if you like, you will not find it."

The Pardoner nodded to the officer who quickly checked Randulf over. "There is no dagger, Sire."

"Well, search the other one. They are in league together."

The officer grabbed at Adam's arm and wrenched it forward. There was a dull thud as the Bible slipped from his hand and hit the floor. The Pardoner's eyes widened.

"Well, well, what have we here?" he mused. "Here is a better prize than the dagger, if I am not mistaken. Bring the book here."

Adam glanced quickly in panic at Randulf, but he turned his face away.

"Oh, it is, it is the Bible!" purred the Pardoner as he flicked through the pages. "Well, Master Payne, this will see you put to the stake, will it not? What a mistake of yours to keep it."

Randulf stared at the Pardoner. "It is not mine."

"What did you say?"

"The Bible is not mine, so you cannot arrest me for it. Was it in my possession? Was I holding it?"

The Pardoner looked confused and mumbled something beneath his breath.

Randulf continued, "No, it does not belong to me, but to this man, Adam Wolvercot." He pointed to Adam.

Adam blurted, "Randulf, you…"

"So it would be better for you to arrest him for possession, and see him burned, don't you think. He is the Lollard and the one who has broken the King's command. He is the one who should burn as a heretic." Randulf kept his eyes fixed on Athelard Drake as he spoke, and well away from Adam.

"So, you seek to preserve your own life, even at the cost of betraying your friend. What a deathly liar you have become, Master Payne. What a Judas. Have you descended so low that you would see your friend die, rather than take the blame yourself. I thought more of you."

The Pardoner thought for a moment, then shouted. "Arrest them both! Let us burn both of them."

Randulf had remained motionless until now, but suddenly sprang to life. He stooped to pick up his sword from where it lay on the ground and then ran straight towards the Pardoner, yelling at the top of his voice. One of the officers lunged with his foot to trip him, but only caught the toe of his boot. Randulf stumbled and barged into the Pardoner, knocking him with an elbow and sending him squealing to the ground. He turned direction and raced for the doorway that lead out of the cathedral as a crossbow bolt whistled past and struck the wall by his head.

Adam tried to follow, but his twisted foot held him back and as he hobbled he felt the strong grip of a gloved hand round his neck and he was dragged to the ground. As he looked up he caught sight of Randulf disappearing through the door and running for his life.

"After him!" shouted the Pardoner, and two of the officers gave chase. One stopped at the wall to load and aim his crossbow. He fired, and then swore as Randulf continued to run.

Adam was jerked to his feet and someone bound his hands behind his back. A thick woollen hood was pulled over his head, blinding him, and he felt the hard prod of a sword hilt in his back, forcing him to walk ahead. He could hear the muffled sound of the guards' voices, laughing and joking, and above them the self-congratulatory whine of the Pardoner. Athelard Drake finally was having his moment of victory.

"We should parade him through the streets before he goes to prison," said one of the guards.

"Do you not realise what day it is?" asked the Pardoner. "I have planned this most carefully. Today is the fortieth day since the Proclamation of the *De Hæretico Comburendo*. The edict was proclaimed here on April the eleventh and today is May the twenty-first. Do you not know what this means? It means that this heretic can burn without trial. There is now no time for him to confess or turn from his sin. He has had forty days to do that, and has not recanted in that time. He still carries his heretic Bible, flaunting it in the face of the people, and of the King. I do believe that we can get immediate authority to see him burn tomorrow. I shall personally arrange it. I have friends in high places who owe me, shall we say … favours." Athelard Drake smiled thinly.

+

Sir Osmund Clarke downed his wine and thumped the glass heavily onto the table. He had come with some secrecy to Ely to find out what on earth was going on. He was a man under pressure. Questions were being asked. The Archbishop was demanding to know what was happening, and Henry IV was asking questions of the Archbishop. So when word reached him in his chambers in London that Adam had been imprisoned, that Randulf had run away and the Albino was nowhere to be seen, he at once saddled his horse and with a small retinue made his way to Ely. He would have to explain the situation at the highest level and his neck would be on the line. Obviously he would land the blame on others, for that is what he always did, but as they were doing his bidding the ultimate responsibility was his and his alone.

How he hated the provinces. He rarely left London and despised the squalor and backwardness of the countryside. His three day journey had been one of dirt and peasants, bad food and soreness in the saddle, so when he finally arrived at Ely he was in a foul mood. He was at least given a fine room by Prior Poucher in the monastery, and fed on some choice cuts and doused with fine wine.

But then two days after his arrival and in the early hours of the morning he was woken with the news that Prior Poucher had been found in his private chapel, stripped of his habit and with a sore head; the prison cell was blackened and burnt, and Adam had escaped and was nowhere to be found. This was a disaster. He called for another glass of wine, and wondered what would happen to him when he reported back to the King.

There was a knock at the door, and without waiting for an answer it flew open. Prior Poucher strode into the room. "Sir Osmund, I have good news, that will cheer your very soul!" he exclaimed.

Sir Osmund looked inquisitively at him through slightly bleary eyes.

The Prior continued, "Master Wolvercot has been captured."

"And the Bible?"

"Yes, that too! And there is more. The decree you sent here has been posted for forty days throughout the town, giving plenty of time for heretics to recant. Adam Wolvercot has not done so, and is in possession of the Bible in English..."

Sir Osmund cut across him, "And so he can quite legally be put to the stake. Perhaps things can turn out for the good after all."

Prior Poucher beamed. He would surely be promoted for this news. He rubbed his hands. "You have the authority to pass sentence upon him?"

Sir Osmund thought for a moment, then decided he needed to end this matter once and for ever. He was the architect of the *De Hæretico Comburendum* after all, and he was here to represent both the King and the Archbishop of Canterbury, so surely he did have the right to sign the death warrant on their behalf. Besides he could not risk losing Adam Wolvercot or the Bible again. He nodded.

"Draw up a warrant and I will indeed sign it. And you Prior will have the honour of presenting the evidence tomorrow."

"But I will need to inform the Sherriff if we are to pass such a sentence as this."

Osmund Clarke sneered, "You will do no such thing. I am the law around here, and I say he burns tomorrow. Is that clear?"

"But, Sire, the Sherriff ... he wanted to know if ..."

"Tomorrow, Prior Poucher. In the name of the King do it tomorrow. I do not have time to waste cooped up in this stinking town. I have affairs of state awaiting me in London. Burn him tomorrow or you too will join the pile."

Prior Poucher was ashen, "Aah, yes Sire. But tomorrow is a Sunday. We surely cannot burn him on the Lord's Day?"

Osmund Clarke drew in a deep breath. "Just do it!"

Poucher looked shocked, but realised his low standing before this Lord of the Realm and mumbled. "I'm sure it will be easy to erect a stake and fetch some wood. I know of a band of woodsmen who would be more than delighted to supply the kindling for this Lollard. I will notify the town immediately and I can guarantee a large crowd for the display. You will not be disappointed Sire. No, we will have a spectacle! Tomorrow Adam Wolvercot burns!"

+

Gelfridus Lyttle removed his spectacles and looked up from his bench in the apothecary shop as the door swung open and a hooded figure came in. The shop was dingy on the best of days and was now growing dark. A few shafts of fading evening light filtered through the grimy cobwebbed window, illuminating the motes of dust that floated wearily in the dank air. The visitor was dressed in black and at first Gelfridus thought he was a monk.

"Can I help you, Sir?" Gelfridus asked. The man said nothing, but his hood turned this way and that as he glanced around the small room. The shelves that lined the walls from floor to ceiling were laden with jars, bottles and boxes, each containing some herb or potion or oil. There were pomegranate seeds for the treatment of digestive ailments, camomile for earache and colchicum for gout. Mallows, honey, wormwood, salt and shavings of ivory vied for a place alongside dried beetles and crickets in oil and a jar of live leeches inching around the lid.

Gelfridus could not see the face of the customer, covered as it was with the large hood, and wondered what sort of disfigurement he was trying to conceal. He often had clients with scars or spots or some ugliness of the face caused at birth, and was used to finding the right potion or poultice to bring a degree of relief. Perhaps it was leprosy, though that was rare these days, or the scar from a blade, or a broken nose or toothless mouth, though these he saw often. He coughed and repeated his question. "Can I be of assistance?"

The man stepped towards him in the half dark. A tallow candle, set on the oak counter next to the scales, flickered as his cloak stirred the air. A voice came from the hood.

"Are you Gelfridus Lyttle?"

"Yes, Sir, I am he. Why do you want to …"

"Thank you," cut in the voice.

The hooded man turned to go and as he did so his cloak caught on a small box which crashed to the floor, scattering dried elderberries across the tiles. He grunted a curse and stormed out, but as he went Gelfridus noted the translucent white skin of the long bony hand that gripped the handle of the door. He thought for a moment and then went to the back of the shop to a little alcove where his companion was counting out seeds.

"Jacob, I think we may need to hide."

His companion looked up with steely blue eyes that were younger than his face.

"Have they come for us at last?" he said wearily.

"I think they may have found us. That man asked for me by name and it was obvious that he was not here for any medicine. He only wanted to be sure of my name. I can see no other reason for that than the fact that they have finally found us."

"Or perhaps he was one of us? Could he have been bringing good news?"

"No, I don't think so. He would have shown his face. This man did not want me to see him. Why? What would have been so distinctive about him that he needed to hide his face so well?"

Jacob sighed and clambered to his feet. He was middle aged, but seemed older as though his body had been beaten by the world. He walked stiffly to the door and squinted through the peephole into the street. On the far side if the road was a man in a black cloak and hood, leaning against a wall and watching the shop.

"Is that him?" asked Jacob.

Gelfridus drew alongside him and peered out. The man in the crow-black gown did not stir.

"Yes. What do you think?"

"He is watching us." Jacob sighed resolutely. "We should go, and quickly."

"I knew this day would eventually come," said Gelfridus. "A man cannot hide forever in obscurity. The powers that be are all too invasive. They have eyes and ears everywhere. I wonder how long they have known about us?"

"I don't know. Surely not since the days when you were a monk, cutting herbs for the hospital?"

"And surely not since they released you from the torture. They would have acted before now if they had known our whereabouts. No, my friend, this is something new, a new danger, and we must flee."

The two men gathered their cloaks and Gelfridus bolted the front door. He took one last loving look at the shop he had created, then they crept to the back of the building and made their way along a passage and out through the rear door into the narrow lane behind. It was growing ever darker, and they were soon lost in the shadows of the town.

Chapter 25 - Redeemed

Adam awoke with the dawn, though in truth he had hardly slept. They came for him not long after the sun had risen above the low tiled roofs and just as the townsfolk were beginning to stir and stretch themselves in readiness for the day ahead. Prior Poucher entered the cell first, accompanied by two sturdy men at arms.

"Arise, Master Wolvercot." He spoke kindly, as though already regretting what the day would bring. He was a man of faith after all, and although justice needed to be done, and he would be handsomely rewarded for it, he could still handle the accused with some sort of civility. Adam stumbled to his feet.

"I'm afraid my orders are to have you tied." The Prior nodded to the men at arms, who pulled Adam's arms behind his back and roughly tied his wrists with a thin rope. His face puckered with pain, but they did not care. They were not as gracious as the man of God.

They led Adam squinting into the bright sunshine. A crowd had just begun to muster and one or two called out to him, "Lollard traitor!" "Rot in hell!"

His legs felt like lead as he was marched the few hundred paces to the castle mound where the windmill blades turned gently in the mild breeze. To all it seemed the perfect spring day. A pair of early swallows flittered overhead, catching flies in gaping mouths, and somewhere beyond the priory walls a dove cooed. Only the tall wooden stake and the piles of kindling and logs told a different story. Adam stared at them. His parched tongue stuck to the roof of his mouth and his mind went numb. It seemed an eternity of emptiness before he pulled himself together and realised he was now in the midst of an ever growing and angry mob. He turned his head this way and that, looking for a friendly face, some sort of comfort, but there was none. Never had he felt so alone. Never had he felt so scared.

Down on the road the crowd parted as a parade of figures appeared around the corner, coming from the direction of the priory. Leading it was a man whose stature and authority was evident by his clothes and his gait. And following on behind him were a number of others, including a man that Adam instantly recognised - the Pardoner, Athelard Drake. He was simpering and wringing his hands with delight at being elevated to such a position, walking in the retinue behind Sir Osmund Clarke, envoy of King Henry IV. Adam felt sick.

Prior Poucher waved his staff in the air and the crowd grew silent. When he spoke it was with a gravity that suddenly fitted the occasion.

"My Lord, Sir Osmund Clarke, townsmen and gentlewomen, we are gathered here today to witness a new beginning for our kingdom, for England and for Ely. This man," he pointed his staff at Adam, "This man has refused in the last forty days, when grace was given to repent, when our blessed King had decreed that heretics should be given a chance to change, this man Adam Wolvercot has refused to repent. He has refused to hand in his heretic Bible, written against the law in the common tongue.

"He has chosen his own fate, knowing full well the sin he was committing against the King and the Church of Rome. He has not come to change his views and is now accused of Lollardy. Can we let such a man live? No! He will pollute all he comes in contact with and will lead many to hell. Because of his refusal to change, even though given many days to do so by our gracious King, he has signed his own death warrant. And the penalty for this is written large on this decree." He held out his hand to a man at arms and was given a rolled parchment. He lifted it high for all to see. "The *De Hæretico Comburendum*, which you have all seen and read, states that by decree of the King, every such heretic must be made a spectacle and burnt to the death at the stake on a high place, on full view to all, as a warning. As a warning, my friends! So be warned. The King and his Holy Church will not tolerate such heresy. We will protect the church! We will protect this land!"

A huge cheer went up from the crowd as Prior Poucher finished his speech. He had certainly warmed to his theme and was now enjoying the adulation of the townsfolk.

"Well said," murmured Sir Osmund Clarke in his ear, then added impatiently, "Now, may we proceed?"

Prior Poucher reddened a little, then wiped a bead of sweat from his fat brow. He motioned to the men at arms who dragged Adam through the crowd and up the incline to where the wooden post was hammered into the earth. One carried a coil of rope, and with this they bound him to the stake, wrapping it from shoulder to waist until he was wrapped like a mouse in the coils of a snake.

"Place the heretic Bible with him. Let them burn together." called out Osmund Clarke.

They placed small twigs and kindling wood about his feet, as high as his thighs, then rested larger branches and logs against these. Adam felt a warm wetness run down his legs, and his mind raced with flashing images. He felt utterly out of control. How had it come to this? Where was his God now? The beams of wood resting against his chest made it hard for him to breath, but his chest still pounded with short fearful breaths. He stared wildly at the ugly faces of the mob that surrounded him. There was no way out.

Prior Poucher turned to face him. "Adam Wolvercot, do you repent, even now? You may have one last chance to enter the fold and turn from your evil ways. What do you say?"

Adam had no idea what to say. His mind was a wordless turmoil, and though he opened his mouth, no words came.

Prior Poucher addressed the crowd. "You see how foolish these Lollards are? They cannot even defend themselves! There are no words for their defence." There was a rustle of tense laughter, broken by an impatient shout from Osmund Clarke.

"Burn him!" he yelled. "Get on with it!"

A flaming torch was set to the kindling. It glowed red and then caught and a plume of smoke spiralled upwards through the pyre. Adam felt the stinging heat coming ever closer, the tips of the flames nipping at him like the stings of a horde of wasps, and he tried frantically to kick the kindling away. But he was bound so fast that he could only move his feet, and the stinging only grew worse.

There was a commotion in the crowd. Someone was pushing through the mob and the sun caught a glint of steel. Sir Osmund Clarke turned to see what was going on, but too late. The steel blade was at his throat and a hand twisted his arm painfully behind his back.

"Untie him!" yelled the man with the knife. "Untie Adam Wolvercot or I will surely slit this throat."

Osmund Clarke croaked something and waved his arms frantically in the direction of Prior Poucher. The Prior hesitated for just a moment and then shouted to the men at arms to dowse the flames.

Osmund Clarke could not see his assailant who was tight behind him, but there was something familiar in his voice. Something too familiar.

"Randulf? Is that you?" he croaked.

There was a pause before the young man spoke. When he did it was full of venom. "Yes, it is me. And I have come for my friend." He shouted to the Prior. "Untie him!"

"Randulf, Randulf, what are you doing?" said Clarke. "Let me go, or there will be trouble."

"There is already trouble," said Randulf. He shouted once again, "Untie Wolvercot or I will surely kill this man and his blood will be on your hands."

Prior Poucher looked from Osmund Clarke to Randulf and back, unsure of what to do. The youth looked half crazed and really would draw that knife across his throat if there was too much delay. He waddled to the stake and began pulling smouldering branches from it. He called a couple of men at arms to help him and whispered something to them. They looked back at Randulf and nodded.

Osmund Clarke spoke. "Randulf, there is something I need to tell you. There is something you need to know."

"Shut up! Or I will use this blade."

"No Randulf, you can't do that. Have you never wondered why you were so special to me?"

"Special enough to make me watch a man burn? Do you know what that is like? Can you imagine the sound they make, or the stench that never leaves your nostrils? No I am not special to you." He pressed the sharp blade closer to his throat and a trickle of blood ran down Osmund Clarke's neck.

"But you are special. I have always loved you. You do not know ... I never had the chance to tell you, but there is a reason you cannot kill me... I am ... I am your father."

Randulf scraped the knife against the skin of Clarke's throat, scratching it over the stubble where his beard was shortest. "I do not believe you," he said.

"It is true! Let me live and I will prove it to you and you will live as my heir. All my estate will be yours to share. I have wealth and power beyond anything you can imagine, and it will be yours, Randulf. It will be yours, my son."

"I have tasted your wealth and your power," said Randulf slowly, "and I have no hunger for it."

"So you would rather be an outlaw on the run, than the master of your own destiny?"

Randulf thought for the briefest of moments, and then made up his mind. He held the knife tight against Osmund Clarke's throat and shouted, "Faster! Get him down faster."

Adam was now clear of wood and with one last glance over to Osmund Clarke, Prior Poucher undid the rope that bound him.

Randulf pushed Clarke towards the stake. "Adam, run!" he yelled. Adam finally spoke, his voice rasping, "Randulf ...?"

"Go, Adam, go! I will be fine. Just get out of here fast."

Adam began to run, first a painful uncontrolled hobble, and then gathering speed until he ran at full stretch down the mound and through the crowd. No-one stopped him. Perhaps they thought this was all a part of the spectacle, perhaps they were just shocked. He tumbled down the street and disappeared around the corner, out of view. There was a deathly hush.

In the sudden silence Randulf caught the unmistakeable sound of a sword being drawn from a scabbard. He spun around to see one of the men at arms lunging towards him. He ducked and the sword hit Osmund Clarke squarely across the shoulder. He buckled under its power and crumpled to the floor. Randulf ran. He leapt to the stake, scooped up the Bible from where it had fallen, and barged his way out of the crowd.

Prior Poucher lunged at him, but his overweight body was too slow, and he slipped and clutched at the stake with both arms to stop himself from falling. As Randulf ran, he turned his head just once to see the Prior fastened to the stake and surrounded by smouldering wood. The Pardoner was shouting something and waving his arms around like the sails of the windmill behind him, but no-one was taking any notice. It seemed as though, at least for the moment, the crowd was confused, not knowing which way to turn or what to do. But Randulf knew he would not have long. He raced down the hill and towards the quayside as fast as his legs would carry him.

There was a small fishing boat tied to a post and Randulf vaulted into it and unwound the rope. He cast off and pulled strongly at the oars, the boat at first juddering under the strain, but soon sliding across the water as silently as a swan. He knew he only had moments before the crowd came to their senses and came after him. He pulled on the oars with all his might, bending and stretching his back as he jammed his feet into the wooden hull to brace himself. He was a few hundred yards out before the first of the townsfolk came into view, and another few hundred yards before one of them decided to give chase. He was a portly man who wheezed as he climbed into his boat, and it was obvious to all that he would never row faster than the escaping Randulf.

Adam watched all this from the safety of a half hidden doorway. He had hobbled to the quay in a state of shock and had ducked into the shadows a number of times to hide from the approach of folk from the town. He had hoped to steal a boat and escape but now there was no chance of that. The quayside was crowded with people, all on the lookout for a limping Lollard. Randulf had abandoned him and run away with the Bible, and now here he was trapped once again on this accursed Isle of Ely. And his life was still in danger.

He wrapped his cloak around him and squeezed into an alleyway between two rows of fisherman's huts, and stopped to think. How was he to get away, and where to? Only a few moments before he was set to pass from this life to the next, but now he had a fresh start, and his heart began to pump faster. Slowly his head cleared and he knew what he had to do.

Randulf was bound to be heading for Thetford, he had to be because his horse was there, and if Adam could also get to Thetford quickly he still might be able to find him, get the Bible and save his father. Gelfridus Lyttle was in that town and he was the answer to the riddle. If only Adam could find him, then he would find his father. It all felt a little ridiculous, but it might just be possible. The only other option was to give up now and return home in defeat, but that was no option at all.

The crowd had thinned as there was little now to see, and Adam slipped out from his hiding place. It was still early morning and there were a number of fishing boats and rowing boats lined up, ready for the day's trade. Some took passengers and some cargo, and some barrels of eels. Most had oars for rowing, but one or two also had sails.

He covered his head and tried not to limp as he wandered as casually as he could over to the boats, trying to decide which one he could take. He knew that he no longer had the power to row; a few months in prison and a crooked foot saw to that. But he also had no idea how to sail a boat. As he was pondering all this he heard a voice behind him. He turned and came face to face with the boatman who had ferried him from Fynchyngbroke Priory to Ely so many weeks ago. The boatman grabbed his arm and led him towards his boat which nestled amongst three others alongside a jetty.

"Jump in quick," said the boatman, and he heaved Adam into the boat. "Cover yourself with this." He handed a rough wool blanket to him. As Adam crawled between two barrels and pulled the blanket over him he heard the boatman say, "I have instructions from a friend of yours to bring you to the Priory – a certain Friar Stephen. He told me to watch out for you and to rescue you if you needed it. I believe he has the same faith as you."

Adam felt a jolt as the boatman cast off and then the gentle pitch of the boat in the water as the blades dipped and rolled.

Chapter 26 - Master Randulf Payne

It took Adam four days to reach Thetford. The boatman dropped him later the same day at Fynchyngbroke Priory where he was met by Friar Stephen and Prioress Moulton. The Prioress, after welcoming him back, quickly mentioned the cost of stabling Beatrix, but Friar Stephen cut in to say that he would meet all the costs. He winked at Adam behind the Prioress's back, and handed him a small bag of coins. There was plenty there for the stabling, and plenty left over.

Adam was led to the stables by novice Imelda and by some animal instinct Beatrix sensed he was coming. She whinnied and stamped her hooves on the straw-covered floor, and shook her mane in excitement. Adam called her name in a soothing voice, and tried to pretend that he was not churning up inside with the same excitement and relief. He had often imagined this day when he was locked away from the world in the prison cell. He had imagined it, but had not dared to believe he would ever see it. And now, as he stroked Beatrix's soft muzzle and looked into her deep brown eyes, he cried.

A day later he was on his way. He rode Beatrix as fast as she would go, keeping the marshlands around Ely always on his left as a marker, and so he rode south and east from the Priory, skirted around Cambridge, and then headed north and east towards Thetford on the ancient Icknield Way. This road was well marked and well used, and, although in places churned and rutted by cart wheels, it was generally in fine shape. Already used for more than a millennium, this major route across England was the lifeline he needed. It took just two days of hard riding to reach the outskirts of Thetford town. And here he alighted and found a place in an inn for the night.

The next morning he took bread and ale for breakfast and then, as he paid for the bed, asked the Innkeeper if he knew of an apothecary shop.

The Innkeeper scratched his head, then replied, "Ay, there is one hereabouts in Nether Row, not far from the old castle ruins. It's run by an old monk and his friend."

Adam left quickly and headed for the castle, the ancient remains of which stood on a high man-made hill near the centre of the town. He skirted around the edge of this and then asked a ragged pedlar the way to Nether Row. He pointed a dirty finger towards a small street, bordered by shops and houses that curled away from the castle. Adam strode towards it, wondering what he would actually do when he reached the shop. What would he say? After all he no longer had the Bible.

As he rounded a sharp bend in the street, he caught his breath and halted. There above a doorway hung a metal hoop encircling a silhouette of a pestle and mortar. But it was not the sign for the apothecary shop that made him halt in his tracks; it was the two men standing beneath it. They were talking with heads close together as if passing on secrets, and seemed totally oblivious to the world around them. One of the men was tall, thin, and cloaked in a black gown that contrasted severely with his pale white face and hands, and the other was very clearly the figure of Randulf.

Adam took a step back and pressed himself into a doorway. The Albino pointed a long bony finger at Randulf, who flicked it away with his hand. Adam thought hard. Who was Randulf? Which side was he on? He seemed to change like the wind. Could he ever be trusted? Only a few days ago he had rescued him from death, and now here he was in cahoots with the enemy. What was going on? He watched a little longer, and then the two conspirators walked away in opposite directions. The Albino headed down the street towards him.

Adam turned his back to him and sidled into a doorway, trying to hide. He could hear the footsteps of the Albino squelching in the mud, coming ever closer. He froze and held his breath. He heard the groan of wooden wheels turning on a wet axel and looked up to see a farmer coming in the other direction pushing a handcart laden with straw. The cart was so full that there was little room on either side of it, and he was leaving strands and stalks on the rough walls as the cart bounced and slewed from side to side in the muddy road. The footsteps behind him stopped and he could hear the rasping breath of the Albino just a few feet behind him. An icy river swept through his veins. The handcart slid in the mud, and the Albino swore at the farmer as he jerked himself out of the way and bounced into Adam. He grabbed at Adam's shoulder to steady himself and then pulled away, shouting at the farmer and storming off down the street.

Adam turned his face from the doorway and watched him go, his heart racing. He waited a few moments before leaving and then followed the cart up the street towards the apothecary shop. Randulf was nowhere to be seen. Adam tried the handle, but the door was locked. He knocked and waited. No response. He stepped to the window and peered in, but all was dark and he could only make out the outlines of a few jars and bottles on the shelves nearest the light. He knocked on the door again. Perhaps he was too early. Perhaps he should call back later in the day. Perhaps he should try and find Randulf. Perhaps he should just hang around and wait.

+

Gelfridus Lyttle led the way through the alley and out into the precincts of the castle. The once magnificent building was now largely a ruin, with just the yard and a shoulder high stone wall still intact.

"Follow me closely," he said. Jacob nodded and hurried his pace to keep up. His stiff legs and bandy gait told of the stretching he had received on the rack, and he winced with nearly every step. His stout walking stick was all that stopped him from falling.

"Where are we going?" he asked.

"There is a place I know where we will be safe for a while, at least until this storm blows over," said Gelfridus.

"You have not mentioned this before."

"I have not needed to. Some secrets are to remain so until they are needed. This one may well save our lives."

For many years there had grown up a cluster of small dwellings and hovels around the castle walls. As the centuries passed some had crumbled and returned to the earth that formed them, and new dwellings were added in their place. Stone replaced mud, and brick and tile were added later and the village grew. Pathways turned into small streets that wound in and out of the settlement and criss-crossed each other at odd angles. The houses had been homes once, but were all now unoccupied, empty and crumbling. The town had slipped away from the castle walls and grown up a little farther away, leaving this area as a ghost town, a distant memory of former times, a waste dump.

And at the centre of all this stood the castle, built on a huge mound that many said had been built by the devil. A large wooden keep overlooked the houses, and the whole was surrounded by a ditch where the inhabitants threw their waste. It was into this purlieu that Gelfridus now led Jacob. They wound their way towards the mound, and then circled the foul smelling ditch to the north until they met the earth ramparts. There were stones here, large ones that had once been a part of the structure, but now lay abandoned and fallen like drunken guardsmen. There was no-one living in this part of the village and the decaying houses were in bad shape. Gelfridus tugged at Jacobs's sleeve.

"In here," he said.

Jacob followed him into a hovel, ducking to miss a fallen roof beam that half blocked the entrance. Gelfridus was already at the back of the room and was scrabbling away at the floor. He had scraped away a layer of mud from a large flat slab of rock and was now marking the edge of it with a dirty finger. As Jacob drew close he could see two metal rings embedded in the slab which would act as handles for moving it. Gelfridus looked up from his work.

"We will need your stick. Can you lift?"

"I don't know. It looks heavy."

"You will be surprised," said Gelfridus with a quick smile.

They knelt down and threaded the walking stick through the metal rings and each took an end. Then Gelfridus grunted, "Lift," and they strained at the slab. It shifted a fraction, then suddenly came free and slid to one side. Jacob gasped. The stone slab was only a finger width in thickness and was resting for strength on a wooden trap door.

"I told you it would not be heavy," said Gelfridus. "The old monks knew a thing or two about hiding places. This one is ancient and I think all have forgotten it is still here, but I came across a mention of it one day in an old manuscript relating to the castle. I did some exploring, pretending to be looking for plants for the hospital, and came across it. It has been my secret since then. Come, I will show you."

He lifted the trap door and eased himself into the hole that had now appeared below the floor. Gelfridus felt around for something and then pulled out a candle, a flint and a firestone and soon had the candle aflame. He disappeared into the darkness below. Jacob swung his aching legs into the hole and discovered the top rung of a wooden ladder than descended into the pit. He cautiously put his weight on it, and then clambered carefully down, feeling each rung through his thin leather soles.

Gelfridus was waiting for him at the bottom, candle held aloft and illuminating a surprisingly well-constructed underground room. He lit a few sconces on the walls and light flooded the underground room. The walls had been lined with masonry and the roof was held up with sturdy stone arches. On the far wall was the opening of a tunnel, leading who knew where.

"What is this place?" asked Jacob, when he had got his breath back.

"I believe it was part of the defence of the castle, built many years ago. A sort of secret hiding place if all else was lost. And now it will hide us."

"And the tunnel?" Jacob nodded in the direction of the dark doorway.

"That leads into the mound, and an even greater treasure. Come, I'll show you."

He led the way, the candle light flickering and dancing on the stone walls. The tunnel was low and they had to walk with heads bent to get through it, but after only a few paces it opened up and they found themselves in a magnificent chamber.

"We are in the heart of the mound, right below the keep." Gelfridus spoke with awe. "Over the years I have made provision here. Welcome to my hide-out."

Jacob stared open mouthed around him. The room was lined with a variety of pieces of simple furniture, each one carried here in pieces and constructed by his companion. There were three chairs, a bench, two tables and a coffer, a shelf against one wall containing books, and a box holding candles and provisions. Two pallets of straw rested against one wall and a water butt stood by, and mugs, plates and knives were stacked on one of the tables. And alongside the tunnel, hanging from the wall was an armoury of weapons; two swords, some daggers, a shield, and a crossbow. A longbow and a quiver of arrows rested on the floor beneath them. Jacob whistled.

"So much for the monk of peace."

"I have not been at peace for many a year," replied Gelfridus. "Let's rest. We are safe here and can stay for several days until all this is over. No-one will be able to find us. No-one."

+

Adam settled himself down with a tankard of ale and looked out of the window of the Golden Crown. He had waited in Nether Row for an age, wandering aimlessly up and down the street and waiting for the apothecary shop to open. The bells had struck for noon and still the shop remained shut. Finally the hunger that rumbled in his stomach persuaded him to give up his waiting and he sought food and ale in the tavern. He sipped slowly on his tankard and wondered what to do. Somehow or other he had to find this man Gelfridus Lyttle. He was the key to finding his father. And then he could go home. Home to Agneta and his mother and Richard. Home to the safety and comfort of his bed and his farmstead. Home to a normal life.

He thought back over the months since he had left on that fateful day in February with Randulf. And now it was May, almost June. He had nearly drowned in the river, had been beaten up and robbed, imprisoned, tied to a stake and almost burned to death. In addition he had killed a man - although arguably in self-defence - and had been frightened witless on more than one occasion.

He trawled through his mind to think of ways of finding Gelfridus Lyttle, but could come up with nothing. The only connection to him was the apothecary shop and that had come to naught. But he had no other option but to keep watching and waiting. He finished his trencher and headed back to the shop.

The door was slightly ajar but as Adam drew closer he could see that it had been forced and splinters of wood lay scattered on the street outside. He slowed his pace and crept nearer. The sound of a table being overturned came from within, glass jars smashing on the tiled floor. The shutters were closed, but the wood had shrunk over many years, producing a slit through which Adam could look unseen.

Randulf was digging through a cabinet, pulling out drawers and rifling through the contents. He pulled out a measuring spoon and threw it across the room with a clatter, then followed it with weights and a small vial of green liquid. He reached into the back of the drawer, searching the corners with his fingers, and then slammed the drawer shut. He turned around and Adam froze involuntarily, even though he knew he could not be seen.

Randulf moved to a shelf and fingered through the books that were stacked haphazardly upon it. He opened each in turn, flicked through it and then discarded it on the floor at his feet. He was almost at the end of the shelf when a piece of manuscript paper fluttered to the ground alongside a heavy tome. Randulf bent down to retrieve it, then straightened and scratched his head. He moved closer to the window and opened the shutter a little to let the daylight in. Adam flattened himself against the wall and held his breath.

"By the blood of the Saints," he heard Randulf whistle through his teeth. "So that is where he is."

Adam turned his back as Randulf stormed out of the shop, slamming the door shut behind him, and headed off down the road towards the castle, the manuscript clutched tightly in his hand. Adam waited a few moments and then followed, keeping close to the buildings and ready to hide should Randulf look his way. Once or twice he stopped and consulted the paper, turning it this way and that and looking around for signs to show that he was on the right track. Then he would stride purposefully on, or change direction at a crossing and head left or right.

The town gave way to the hovels that encompassed the castle and soon Adam found himself squelching ankle deep through the wet mud and slops that circuited the ditch. He was more cautious now that the buildings were closing in on him and as they twisted and turned he needed to draw closer to Randulf to keep him in view. And then Randulf disappeared.

Adam hurried his pace, cursing his limping foot that slipped so easily in the mud, and looking through each hovel door for movement. The smell from the offal ditch was overpowering and tainted the air in the narrow lanes. It hung like a reminder of the pestilence that had so ravaged the towns and villages until recently.

A strange creaking sound alerted both Adam and Gelfridus to the opening of the trapdoor. Adam moved as stealthily as he could and arrived at the hovel entrance just in time to see Randulf's hood disappearing from view below the ground.

Gelfridus was seated opposite the tunnel entrance, a position he often used as it meant he could guard the only way in and out of the room. He stayed put but motioned to

Jacob to cross the room and hide beside the tunnel. Jacob sidled against the wall, keeping out of sight of the entrance and plucked the crossbow from its mounting on the wall. They could hear boots in the antechamber and as Jacob loaded the crossbow, Randulf burst into the room. He flung himself towards Gelfridus, a dagger in his hand.

"Your name, Sire! Give me your name." Randulf's voice was tight.

Gelfridus fixed his eyes on him, hoping to keep any attention away from the tunnel and Jacob.

"So you have found me. That was clever. Or perhaps I was stupid. I see you have the manuscript." He pointed to the paper that Randulf still held scrunched in his hand.

"So you are Gelfridus Lyttle?"

"If you say so."

"Then this is for you." Randulf moved his dagger arm swiftly backwards.

There was a clatter of iron on stone and Adam ran into the room from the tunnel, sword in hand. "Randulf, stop!" he cried.

Randulf swung around. "Stop, Adam? Stop what? Do you think I have come here to finish him off? Do you think I am in league with the devil? Is that what you suppose?"

"I no longer know what I think. One day you are on my side and the next you betray me. What am I supposed to make of that? Who are you? Who are you really?"

Randulf thought for a moment, and then said, "I am not the man I thought I was, Adam. I have changed. You have changed me, this journey has changed me. This book has changed me." Slowly he drew the Bible out from inside his shirt, where he had kept it hidden next to his heart. He turned to Gelfridus.

"Gelfridus Lyttle. This is for you. I know you have waited many years for it, but now it is yours. Preach from it carefully."

Randulf Payne held out the Bible on his open palm. Gelfridus looked wide-eyed at it. Randulf nodded and Gelfridus reached over with a shaky hand and gently took the book from him. He opened the cover, then smiled and clutched it to his chest.

"Thank you," he whispered.

"Not so fast!" The voice came from the passageway. Gelfridus looked across the room to the doorway as the white-faced man ran into the room, his crow-black gown rippling behind him and a sword in his fist. He shouted angrily, "Randulf get away from him. He is mine now! I will see him burned for this treason! The heretic Bible too. Our job is now done. Get away from him Master Payne."

The crossbow bolt entered his leg from behind, just above his knee, slowing in its pace as it drilled through bone and sinew, but still with enough power to force the sharp arrowhead and half the shaft out the other side. The Albino shrieked and dropped his sword as he clutched at his leg. Jacob came out of the shadows. "I think we should go now," he said in voice full of relief.

Gelfridus rose and made for the door, steering Randulf past the collapsed figure of the Albino, and gathering Adam along the way. They entered the tunnel and Jacob followed on behind. Nobody spoke. They closed the trapdoor on the Albino and lowered the stone back in place.

"When we are far away I will send someone to rescue him, for this is charity," said Gelfridus finally. "Jacob, he must be a tortured soul, and as such is in need of mercy."

Jacob! Adam felt his pulse quicken at the name. He looked at the man in front of him. Could it be? Could it really be him? He looked so old and so gaunt and so haggard, not at all the way he remembered him.

"Jacob de Wolvercot? Are you Jacob, my father?" Adam's voice cracked as he spoke the words.

There was a moments silence while Jacob looked Adam over, trying to see if the man who stood before him just might be the boy he last saw over ten years ago. But there was no mistaking those features, the piercing blue eyes and straw-coloured hair, his mother's lips and the reflection of himself in the way he spoke. Jacob held back a tear and then threw his arms around his son, hugging and kissing him.

"Adam!" he cried, "Oh, Adam, how I have longed for this day. I knew you would come eventually - I knew you were smart enough to find me. But I have waited a long, long time. My son, my son, you have found me."

+

A young girl ran before them as they walked sore-footed into the village of Wolvercot. It was a raggle-taggle company; a young man in fine colourful clothes leading a fine white palfrey of some breeding, an old man with wire framed spectacles riding the horse and muttering prayers, another in his fifties astride an old nag that was being led by a young man who hobbled with a twisted foot.

They had travelled far, that was evident from their mud-stained clothes and the hunger in their faces, but there was a glint of hope in every eye. They passed by the old oak tree and a small child whistled a minstrel tune and showered them with twigs. Laughing, he jumped from the tree and joined them in their parade. A dog barked in the manor grounds, and for a moment the young man with the limp paused, then collected himself and moved on.

The child ran ahead and knocked on the door of a cottage, hammering at the wood until it flew open. She went inside briefly and then led a middle-aged lady out, followed by a girl who was cradling her swollen belly as if to help carry the weight. She looked over to where the child was pointing and clasped a hand to her mouth, then ran, arms aloft and shouting towards the travellers.

Adam let go the reins of his horse and stumbled to meet her. She threw her arms around him and they embraced, clinging tightly to each other, until Isabel broke them apart and hugged her son. Jacob dismounted from Beatrix and walked with his awkward stretched gait towards them.

"Isabel," he said quietly, "It is I, Jacob."

She spun round and studied his features. Could this really be him, this man with an aged face, drawn with lines of pain and suffering, and moving with such difficulty? Was this her

Jacob, the fit and handsome husband who had disappeared so long ago? He held out his hand, and suddenly she could not control herself. Her head filled with lightness and the world swam before her, and before she knew what had happened she was in his arms and kissing his cracked lips, and whispering "Jacob, Jacob" over and over again.

Adam glanced around him. "And where is my brother, Richard? Is he out in the fields, or with some pretty girl?"

Isabel looked in desperation at him and shook her head. "I am so sorry," she murmured, "he never recovered from his sickness. The fever took him soon after you left."

Adam looked piercingly at Randulf. "Why did you not tell me?" he snapped angrily.

Randulf reddened, "How could I have told you? You would not have been able to cope. Not there, in that prison cell."

"But I should have known…"

Randulf jerked Henry's reigns and spun him round to leave. He tapped Gelfridus on the shoulder and said, "We should be off now. There is no more we can do here. Come on, let's go." He seemed edgy, as if his presence there was awkward, and as if he would rather be anywhere else at that moment. He said, "We are leaving. Farewell to you all."

Adam called out, "No, stay. Stay with us for the night," and Isabel smiled and opened her arms as if to welcome them as family.

"No, I think it best that we go now, and leave you be. I am sure you have much to talk about. Come Gelfridus, we should be on our way." He tugged once more at Henry's reigns.

"I will not have it," said Isabel. "You are to stay at least overnight and rest before moving on – that is if you really have to go. Why not stay here with us a bit longer. You could settle down and make a home."

"We are hunted men. We cannot settle down," interrupted Gelfridus.

"Then where will you go?" asked Jacob.

Randulf shrugged, "Here and there. A long way from here. Wherever we can find a bed and safety."

"And someone to preach to," added Gelfridus with a smile and he patted the Bible in his hand. "It seems my young friend is in a hurry to go. Perhaps he has trouble with partings. I think it best we leave you be."

Gelfridus hugged Jacob and held him for a long time. "We do not want any more trouble to come to you. You have seen enough of that. No, we will be away. There is much work to be done and much preaching to do. I will look after this young scoundrel and teach him all I know." He pointed with his chin at Randulf.

"And I will keep this old man safe," added Randulf with a grin. "Farewell to you all. I am in your debt." He took Adam by the hand and shook it firmly, then gripped him to his chest in a hug. He whispered in his ear, "And to you my friend, I am sorry."

Then Randulf pulled at Henry's reigns and led him westwards along the lane that led far from Wolvercot. Adam held Agneta tight as they watched them go, and then kissed her once again.

Epilogue

Two years had passed since they returned home. Agneta gave birth safely in the September of that year, proving once and for all that she and Adam had had more than one time in the hay. They called their son Richard, and she was now heavy with child again.

Adam married Agneta soon after his return in a short ceremony at the church, with Jacob standing at his side. Isabel took Adam's hand and placed it on Agneta's as the Priest gave the blessing, finally giving hers in that same instant to both her son and his new wife. Agneta's own mother refused to attend, saying that she no longer had a daughter.

Adam began to work the small plot of land owned by his parents and soon became adept at growing peas and beans and cabbage. He sold some at market along with eggs collected from the hens and was planning to keep some money back to buy a small plot of land and build a home for his growing family. Isabel wanted him to add a room onto their cottage instead, and in reality this was all that he would ever be able to afford.

But the simple life pleased him. He had seen enough of danger and adventure, and was happy to grow old at home where it was safe and where he could best provide for Agneta. It seemed to him that life was at last returning to normal. He had not heard from Randulf or Gelfridus in all this time, and had no idea where they might now be.

Jacob rested much, and had constant pain in his joints. He felt old, even though he was not. He spent much time just gazing at Isabel, at Adam and Agneta, and holding his grandson, Richard. He prayed often and fervently.

And from time to time, from a hiding place in the lonely shadow of the woods, they were watched by a pink eyed albino dressed in a crow-black gown.

Historical Notes

This tale, although fictional, is based on actual events that took place in England in 1401. Some of the characters here are real and lived and breathed during this turbulent time of English history; others are pure invention. With regard to the actual historical figures, I have created personalities and character traits that may not be entirely accurate. In so doing I have probably made them less likeable than they may have been in real life. I ask forgiveness from their descendants!

The towns and places these characters inhabit are depicted as accurately as my research would allow. Much has changed in the last six hundred years, but in some cases there are still well-documented details, including names of streets and inns, and even records of the people who lived in a particular town. I have to say that I have enjoyed the research almost as much as writing the book!

Adam, Isabel, and Jacob are all fictional, but the village of Wolvercot that gave them their name existed in the medieval period. It was edged with a common ground, and still lies just a few miles from Oxford.

Merton's College had a bursar by the name of Peter Radle at the time of the break-in and was the foremost library in England. John Wyclif spent much of his life at Oxford and was a theologian at the university. For a part of this time he worked at Merton's College. He died at Lutterworth two days after having a stroke while preaching on Holy Innocent's Day, 1384. I have quoted (*in italics*) from his translation of the Bible.

Sir Osmund Clarke, the Albino and Randulf Payne are figments of my imagination, however the Archbishop of Canterbury, Thomas Arundel, and the king, Henry IV are not. The *De Hæretico Comburendum* was signed by Henry IV on March 28th 1401 after he received a petition from the Archbishop on February 26th for the burning of William Sawtrey. I have quoted (*in italics*) from the authorisation Henry IV made in response to the petition in the chapter called The Petition. William Sawtrey was martyred for his beliefs on March 2nd at the livestock market at Smithfield in London.

Catherine Multon was the Prioress of the small Priory at Fynchyngbroke in 1401. I do not know about the novice Imelda. I need to thank Geoffrey Chaucer for the loan of some of his characters from the Canterbury Tales, written at the end of the fourteenth century, for my nasty bunch of companions who robbed Adam, and especially for his description of the Pardoner. What a wonderful character!

John Brevetour, the poor preacher whose body they discover at Prickwillow (another name I could not refuse) is again fictional, but his name is found in the record books for Ely at that time. Brevetour means someone who was 'skilled in monastic craft', and therefore seemed a suitable surname to use.

All the other characters exist only in this novel, and for that I am saddened, because I believe they would have made wonderful friends.

I would love it if you would leave a review of this book at Amazon.

I have a facebook page at
www.facebook.com/andrewmartinwalker
and a website at www.andrewmartinwalker.com

Printed in Great Britain
by Amazon